T0319130

Scandal is his chosen path—until this infamous Shaw surrenders to love...

When Lady Charlotte Engles receives an offer of marriage from an eligible suitor, she's finally ready to let go of her long-held hope that her engagement to Lord Valentinian Shaw will result in marriage. For despite the betrothal their families made between them, Val shows no interest in leaving his reckless life behind in favor of one with Charlotte. But when her plea to end their arrangement ends in a heated embrace, suddenly Val seems reluctant to let her go . . .

The last thing Val wants is a wife, despite how desirous his lovely bride-to-be has become. But when he discovers sweet Charlotte is planning to marry a dastardly man, he feels duty bound to keep her safe, even if that means making good on his marriage pledge. Then Charlotte is taken hostage by her dangerous suitor and suddenly Val is ready to risk everything for the woman who has won his heart . . .

Books by Lynne Connolly

Emperors of London
Rogue In Red Velvet
Temptation Has Green Eyes
Danger Wears White
Reckless In Pink
Veiled In Blue
Wild Lavender

The Shaws
Fearless

Published by Kensington Publishing Corporation

Fearless

The Shaws

Lynne Connolly

LYRICAL PRESS
Kensington Publishing Corp.
www.kensingtonbooks.com

Lyrical Press books are published by
Kensington Publishing Corp. 119 West 40th Street New York, NY 10018

All Kensington titles, imprints, and distributed lines are available at special
quantity discounts for bulk purchases for sales promotion, premiums, fund-
raising, and educational or institutional use.

To the extent that the image or images on the cover of this book depict a
person or persons, such person or persons are merely models, and are not
intended to portray any character or characters featured in the book.

Special book excerpts or customized printings can also be created to fit
specific needs. For details, write or phone the office of the Kensington
Special Sales Manager:
Kensington Publishing Corp.
119 West 40th Street
New York, NY 10018
Attn. Special Sales Department. Phone: 1-800-221-2647.

Kensington and the K logo Reg. U.S. Pat. & TM Off.
LYRICAL PRESS Reg. U.S. Pat. & TM Off.
Lyrical Press and the L logo are trademarks of Kensington Publishing Corp.

First Electronic Edition: August 2017
eISBN-13: 978-1-5161-0247-1
eISBN-10: 11-5161-0247-9

First Print Edition: August 2017
ISBN-13: 978-1-5161-0250-1
ISBN-10: 1-5161-0250-9

Printed in the United States of America

Chapter 1

Charlotte spared her betrothed a glance but took care not to linger. People might notice her looking. Val was talking animatedly to a group of friends, standing at the rear of the garden. As if he felt her regard, he turned his attention to her and returned her look, the corner of his mouth tilting so slightly she wasn't sure she'd seen it.

Then he returned his attention to his friends.

Of course he did, because that was what he always did. Indeed, why should he not? They might be affianced, but their attachment was not a romantic one. At least, it was not supposed to be.

Lord Valentinian Shaw and Lady Charlotte Engles had entered into an arranged marriage, brokered by their parents. What was so unusual about that?

Only the secret Charlotte held closely to her heart. Fortunately she had practiced at hiding her emotions, so only she knew the truth.

Charlotte gave the lady chatting to her a broad smile, not at all sure what she was talking about. Lady Duckworth had the proud reputation of boring for England, as Val had said once, but she meant well. Fortunately, all she required was an audience. Responses were optional.

She shuffled her toe in the gravel but kept the smile in place, listening to Lady Duckworth's conversation long enough to agree with her proposition that all satirical poets should be forced to debate their absurd propositions. Then she returned to her private thoughts.

She should be grateful for the brilliant match her father had contrived. People kept telling her, therefore it must be true. When Val had asked her to marry him, he'd done it formally, with a kiss on the back of her hand when she duly accepted. The betrothal was perfectly conventional. Nobody had asked for Charlotte's opinion. If they had, she might have begged for him. She had fallen deeply in love with her betrothed.

Her guilty secret accompanied her everywhere. She had agreed to the proposal as a way of getting away from her home, a way her father had agreed upon, but once she'd met Val, her opinions had changed. She wanted Lord Valentinian Shaw so badly, she'd even become his respectable companion while he roistered and scandalized society. She had continued with the arrangement as a way of providing a new home for herself and her sister, but after an inordinately long betrothal, she was forced to think again. She had to get away from her father's house and provide a place for herself and her younger sister.

A masculine voice broke into her thoughts. "Lady Charlotte."

She tilted her head, which would have meant she was staring directly into the sun, but someone was shielding her from it. The sun blazed on either side of him, leaving the man in darkness, as if he were a visitor from the heavens.

After bowing over Lady Duckworth's hand, the man begged her to grant him the favor of allowing him a few moments of her company.

Charming, elegant and smooth, Lord Kellett had shown her flattering attention of late, but Charlotte found him less daunting, more approachable than her future husband. He listened to her conversation, he sought her company at balls, and if she had not been spoken for, she would have given him even more attention. However, he had never stepped over the rules of propriety. He behaved to her like a friend, as he was doing now.

Having seen Lady Duckworth to another group of people she could bore, Lord Kellett offered his arm. Charlotte took it with a smile.

"You should smile more often," he said. "It suits you." He led her on a gentle stroll across the width of the terrace and then down the stairs at the end. The stone staircase led to the main part of the garden.

Rosebushes massed in pleasing abundance, trained well away from the paths. The fragrance surrounded them, perhaps a little too sweet for Charlotte's taste, but the effect was heavenly. "Whoever the gardener is, he deserves a medal for pruning the bushes so carefully."

"Hmm?"

Lord Kellett didn't sound interested, but Charlotte plowed on. "Sometimes negotiating a rose garden is more like fighting through a thicket."

He frowned, but gave her no response.

Charlotte sighed. "Never mind."

"You have a droll sense of humor, my lady," he said then, and laughed.

She hadn't meant her comment humorously. The gardener really had considered the width of ladies' hoops and taken the full skirts of a gentleman's coat into consideration too. The thorns did not discommode her wide skirts at all.

"Thank you." She consoled herself with the knowledge that he meant well.

They moved along the path that led to the next part of the garden, still well in view of the house. Her aunt, who acted as her chaperone, was somewhere indoors, so Charlotte had relative freedom. One would have thought that at her age her father would have allowed her more discretion, but they did not. Not many people had a father like hers, though. They should thank heaven every day for that.

Charlotte could relax and allow his lordship to take her for a little perambulation around the lovely gardens attached to this equally gracious London house.

The house belonged to her betrothed's family, and if she married him, she would live here, or Val might even lease an establishment of their own. The Shaws were a large family, sprawling, noisy and somewhat uncontrolled—all things her father detested. But he had agreed to the betrothal, because few people ever denied the Shaws anything.

Frankly, the family of the Marquess of Strenshall, and the extended family known in society as the Emperors of London, unnerved Charlotte, but she could hide behind her proper mask and smile and nod. She was perfectly aware that people thought she was dull, but she had little choice. So she smiled and nodded, just like always as Lord Kellett asked her about her favorite pieces of music, and the uncomfortably warm spring weather.

Charlotte was tempted to tip her head back and hold her face up to the sun. However, that would dislodge her hat and draw attention to her. She refrained, as she always did, from succumbing to temptation.

"I find the Italian operas somewhat too dramatic for my taste," she confessed.

"Indeed, ma'am? I must introduce you to the great Sodrendo. His tone is divine."

"A good countertenor is a marvelous thing." Not that Sodrendo was a great countertenor. He sounded as if he was imitating the pure tone of the greats. The passion for the high-toned male voice had led to much mutilation of young boys and a few men who had remained intact but could sing in the higher range. For Sodrendo's sake, Charlotte prayed he hadn't sacrificed his manhood for an inferior voice. However, she wouldn't dream of saying that out loud.

"Indeed, sir. I will ask Lord Valentinian to escort me and my chaperone one night."

"Now that," he said softly, "is what I would particularly like to talk to you about."

With a swift left turn, he rounded a hedge and kept going, taking her to a small building at the end of the path. Nobody could see them if they entered. Greatly daring, Charlotte allowed Lord Kellett to take her between the twisted columns into the cool space within.

He escorted her to one of the hard wooden benches lining the white-painted walls, and she sat, her smile fixed in place. He sat next to her, as close as he could get, gazing at her.

He glanced down and then back up at her face. A small crease marked his smooth forehead. "Lady Charlotte, I find you charming and a delightful companion."

If she didn't know better, she'd think he was making a declaration. However, he could not intend that. "Thank you, sir. I confess, it is delightfully cool in here. How clever of you to find it." She laid her fan on the seat next to her and folded her hands in her lap. "The garden is beautiful from this aspect."

He barely spared the vista a glance. "I prefer the view from where I am sitting."

"Sir—" She got no further.

"Madam, my lady...Charlotte. I have done my best to quell my feelings for you. But I can bear no more."

He paused, seemingly at a loss for words, catching his bottom lip between his teeth. Although his words made her uncomfortable, Charlotte stayed to listen. "Lord Kellett..." She laid a gentle hand over his, which proved a mistake, because he captured it in both of his.

"Hervey, please call me Hervey, at least in private."

She should not, but she'd do it to pacify him. "Hervey, then. You are aware I am betrothed?"

"Yes, and I am also aware that I am transgressing, not only with you, but with the hospitality of Lord Strenshall and his family."

She nodded. Being in their house, he most certainly was.

"I cannot hold my emotions back any longer. Lady Charlotte, why do you allow Lord Valentinian to treat you so?"

Now it was her turn to frown. What on earth did he mean? "He treats me with respect."

"I would not say so!" He spoke with such passion that she moved back. However, he did not let go of her hands. "He treats you with a great deal of carelessness. He is happy merely to have you in his sights, although he makes no move to further his connection with you."

"We like one another well enough, but we prefer not to live in one another's pocket." Wistfulness infused her. She would like to know what that felt like, to have a man devoted to her, one who could not wait to marry her. Val had enjoyed a number of mistresses. She had no idea if he had one now. The thought did not sit well with her, but she would have to endure many such once they married.

Her mother had tolerated many before her death, but her father kept his women carefully closeted. There was never any scandal. He never used a society lady and he paid off his mistresses with enough of an annuity to keep their mouths shut. Charlotte only knew because she'd heard her brother talking about it with a friend. "My father has to pay for his pleasures because of his proclivities," George had said with a sigh. George sent abroad for that transgression, to tour Europe with his tutor. Not that it proved any punishment, because he was soon setting Versailles on its ear.

"You have been betrothed for an age," Hervey gently pointed out.

As if she needed reminding.

"Two years," she said, setting her jaw. In all that time Val had treated her more like one of his sisters than his betrothed, and he had never broached the subject of setting a date for their wedding.

"Will Lord Valentinian not come to the mark? Because if he will not, there are plenty of people who will."

Was he speaking to her as a friend? He was caressing her palm with his thumb, which she found distracting. She wasn't at all sure she liked it. His gesture made her want to scratch her hand. "I haven't noticed a preponderance of men flocking to my door."

"You only need one. May I be frank, Charlotte?"

She allowed the use of her first name. Intrigued, she nodded.

"My dear, I have become very fond of you. More than fond, if truth be told."

"We have only been acquainted for three months."

"I only needed an hour." His fervent voice echoed around the hushed space, bouncing off the roof and back to her. "I have tried to remain silent, but I can do so no longer. I adore you, Charlotte, and I would love nothing more than to offer you my hand and protection in marriage."

Shocked, she stared at him. Was he truly saying this? She'd had no idea he felt so strongly toward her. His blue eyes were wide and his mouth partially open, even though he had stopped speaking, revealing the gleam of sharp, white teeth. "I can say nothing, you know that." What else could she say? The experience of having a man wildly in love with her had never come her way before, and she floundered, not knowing how to respond.

She found his fervency somewhat alarming, but all the same it fascinated her. "How can you possibly know you want me?" She bit her lip, wetting the suddenly dry, delicate skin.

"I know, dearest Charlotte. Believe me, I know. Is there any way our love can be fulfilled, or are we doomed to watch each other from afar?" He lifted her hand to his lips and kissed it, letting his tongue dip between her knuckles with a flicker she wasn't sure of until she saw the flash of pink that went with his gesture. He had tasted her.

Charlotte knew her duty. "We cannot, sir. I have always been obedient, never gone against what my father wished..." Indeed, how could she? Unlike her sister, who she had not seen in over a year, the sister she was forbidden to talk about. A tinge of sorrow touched her when she recalled Sarah, her laughing face and the daring ways that had eventually led to her downfall.

"You are a good and obedient daughter," he said in an approving tone. "I have spoken to your father, told him how irresistible I find you."

Charlotte quailed. "Did he not forbid you?"

"Not precisely. He reminded me of your contract to Lord Shaw, but he gave me permission to speak to you. However, he said the choice must be yours. You must speak to him yourself."

Her father was actually amenable to this change?

"Will you not ask your father on our behalf? Surely he does not wish to see his daughter dwindle into an old maid while her betrothed gads about with not a care to his responsibilities?"

Should he be talking about Val like that in front of her? But he had cause. However, honor demanded that she remind him of the proprieties.

A bee buzzed by her nose, circling her, probably after the roses in her hat. It was doomed to disappointment, since they were made of silk. "Sir, Lord Valentinian and I are considering our wedding date." They weren't, but it didn't hurt to say so.

With his free hand, he made a grand dismissive gesture worthy of an actor. "Pah! Lord Valentinian is deferring his wedding for all he is worth. If I thought there was true feeling between you, that you were devoted to each other, I would never dare speak, but that is not the case, is it, dearest Charlotte? I can make you happy. I swear I can. I will devote my life to you and consider it well lost!"

His fervency spoke volumes. Had he really lost his heart to her? Did she dare to believe that she, dowdy, quiet Charlotte, had engendered passion in a man?

More importantly, his estate assured Charlotte that he was no fortune hunter. The fervency of his declaration and the suddenness with which he made it could have made her suspicious. Society took her for granted, gave proper due to her status as the daughter of a duke, but nobody took much notice of her.

Or did he want a wife with status? Lord Kellett was a peer in his own right and possessed of considerable wealth. So no, he would not need her standing in society or her fortune, which, for a duke's daughter, was relatively modest.

He had brought her here for a private conversation, but he could easily have chosen this place to compromise her and force her decision. If she'd thought he'd have any degree of success, she would never have accompanied him to this secluded spot.

Charlotte was no naive society miss with feathers for brains. Moreover, if he sought to compromise her, this was not the house for it. The Shaws had their own scandals, most of which society forgave, because the Emperors were society's darlings. She stared at Hervey, a million different thoughts sparking in her head.

Had he really lost his heart to her? That would make a refreshing change. She'd waited a year to see if Val would see her as more than a convenient excuse. When they had become betrothed he'd been frank, asking her to allow him some freedom before pressing him for a wedding date. He'd proceeded to use her as a useful way of dissuading the more importunate matchmakers who clustered around the Shaw family every season.

Charlotte had allowed it. In the back of her mind, she'd waited for him to fall in love with her, or at least show her some affection, but he still treated her with the same careless but polite indifference he used with everyone else he knew.

Hervey was handsome and passionate. She was sure she could come to love him in time. He would be hers, devoted to her. Moreover, she did not feel the same despairing love for him. She liked him well enough, in a way that could, she imagined, easily turn to love as time passed.

Yes, she would do it, on one condition. "Would you offer my sister a home?"

He gave her a quizzical look but nodded after a moment. "I would be honored to do so, should she be in need of one."

That was the answer she needed. Resolution took her. She could not continue as she was, with her sister and herself under their father's thumb and with no prospect of actual marriage to Val. She had to move on with her life. If possible, she would take this man.

Ever since he had appeared in London at the start of the season, Hervey had paid her particular attention, so his regard, while premature, was not totally unexpected.

He clasped her hands, tightening his hold. "Please, my dearest one, give me an answer. If not now, tell me when you will be free. If you tell me to leave, I will never mention this again!"

"You had better not," a voice drawled from the doorway.

Chapter 2

Charlotte had been so engrossed in Hervey's declaration she had not even noticed the shadow falling over the tiled floor. Normally she was very aware of her surroundings, knowing that alertness mattered even more than most people would suppose. She gasped. "Val!"

Hervey sprang to his feet and executed a perfectly elegant bow. "Lord Shaw, I will not apologize. I cannot imagine what has made you deny this lovely creature for so long."

Valentinian's amused gaze traveled over Hervey's stiffened, bristling figure. He took his time, traversing him several times before he finally straightened and bowed his head in an almost insultingly small gesture, returning the flourishing bow with a barely there nod. "You have an interesting turn of phrase, sir. I could listen to you all day. Pray, don't let me stop you." He lifted his hand in an elegant, arrogant gesture. "Do go on. I will act as Lady Charlotte's duenna, although I admit my experience in that area is paltry." He took a few steps, his shoes rapping on the terracotta beneath his feet. "Such eloquence deserves an audience."

Now he had moved out of the sun, Charlotte spotted the signs of his displeasure. Val was smiling, but his brilliant blue eyes were hard as sapphires, and his square jaw was set. The soft sensuality of his mouth deceived many into looking no further, but Charlotte had learned better. Charlotte was far more observant that most people supposed. She had to be. If Val wanted something, he got it. He was not happy right now.

He took a circuit around the pavilion, hands behind his back, ending by staring out at the garden with his back to them. "My mother loves it here. She has created a veritable oasis in the midst of strife." He shrugged, his shoulders moving slightly under the beautifully cut dark red cloth coat.

"I'm mixing my metaphors a trifle, but you understand my meaning, I'm sure." When he turned back to them, his face was wiped of expression. "Madam, your lady aunt has arrived and is asking for you."

With a strangled yelp, all her grace gone, what there was of it, Charlotte sprang to her feet. If her aunt reported her transgressions to her father, she would be in trouble.

Val gave a small shake of his head. "We are dealing with her. Please, don't alarm yourself."

"She will expect to see me." They all walked a tightrope, Charlotte, her sister, and their aunt.

"And she will."

When she reached him, Val drew her to his side, as if he had a right to do so.

Slowly, Hervey got to his feet. "I will take my leave. But this matter is not over." He bowed, ensuring Charlotte was the recipient. "We will speak again."

Charlotte didn't know what to say. She covered her confusion by curtsying. "My lord."

She stood in frozen silence with Val until Lord Kellett's footsteps ceased to crunch on the gravel path.

Letting out a small sigh, Val turned to Charlotte. "I swear, we're handling your chaperone. Dru will meet us here in ten minutes. She's avoided this party by hiding in the library, but I pushed her into action. As far as your aunt knows, you are walking with my sister in the garden."

That would serve their purpose well. "Thank you!" Her relief was so profound she almost fell on him, her knees giving way for a second.

He caught her elbows and held her up, turning her to face him. "When we were first betrothed, your father said you were his dearly beloved daughter, yet he treats you with scarce interest, and you are obviously in fear of him. Why would he do that?"

"You never asked me that before."

"You are usually more circumspect. I have never seen such an extreme reaction in you before."

She had thought of asking for his help in her dilemma, but he had never shown an interest. She would not go to him as a petitioner if they were to part. Her pride would not allow it. "He disowned my older sister." When her heart sank, Charlotte hid her emotion as she did every time the subject came up. "She was warned, but she went ahead with her plan."

"He has made society aware of that. Was it so hard for you?" His voice softened, became as intimate as she had ever known it.

She bit her lip. She had given away too much and he was angling for more. "I love Sarah, but I never see her. He threatens to cast me off if I behave disobediently."

"And you have a younger sister."

He was getting too close. Her natural protective instincts came to life. "She is not yet out." Nor ever likely to be, but she wouldn't tell him that. "I am the only daughter in society."

"Are you the only beloved daughter?" Her father frequently referred to her in that way. "I doubt it." She tried to smile, but it fell short. "I am cared for, most certainly." Perhaps if she weren't requesting an end to their relationship she could have said more, but as it was, she could not. The Shaws gossiped. They did not have loose tongues, but amongst themselves they chattered and exchanged information. She would not allow her family to be the subject of gossip, however circumspect. Charlotte did not know all Val's cousins, so she could not assess them all.

His voice softened. "Your father has a certain reputation for the way he runs his household. Is it worse than that?"

Immediately, without pausing to think, Charlotte shook her head. "Of course not. He is strict, but so are many parents." Her father preferred private matters to remain so.

"I wish you would tell me, my dear."

Very few people saw Val like this—compassionate, his gaze direct, and no sarcastic smile curling his lips. He made Charlotte feel privileged because he was letting her in. The family members surrounded themselves with an invisible fortress, as impregnable as any Norman castle. She'd had tantalizing glimpses of it—this large, loving family who tolerated each other's foibles and follies—and wondered what it could possibly be like.

Charlotte didn't have any follies.

She shook her head, lowering her gaze.

Val tucked a finger under her chin and gently tilted it up. "I won't ask if it distresses you."

"It's not that." Wildly she thought of an excuse. "It would feel disloyal." He would understand that.

He gave a slow nod, but he narrowed his eyes, turning perceptive. "I see."

She feared he saw more than she wanted him to. She met his gaze and let him look, to try to pierce the mask she donned every day before she left her bedroom. She swallowed, but she said no more. If she did, she might never stop.

Val smiled. Not his society smile, the one that could be supercilious or sarcastic or even devastatingly reckless, but warm and friendly. "Now, about what I interrupted. Was Kellett upsetting you?"

"No." At least she could be totally honest about that, but when she came to the point, she found words hard to find. "He wants to marry me, Val."

He raised a brow. "Did you remind him that you're spoken for?"

"I did. But, Val…you've kept me for a very long time." Releasing his hands, she moved away, pacing the small space, her skirt swishing, adding to the sounds of the birds singing joyously and that wayward bee that still couldn't find an exit. She knew how it felt.

She turned back to him, ignoring the way her skirts wrapped around her legs before unwinding themselves. Her aunt would reprimand her for her inelegance. Her father would probably order her to stand for an extra hour.

Charlotte was one of the few people who could have become a lady-in-waiting at court with no problem. Ladies-in-waiting were required to stand silently for hour after hour. She could accomplish that with no problem at all. Perhaps when the country had a queen again, she would consider asking her father to find her a position for her. After all, the King had daughters. One of those might want a lady-in-waiting.

Again she was thinking of escape. She had dreams about running, and woke up out of breath sometimes.

"Val, you don't want me, do you?"

"Charlotte."

His voice was so gentle that tears formed in her throat. She had started on her path now; she had to finish it.

"You are a delightful girl."

"I'm not a girl. I'm twenty-five." She swallowed. "Val, I want to marry soon."

What would he say to that?

She watched the expressions flit across his face. Val let out very little, but that door he'd opened for her enabled her to see in a little further than most people. That slight twitch of his eyelid and the way his eyes seemed to darken in color told her more than he probably imagined. Or perhaps he let her see. She never knew with Val.

"I had expected not to." He sighed. "But I have seen nobody I would rather marry than you."

Damned with faint praise. She tucked her hurt away, prepared to deal with it another time. "But that's the problem." She walked closer to him. "You don't want to marry anybody. There's no reason why you should."

He was a second son, and his brother was busy creating heirs for the estate with his new wife.

"Ah, but there is." He scratched a spot just above his ear. He did that when he was dealing with a tricky problem. At least he found her tricky. Maybe she should be grateful for that. "My father treated me to a lecture today," he went on. "He does that rarely, but he said that we had to set a date for this year. He pointed out that you are supposed to keep me on the straight and narrow path. The path of respectability and sober behavior. Do you think you can do that, my sweet?"

"No, I do not. But I can lend you respectability."

That was what her father told her to do. "It's no use my asking you to guide him," he'd said. "Women rule from the bedroom, and I do not imagine for one moment that you will ever develop the skills that would hold a man as wild as Lord Valentinian Shaw."

Not that she would tell Val that.

"Would you be willing to stand by while I have wild affairs, visit the worst gaming hells and clubs, and generally drag my family's name in the mud?" His mouth twisted. "Those are his words, by the way."

She swallowed. "That is why I'm asking you to release me. I can't stand to see you do those things."

"We have signed the marriage contract." The contract was the result of hours of careful negotiation.

"We could have it broken."

He shook his head slightly, regret shading his eyes. "I'm not being fair to you, am I? You should be married and a mother by now. But for the past two years, we—the family, that is—have been engaged in something—" He looked up at the dark wood ceiling, as if to gain inspiration there. "I cannot say. I would break too many confidences." He laughed harshly. "And none of this is making sense to you. No matter, it's in the past."

She was close enough for him to gather her hands in his again. His warmth enclosed her, and she melted. She always did when he touched her. However often she'd tried to suppress her reaction to him, when he touched her it started all over again.

Women were carefully chaperoned for this reason. Val Shaw—that was the reason.

"My dear, if you wish, I'll talk to my father."

She nodded, beyond words. Inside her, horror lurked when she pictured the life Val had laid out. To sit and smile while he was indulging in all kinds of debauchery. "Do you really do that? All those things?"

The corner of his mouth quirked. "Some of them."

"Then yes, talk to your father." Because if she married him under those circumstances, she would run mad. Rather than that, she'd give him up altogether. She'd waited so long, dreaming foolish dreams about domestic bliss. She couldn't bear the mistresses, gambling, and drunken behavior society credited him with. Especially the mistresses. "Do you have a mistress now?" She would have clapped her hand over her mouth, but he had both her hands in his.

"No, I do not. And before you ask, yes, I have had mistresses in the past. Why, were you considering taking the position? Because I have to tell you that you disqualify yourself."

"Why?"

"You're too well-born, too innocent, and far too pretty."

The last made her eyes widen. Pretty? Her? "You don't like your mistresses pretty?"

"They are lovely, lush, generous," he said. "Not like you."

That hurt. "I see." She tried to pull her hands away, but he held them fast. "I think I'd like to go back to the house now."

Instead, he drew her closer, so close his body heat reached her. She wore only a thin silk gown, and her arms and bosom were barely covered. She wanted to rub against him and gather more. Which, of course, she was not planning to do, but she recognized the urge.

"You don't see, my dear. Not at all. Mistresses tend to make the most of their assets. You do not." He glanced down at her fichu-covered bosom and her respectable gown, the blue one she'd worn to many events this season. The embroidery was understated and her robings were plain, folded back to display a hand-embroidered stomacher and a matching petticoat. "You are neat to a pin, but not alluring. You could be, you know." He smiled at her amazement. "Believe me, you could. You should stop powdering your hair, let us see that glory."

She scoffed. "It's brown. That's all."

"Chestnut," he insisted. "It would suit you more than that dead white."

Val wore his own dark hair, so brown it was nearly black, tied back neatly. The Emperors were setting a new fashion, yet another way they dictated to society.

She already knew that, but her maid powdered her every morning and topped it up for the evening. She didn't always wash it out at night, and the stuff itched. But her father insisted on the formality of hair powder.

"That is my concern, sir." She put up her chin.

"So it is. But you did ask. I feel you do not see yourself as I do. You could make yourself a raving beauty."

"That is utter nonsense." How could that be, when men did not exactly crowd around her? If they did, she would not have this problem.

He smiled. "I think that is the first time I've seen such spirit in you. You should cultivate it. It puts fire in your eyes. However, my sweet, I will release you if you wish it."

"Thank you." Sadness swept over her in a suffocating wave. Charlotte forced herself to breathe. After all, she had asked him, had she not?

"I ask one favor before we say goodbye. Because this will be goodbye, Charlotte. I will seek an interview with my father, and you must speak to yours. They will negotiate how best to break the contract, and then it will be over. You'll be free to marry your Lord Kellett."

She closed her eyes and swallowed. Yes, she would. "Could I ask my father first? Will you give me a few days?"

"Of course. We shall say that my behavior is too much for you to bear. That is only the truth, after all."

He saw too much, but she would not deny it. "Yes." Her stomach tied itself in knots at the thought of the ordeal that lay ahead. But she was set on the path now and she would see it through. At least she could offer a substitute husband, one who wanted to marry her immediately.

"I'll always be your friend, Charlotte. You must come to me if you ever need help."

He didn't say it, but he inferred that her brother was no use. That was not strictly true, but as yet he was too young to have any influence on their father. In time he would make a fine duke, but to rely on a man five years younger than she… No, she would not think of it.

Normally she would have said thank you, drawn her hands away, and asked him to take her into the house. Today she wanted one more thing. "I want us to part with a kiss," she said, but her voice shook on the last two words. Just once she would know what he tasted like, why women went wild for him.

He stared at her, eyes wide and dark.

"Never mind. I didn't mean it."

With a swift movement, he dragged her forward, tipping her off-balance so she fell into his arms. "Oh, yes, you did." His voice deepened to a growl as he settled her against his shoulder. "You shall have your kiss, Charlotte."

When she opened her mouth on a gasp, he brought his lips down on hers.

Charlotte had imagined adult kisses—of course she had—but this was her first. That was why she'd wanted it from Val. He knew how to kiss. He must, with the numbers of lovers he'd had.

She wasn't wrong. He brushed over her lips in a gentle caress, moving from one side to the other before settling in for a firmer touch. Unthinkingly, she reached up and curved her hand around the back of his neck. Under the crisp white neckcloth, his bare skin waited for her. Inching a little higher, she discovered the nape of his neck.

Was it her imagination, or did he shudder?

He had his hands spread over her back. Even through her shift, stays, and the heavy back pleats of her gown she felt them burning, touching her as if she belonged to him. They held her firmly, giving her the entirely erroneous impression that she was safe with him. Charlotte had never been safe from Val.

When he crushed his lips against hers, she moved closer, curving her body to press against him. Despite the many layers they both wore, their proximity made her melt. His breath was hot on her cheek, and the stubble she could not see, only feel, rasped with delicious roughness against her chin.

He touched her lips with his tongue, delicately tracing. With a little gasp, she opened. His grunt was like nothing she'd ever heard from him before, unguarded and essentially masculine.

Firm, slick wetness caressed her when he touched her tongue with his, stroking her, exploring her mouth, delicately at first and then with more firmness, taking all she offered and demanding more.

When he sucked in a breath through his nose, she realized she'd been holding hers. She followed suit, breathing through their kiss, letting him take her where he would. His moan vibrated through her mouth, and she swallowed it, hungering for more.

Was she really letting this man go? She should have hung on, demanded more, because she ached to know what came next.

* * * *

For the first time in his adult life, Val lost control. Most of his friends and acquaintances would say they'd witnessed him doing exactly that many times, but they'd be wrong. He always retained a soupçon of sense, never lost himself completely.

He'd been trying for years to do exactly that, and now he'd found delicious oblivion in the most unexpected place.

Val began the long seduction of this woman who tasted like no other. He would never get the flavor of sharp apples out of his mouth, especially when accompanied by the faint perfume of sweet lavender.

He released her with one hand and trailed his fingers up the irritatingly all-encompassing fabric of her gown in search of flesh. He found it at her neckline. A thrill went through him when he discovered soft skin, delicate wisps of hair stroking his fingers as he touched that small patch of skin. Apart from her forearms and throat, he would uncover no more bare skin until he had her unhooked and lying deliciously naked in the nest of her clothes. That became his only aim.

Val lost sight of where he was and what it would mean if someone discovered them. His sense of self-preservation melted away as if it had never been.

Her unique flavor drew him in, and her kiss took him further. She followed his lead, but when she added shy little touches of her own, triumph and joy filled him. To coax that response from her meant more than a ship filled with gold coming into port.

Predictably, his body responded with ironclad need, his cock demanding attention, pressing against her as if to find a way out of his clothes and through hers. To touch her, to feel her nakedness against his own became his only ambition. Glancing up, he assessed the possibilities of the narrow benches lining the summer house, the thoughts fleeting through his mind even as sensation swamped him.

No, the floor would be better. With their clothes to lie on, they would be comfortable and have the room to spread out.

Sheer animal want charged through him with the speed of a fire in a forest on a dry day, scorching all reason. He was no longer entirely steady, his body reacting to the strength of his desire. Fine tremors made his hands shake as he pushed his fingers into her kerchief, searching for a way of tugging the fabric clear. He hungered for her skin.

He dared not release her lips. If he did, she might utter the words "stop" or "no," and that would kill him.

Instead, he continued to kiss her. Taste and smell combined to drive him higher. As gently as he could manage, he sucked her tongue into his mouth, owning it, lavishing it with sweet caresses. Her moan told him she approved. Emboldened, he initiated a deeper, stronger kiss, one that would take them past the point where neither of them could turn back.

Footsteps crunched on the gravel.

He cursed. He would not have objected to anyone discovering him with his betrothed. Except she would not be his betrothed for much longer. He had to do her the courtesy of giving her the choice. If they were discovered in this state, their marriage would follow as fast as their parents could arrange it.

With a convulsive move, he released her and turned his back, striding to the other end of the pavilion to give her space to restore herself to rights.

Standing here, he would block anyone approaching them from seeing them. Her delicate steps echoed as she hurried in the opposite direction.

"Drusilla, there you are," he said with relief.

His sister's voice echoed around the space. "Ah, is everything well?"

"Yes," Charlotte said coolly, coming forward, "I merely wanted to chase this foolish bee out. You want him pollinating your plants, not making himself dizzy in here."

Charlotte sounded cheerful, her usual self. She had recovered remarkably quickly. As he ran his fingers over his disordered neckcloth, restoring it to some kind of order, Val wondered at that. Her facade must be very good indeed. He knew how much he'd affected her—as much as she had affected him. He'd felt her shiver under his touch, knew her passionate response was real.

He had never realized her society mask was so rigid before. He had assumed her calm demeanor was the essence of her. He should have known better. He'd detected fierce intelligence a few times before, and intelligent ladies were not in as much demand as the pretty, easier ones. He considered himself an expert at detecting falsehoods and carefully constructed personalities, but the depth of the passion he'd found in his affianced bride had completely sideswiped him.

Need clawed at him, and with a sinking feeling, he recognized the sensation. His twin would recognize it in him, too. Obsession, the force that drove him, the need to master a new situation, solve a problem.

He wanted to discover the person Charlotte was so eager to conceal. He was capable of jettisoning everything else in its favor. Only this time he could not afford to do so. He had agreed to release her to someone else.

That meant he had a fight ahead, a struggle to relinquish her and to let her move on. How could he do anything else?

Dru shot him a curious glance when he turned around, but he merely gave her an urbane smile. "Charlotte insisted we free the poor creature. I think we succeeded." He hadn't even noticed a bee. He was collected enough to offer his arm to his betrothed. For the first time since their engagement, he paid her the notice she deserved. Her hand was perfectly steady on his sleeve, and she reflected nothing but happiness at seeing Dru, where Val wished his beloved sister anywhere but here.

He might never get another opportunity to explore the fascinating enigma that was his betrothed, because she would not remain so for much longer.

Charlotte's aunt was indeed waiting. Val's mama calmly ordered another cover for dinner and treated Lady Adelaide as if she were the most honored guest in the house. Very little put his mother out, and it would take more than uneven numbers at dinner to do so.

The afternoon guests had departed. The dinner guests went through to the drawing room for the late afternoon ritual. Later they would go to the theater, and later still, attend a ball or two, which Val had decided to miss. He might change his mind about that if Charlotte was headed to one.

However, Charlotte was hardly dressed for a ball. Her gown was too plain even for her simple and unpretentious style, the neckline nowhere near low enough, although if he'd succeeded in removing the maddening kerchief, that would have been remedied.

For someone to hide all that passion from him for so long spoke of skill indeed. What had happened to her, that she felt the need to cover her true self so powerfully?

He would find out, he vowed. Even if their betrothal was at an end, he would discover more about the elusive person Charlotte had turned out to be.

Chapter 3

Standing outside her father's study, Charlotte felt her fear and accepted it. She would do her best to overcome the sheer terror that enveloped her every time she was the recipient of his entire attention. This time she had asked to see him. He'd kept her waiting two days before he'd granted her an audience.

His grace the Duke of Rochfort was acutely aware of his station and his importance and made no bones about informing everyone who might be interested of that fact. Those people included his daughters and his son. He was the same in private as he was in public, and he expected the same standard of behavior from everyone he deigned to meet. He had been brought up that way, he told them, and the experience had made him a better father, husband, and more importantly, duke.

Everything was subservient to the dukedom and its needs. They served it as if it were more important than the King, and since her father was its embodiment, they served him in the same way. His punishments were severe and his rewards nonexistent, so his children had learned to obey him without question. At least, until they cracked under the strain.

Anxiously, Charlotte checked her appearance in the spotted mirror by the door. Her linen cap covered most of her hair, except the curl she hastily shoved under it. She changed the plain linen one for a modestly lace-trimmed one when they opened the house to visitors or she went out. Her gown was of good English cloth, and her apron spotless. Ladies wore aprons as fashionable accessories, and this was no different, so fine the color of her gown was easily visible under it. But it had to be creaseless and spotless, or her father would not accept her presence. The ribbons in her hair were all ironed and tied without a fault, even though they were out of sight. Even her shoe buckles were tightened to the correct degree. The duke demanded neatness and orderliness, especially when he'd granted a personal interview.

His secretary opened the door and found her two paces away from it. He inclined his head. "You may enter, your ladyship."

Doing her best to glide, as fashion and her father dictated, Charlotte entered.

Her father looked up, a welcoming smile on his broad features. Or what passed for one, though they rarely reached his eyes. However he appeared in good heart today. While the Duke of Rochfort was overburdened with avoirdupois, he was no more generously endowed than many men in society. He kept to the full-bottomed wig of his youth, carefully powdered and neatly disposed in the correct fashion about his shoulders. He wore his blue velvet coat with silver buttons, and his waistcoat reflected the style and consequence of his position. He folded his large hands on the desk before him as Charlotte made her curtsy.

The duke's study also reflected his grandeur. Mahogany and gilt furnishings dominated the large room. The bookcases contained beautifully tooled leather-bound books that contained the business of the dukedom together with a few improving volumes of sermons and books of information about crops and farming.

The room smelled of nothing, except perhaps a faint odor of masculinity. Not the intoxicating kind she recalled from Val, but the other kind— perspiration and hair powder. The kind she was used to.

She dipped to exactly the level a duke demanded and rose without a tremor. The secretary closed the door quietly behind them but did not leave the room.

"Good morning, Father. I trust I find you well?"

"Tolerably, thank you. Have you found London to your liking?"

"Of course, your grace. I am delighted you chose to bring us with you."

"Us?" The voice was sharp.

"Myself and Louisa." She waited for the explosion, her stomach tightening.

"Ah, yes. Louisa." He rarely referred to Charlotte's younger sister. Every now and again he asked after her, but nobody was sure of his intentions toward her. In fact, that was the problem. He occasionally said he would set up a trust for her, but if she displeased him, which was often, he threatened to have her "put away." He preferred to ignore Louisa's existence, but as long as she was quiet, he was content to allow her to remain in the same house as him. "She is behaving herself?"

"Yes, Father." Not wanting her father to see the anger that sparked in her eyes, Charlotte lowered her chin.

"Look at me, girl!"

She jerked up her chin. By the time her eyes met his, they were again tranquil. She knew because she had practiced the expression before the mirror until she had it perfectly.

He gave a satisfied nod. "I am glad you came to see me this morning, for I wish to discuss your situation."

She knew better than to interrupt him.

"You are sadly lacking in womanly wiles, but even taking that into consideration, your progress with Lord Valentinian Shaw has been disappointing."

Humiliation washed through her. Her father's criticisms always hit the mark and never failed to pierce her. Even when she told herself she did not care what he thought, he could always find a way to hurt her.

She had tried to develop womanly wiles, but not knowing what they were held her back. When she tried to flourish a fan, she merely appeared foolish, and if she tried to engage a man in witty conversation, he would invariably wander away.

The servants reported her movements to her loving father, if he was not near. And Charlotte ended by hating herself.

"Lord Valentinian has been perfectly content with our arrangement, sir—your grace."

"Humph! So he should be. Not every second son snags a duke's daughter."

He did not mention Charlotte's character or appearance. Of course he did not, because her only claim to attractiveness was her status in society.

Rochfort stared at Charlotte for a full minute. She knew better than to break the silence.

Eventually, he nodded to Mr. Webb, who went to the sideboard and poured the duke a glass of burgundy, which did not help his gout. The last physician to suggest he change the frequency and even the type of preferred refreshment had left the house in disgrace, despite his long service to the family. His present medical attendant agreed with everything he did.

The duke took a long sip from his glass, never taking his eyes from his daughter. Used as she was to this treatment, Charlotte nevertheless felt her skin crawl. He could be perfectly civil, or he could roar her faults for the entire house to hear. It depended on his mood.

"Our original agreement with the Marquess of Strenshall was that you should keep his lordship's excesses in check. You have been singularly ineffective in doing so. Do you have any explanation for this?"

The question put her in a dilemma. She could find shelter in craven excuses, passing the blame on to anyone else rather than herself, but

Charlotte refused to do that. "Lord Valentinian is not ready to set a date for the wedding."

"That is entirely your fault, madam!" He jabbed the table with his forefinger. "Lord Valentinian is a wild youth, but a real woman would bring him around her finger. Such men are easy to contain, if a woman exerts herself."

Charlotte didn't have a clue what he meant. He could not intend that she seduce Val, surely? Why would he want that?

Because he wanted the influence the Emperors of London could bring him, of course. To the duke, Val's family were mere pawns in his quest for power. Since the death of the Prime Minister, Lord Pelham-Holles, brother of the vastly wealthy Duke of Newcastle, politics had been in turmoil. Men were fighting for the right to be cock of the heap. Some would win for a time, only to have another cast him down. The factions were vicious, at each other's throats.

The duke expected his womenfolk to take little interest in public matters, but of course they did. They did not discuss it, though. He did, however, expect them to miraculously assimilate his opinions and repeat them when necessary. For the most part, they did so. Life was simpler that way. His political opinions were carefully moderate, so they were safe enough to repeat.

He would tell them what to think, which he did frequently.

"Father, I have done my best," she said, judging it the best thing she could say, under the circumstances. However, instead of promising him to do better, she broached the subject she had come for. "However, I feel it proper to inform you that another gentleman has approached me."

"In what way?" His words were sharp, barked out loudly.

Charlotte could not refrain from jumping, startled by the sudden change in tone. But it was a reflex action only. She would remain on course. "In a perfectly honorable way, your grace, and of course I informed him that I was contracted to marry another. He suggested that I approach you, and if I did not, he said he would do it himself. The gentleman has spoken to you, he says."

"And the name of this man?" This time his words were quiet, far too much for comfort.

She met his gaze. His pale blue eyes narrowed in speculation.

"Viscount Kellett." She lowered her gaze, but kept her attention on him. Charlotte had become adept at that trick, her humility only surpassed by her watchfulness. "He approached me at Lady Strenshall's the other day and declared his interest when we took a walk in the garden."

Silence. Her father finished his wine, his slurp echoing off the walls. The stamped leather coverings and the big painting of the family seat, with her father prominently in the foreground gesturing grandly at his mausoleum of a country house, had different sounds. Even if she weren't looking at him, Charlotte knew where her father was in the room. He could be quiet sometimes, just before the blow. Her father was not a believer in sparing the rod.

"You did not encourage him improperly?"

"No, Father. I swear I did not. I was but polite to him."

"Humph. At least I won't hear that you are a shameless hussy, flirting with every man you meet. Did anyone notice?"

She shook her head and dared to lift her chin. "No, Father. His proposal shocked and unnerved me, but I thought I should tell you of it. I spoke to Lord Valentinian later that day, and he says that he will wait for you to speak to him. His brother suspects him of using me to hold other ladies off. I heard him say so later that evening when he believed I was not by."

"I told you never to speak to Lord Darius," her father said softly.

"I have not sought him out," she said. "But he is my betrothed's twin, and I cannot ignore him without raising the anger of his family." Her knees shook, but she remained steady, willing her tremors to cease.

Her father had spent hours animadverting on the will of society to allow such blatant behavior as that shown by Lord Darius. He had sworn to put evidence before the courts.

Lord Darius was a sinner, a twisted example of mankind. He had offended the laws of God and man, and he would be punished in this world and the next. For Val's twin preferred men to women for bed sport.

When she had learned Darius's secret, Charlotte had been afraid of him, but soon learned otherwise, especially when her father ranted and raved about him. Anyone her father held in that kind of regard could not be all bad. Darius was far more discreet than his twin, and if someone had not told her, Charlotte would not have known at all.

So while Val gallivanted around London bedding actresses and women of the night, sometimes two or more at once, getting drunk on a regular basis and losing thousands at the gaming tables, his brother was the real villain, according to Charlotte's father.

Charlotte liked Darius. He was steadier than his brother, for one thing. If he did have a lover, he kept the man very secret. His discretion knew no bounds. Of course, if he were caught in delicto, he could receive the death penalty, though few would dare to challenge the Emperors in court.

She had placed her reference to Darius's family carefully.

Her father gave a dignified nod, his jowls creasing under his chin. "I fear the family is too rackety. If they continue in this fashion, they will not hold their position of superiority much longer."

That was the nearest he ever came to telling her she was right. Charlotte took what she could get where her father was concerned. Too wise to interrupt, she waited for him.

"I will certainly look into Lord Kellett's suitability. I have met the man a time or two." He averted his gaze, staring at a stack of papers as if gaining inspiration there. "He is a peer in his own right, something Lord Valentinian will never be. He is wealthy, too, and not without influence." He looked up, his expression steady. "Very well. Do nothing unless I instruct you to do so. You may leave."

Every time he interviewed her, the duke dismissed her like a servant. It hurt every time. Charlotte once supposed she would get used to it. After all, what was that in the face of all the other humiliations she accepted every day?

"Sir, I have another matter," she ventured.

"Well, girl, what is it? I don't have all day!"

"My sister. Will she be allowed to attend a few parties this season?"

He sighed. "No. Do not bring the matter up again. The answer will be the same."

She dropped a curtsy. "Thank you, your grace."

She left, taking the main corridor to the music room and then slipping through the job door to take the shortcut to her own bedroom.

The only way to survive her father was to agree with what he said and obey him. Every time she did so, Charlotte hated herself for not having the courage to stand up to him, but there was no other way. Her father punished his children for every small transgression, and he did it in a singular way, one designed to evoke the greatest amount of pain. Charlotte kept her inner-core well hidden. When she escaped her father's influence, she would break free. She'd always promised herself that.

That was why her marriage was so important. She had to marry someone who could resist her father. Val had been ideal. His rackety ways were not, but she had not cared until her attraction to him veered out of her control. It had taken her by surprise, her inability to control her response to him. Before yesterday's kiss, she might have had a chance of letting her love for him fade, but with that shocking, unexpectedly passionate embrace, he'd snared her.

She would be in thrall to a man who moved from woman to woman like that blasted bee in the pavilion had buzzed around looking for an escape.

He would hurt her unimaginably if she were forced to witness that, loving him but unable to keep him. She would have to wear her thick armor until the day she died, and she wanted free of it. Her feelings for Lord Kellett were much more controllable.

Reaching her room, Charlotte crossed to the window and gazed down at the passersby. Even here, in her own room, she had no privacy. The maids reported to her father, and they wouldn't hesitate to tell him if they found anything they considered she would not have. Hunter, her own maid, dressed her according to her father's wishes.

Charlotte had a secret longing for outrageous fabrics and laces, to wear the height of fashion. That would never happen. Opening her clothespress, she eyed the safe colors and modest garments. And sighed.

When would her rebellion come? How could she escape this trap? Her brother had managed it by going abroad. She felt sure he had driven their father to agree to his Grand Tour by behaving in a way he did not wish her to. Women did not go on trips abroad. They remained as helpmeets and obedient daughters.

As she stared at the depressing clothes, an idea sparked in her head. She had no notion where it had come from.

She had pin money saved. The least she could do was own something outrageous. If she concealed it and perhaps wore a piece here and a piece there, she could get away with it. She would have something she had chosen herself, something she could look at and, perhaps, if her father found Lord Kellett acceptable, wear at her wedding.

She rang her bell.

Chapter 4

The following Tuesday, Charlotte, her aunt, and her maid visited the mantua-maker. Usually her aunt arranged that they came to her home, but Charlotte insisted on the visit, saying she would appreciate taking the air in Green Park afterward.

She dropped the hint carelessly, knowing her aunt would take her up on it. Aunt Adelaide was sweet on a gentleman from Hampshire who was presently visiting London. Charlotte's suggestion that they visit the park was tantamount to giving Aunt Adelaide permission to discreetly let him know where she would be.

That was the first part of her plan.

The mantua-maker was probably the stuffiest in town, but she had served the late queen, and Charlotte's father, cognizant of his consequence, insisted on his daughter using her. But Miss Wilson's establishment was in Bond Street, close to many others, including drapers' shops.

For once, Charlotte would do what she wanted. She would not wait for the menfolk to make up their minds to allow her to do something. This was her time and her day. Even if she only had one day in her life where she did as she wished, she would have it and take the consequences.

Whatever they were.

When they arrived at the bottom of Bond Street, Sir Lucas Shapcott was loitering outside, as if browsing and passing the time of day. Charlotte had discreetly encouraged the burgeoning but promising romance between the pair. Her father's sister was as intimidated by him as everyone else, but the moment Sir Lucas had seen her, he had made a play for her. Rejections turned to gentle conversation and a tentative friendship, so knowing she needed a distraction today, Charlotte had conveyed a discreet note to him, informing him where they would be. Taking a walk in the park, she'd found a boy who, for a shilling, had taken her note. She was glad to see the baronet. For all she knew, the boy could have taken the money and dropped the note in the nearest gutter. But all was well.

As the carriage stopped, he glanced at the shield on the door and then took a closer look before smiling broadly and striding forward. Charlotte sucked in a breath and then carefully controlled the way she breathed out, lest her aunt notice.

That was the first part of her plan. Charlotte was not adept at such complex devices, but she had worked out every step, carefully planned it. An element of risk remained. Risk made Charlotte nervous. She had five guineas in her pocket to bribe her maid with, but Aunt Adelaide needed a bit more managing.

After a deal of chitchat, Charlotte brought up the topic she wanted to address, praying Sir Lucas took her carefully dangled bait. "I wished to go to Green Park when we had finished at the mantua-maker's. It is such a fine day, do you not think?"

"It is a very fine day. I would be happy to accompany you," Sir Lucas said promptly.

He would be an excellent match for Aunt Adelaide. Sir Lucas was a widower with grown children who no longer demanded his time. All he required in a wife was companionship. He was tall and a little on the portly side, but he could chivvy Aunt Adelaide out of one of her melancholy moods. Charlotte rather liked the idea of playing matchmaker. "You could go now. My maid is with me, and if I go directly into the shop, we may walk up to meet you afterwards. Nobody would object to that." Green Park lay very close to the shop. She flicked out her fan and plied it vigorously. "The day is warm, and likely to grow hotter. The fresh air will do you good, Aunt Adelaide."

And her aunt would not be there to report what Charlotte did to her father. Because Charlotte was about to misbehave.

Charlotte reminded her aunt of the headache she had woken with that morning and how tonight would be a very long one, with the opera and two balls afterward. At the end of ten minutes, they had finally persuaded Aunt Adelaide to allow Sir Lucas to take her to the park.

As Charlotte watched her aunt go off with her beau, triumph curled through her. She had done it. Small deceptions apart, Charlotte was a good and obedient daughter, but the effort was killing her. She needed these victories to remain sane and healthy.

Turning, she very nearly cannoned into a broad silk brocade-clad chest, the gold threads dazzling her in the bright sunshine. Only his hands on her forearms prevented her from doing so. Her heart pounded as she looked up into the face she knew she'd find. "Lord Valentinian!" Already she knew his touch.

He stepped back and swept a low bow. When he rose, he was smiling. "My dear Lady Charlotte! You are well?"

No breathlessness or surprise covered his features, but for a bare second, she had let her mask fall. She knew it, and knew he had seen it. No matter. Val would not let her down and gossip, even if he had noticed her discomfiture. "Perfectly, thank you, sir. I am going to the mantua-maker's."

He glanced around and pulled a face. "Not this one, surely? Miss Wilson caters for the…more mature lady, does she not?"

"She served my mother, and now she serves me." She let him see her opinion on that, pulling down her mouth and giving an infinitesimal shrug.

He laughed. "If you will permit, I can show you the establishment my sisters frequent. It is but a few doors away."

She frowned, shooting a glance at the shop she'd selected. The windows held drapes of fabric, and a few people had quoted it as their dressmaker. "I was going there…" She waved a hand.

"An excellent choice, but my sisters use Cerisot."

A gasp escaped her. Why did this man always take her off guard? "But she doesn't take everybody. She has a careful selection of clients. Last month, she turned away a duchess!" And she was expensive. Although Charlotte had been hoarding her pin money, she doubted she could afford Cerisot.

"Of course you can visit her." He leaned forward. "You will soon be a Shaw. We have discounts."

The low voice, his breath against her cheek vividly brought back their encounter in the garden. The scent of roses, heady and seductive, swam into her senses, and she sucked in a gust of air.

He retreated. He appeared perfectly normal except for the darkening of his eyes.

"Then I would be honored." Still breathing a trifle too quickly, she let him guide her to the shop while her maid scurried behind them. When Charlotte glanced behind, she smiled sweetly. Hunter glared back.

"I will take the blame," Val said calmly. "Have the bill sent to me."

"No indeed! I will pay!"

To her relief, he didn't argue. "Then I will send it to you, if you wish. That isn't the point. If I choose to present you with a gift, I am perfectly entitled to do so, in the eyes of your father. We are still betrothed, my dear."

Yes, they were. She bit her lip. "I spoke to my father."

"Then I will speak to mine." His voice had gained distance. "I didn't wish to anticipate you. It will be you who cries off. Don't worry. I will contrive to create a scandal your father cannot bear to accept." He laughed, but it sounded forced to Charlotte's ears. "I wonder what it should be? Perhaps I should consult you. What would annoy your father most?"

"Shh!" She jerked her head to indicate Hunter.

His gaze turned sharp. "She spies on you? But she is your maid."

"I know." She gave that infinitesimal shrug again, knowing he would notice and understand.

A few lengths of fabric decorated the window of Cerisot's establishment. The materials were so beautifully exquisite they did not need abundance to make their point.

He opened the door for her and stood aside. "If I never get to wear what I buy today, I will still die happy," she said, breathing the words so quietly she was almost sure nobody heard.

He came in behind her and leaned close. "You will wear it."

Charlotte shuddered at his proximity, reminded of their kiss. "You cannot promise that."

He said nothing, but he might as well have said, "Yes I can," because she heard the words deep in her mind. In the most private place of all where nobody penetrated.

The proprietress herself glided forward to greet them. "My lord." She swept Charlotte up and down with an all-encompassing glance. "At last you bring us your betrothed. I have been waiting for the day." She spoke as if people were not lining up for her services. She didn't wait to ask what they wanted, as any other mantua-maker would have done.

Her French accent came and went, as if she had to remember to apply it, but Charlotte found it delightful. In any case, she wouldn't dare upset the lady. She smoothed her hands down her skirts, suddenly nervous about her appearance.

"If you will come this way, I can assure you a private space to discuss your needs."

She led the way to a private room. Inside a graceful sofa awaited, and a long table with several large books resting on it, as well as a gleaming mahogany tantalus containing a set of three cut-glass bottles filled to the brim.

"Burgundy, my lord?"

"Claret, if you please," Val said. "The day is too warm for burgundy."

"Of course." She poured for Val and Charlotte, her movements neat and precise. She was a small woman, but gave the impression of being taller, as her posture was ramrod-straight. Then she gave Hunter a considering study before turning back to Val. "You may leave, my lord. Return in an hour, if you please."

Val took the wine with a murmured word of thanks. "Oh, no, you don't. I will stay. My betrothed needs my advice."

Cerisot glided to the table, as if she were rolling on wheels. If it weren't for the above-the-ground day gown that gave a glimpse of her delicate blue silk shoes, Charlotte wouldn't have believed she had feet at all. She opened the first volume, grunted, and closed it again. She picked up the second as if it weighed nothing and brought it to the smaller table next to the sofa. "If your ladyship will care to give this your attention, I will show you the colors I consider best for you."

The book contained samples of fabrics. Charlotte caught her breath and reached out to touch a printed blue silk. "That is lovely."

"But not quite your blue, my lady. Here." She flipped half a dozen pages and touched a square at the top. "I would make you a robe francaise of this, with a petticoat of ivory."

For the next hour, Charlotte lost herself in a world of wonderful fabrics and designs.

Val interrupted occasionally, pointing out thread and lace he wanted her to have.

Only when her pocket watch chimed did Charlotte recall herself. She sprang to her feet. "I must go. I'm so sorry, but my aunt is expecting me."

Val rose and nodded to the dressmaker. "We are deeply indebted for your time. How long will the gown take?"

"Do you have an event in mind?"

Charlotte shook her head. "The season is filled with events. I do not have a spare evening until the end of June."

"A week," Val said firmly. "Send the gown to Lady Engles's London address and the usual arrangement for the accounting."

"It is my pleasure, my lord."

Her head spinning, and not from the two glasses of claret she had consumed, Charlotte left the shop.

Val accompanied her to Green Park, a tight-lipped Hunter scuttling behind them like some kind of big beetle. When Val made that comment to Charlotte, she barely suppressed her snort of laughter. "You are bad for my self-control, sir."

"Then I am a success at something in life," he said. "I will not leave a completely barren legacy behind me."

She disliked that. "You are clever, handsome, witty…" She trailed off when she saw his broad grin. "You were joking." Misery crept sluggishly through her veins. "I'm sorry. I cannot always see jokes."

"You have not had the practice." He guided her through the gates.

Of all the parks, Charlotte liked Green Park best. St. James's had a beautiful waterway, where ducks and wildlife gathered, but Green Park was unpretentious. Especially with the small herd of cows kept there for people to buy a glass of milk straight from the animal. Business flourished, especially in the summer months. Charlotte twitched her hat to shade her face from the sun and searched for her aunt. "There she is."

"With Sir Lucas Shapcott, I see," Val said. He slowed his pace and turned his head to glare at Hunter. "Keep your distance."

Hunter's nostrils flared. Nobody spoke to her like that. Charlotte had another moment of triumph. She would miss Val.

"Thank you for today. I intended to make the purchase myself, even if my father sent the gown back, which he probably would have done once he saw it."

"Then don't let him see it until you wear it. Until it's too late for him to change his mind."

Her laugh rang around the park, and her aunt looked up. They were too far away for Charlotte to see her face, but not the way she was eagerly turning to her escort.

"You do not know my father," she said bitterly to Val. "His word is law. He would slice the gown off me if I tried such a trick."

"It's not a trick. It is your choice to dress as you wish. What is wrong with what you have chosen?"

It was good of him to say her choice, but he'd had as much say as she, only because she had little experience at such matters. Choosing her own clothes was exciting but daunting. The difference was Val had ensured she was happy before she made the choice. She'd have ordered half a dozen and hang the expense, if she'd dared. That would have put her in hock for years, but she didn't care.

Most of her larger bills went directly to her father. Consequently, her pin money did not amount to much. She had enough to buy stockings, gloves, shifts, and other necessities. The jewelry she had was mainly from the family vault and consequently old-fashioned, far too grand for most purposes these days.

"It is extravagant," she said to Val, recalling her father's strictures on other ladies. He would go home and dissect them all, before he turned on Charlotte and picked her appearance apart. "He will say that it is not a practical fabric, and it will have to be cleaned far too often. It is too fashionable and it will have to be remade next season. The fabric will not date well. It is far too extreme. It is too tight, the lace too fine."

Val held up his hand. "Stop! I see his reasoning and condemn it all. You must not tell him I said that, if you please. However, I do not scruple to tell you that your father is far too much the great lord. He is a duke, it is true, but he must relax sometimes, surely."

A year ago, Charlotte would not have noticed Val's agitation, but now she did. His blue eyes sparked, and fine lines appeared at the corners of his mouth. Even her recounting of her father's less harsh behavior had driven him to that. She did not dare tell him of the rest.

"Not that I have seen." She bit her tongue before she told him how much time her father expected her to lavish on him. She would be back on duty when she returned home, attending him during fashionable visiting hours. Some thought him a doting father because he insisted on being such an important part of his daughters' lives. Charlotte knew better.

Her shiver made him draw her closer. "What is wrong?"

"Nothing. A chill, that is all. I am perfectly well, sir."

This man was far too perceptive. He had never been so before, had left her to her own devices during their long betrothal. What had raised his curiosity now?

The kiss. That kiss had opened her up. One touch of his lips had turned her into a wanton, someone she hardly recognized, except that the person who had responded so fervently to his embrace had been buried deep inside her. He'd woken her.

She would not wear the gown. She would send it back to Val unworn. That would appease her father and perhaps persuade him to expedite discussions with Val's father to sever their connection.

So why did her heart sink at a prospect she wanted so much?

The bright day and the pleasure of her trip out melted away in the face of her unexpected sense of devastation at the prospect of losing him. She could not let herself grow even fonder of him than she had already. The disgraceful scion of a great house would go on his merry way and never realize how much letting him go had cost her.

She would make sure of it.

Chapter 5

Val strolled down the stairs at the family's London house, glancing in the pier glass as he passed to ensure his neckcloth was neatly arranged.

Pausing, he looked at the small portrait of Charles the Second hung on the wall halfway down. He touched two fingers to his forehead in a mock salute. The old roué was rumored to have fathered the Third Marquess, although he never formally acknowledged it. He probably didn't want to upset the Second Marquess, who was not an even-tempered man.

Unlike Val's own father. The current Marquess, the fifth, was a much-loved father, with what Val would term a measured temper. He could usually control it, although Val wasn't sure how he'd take his current news.

Having ascertained from the footman in the hall that his father was in his office, Val tapped at the door. The impatient "Come!" didn't sound promising, but he went in all the same. He had promises to keep.

The leather-and-brandy smell greeted him the way it always did. The room hadn't changed in his lifetime. A worn oak desk, glass-fronted bookshelves warped with age, filled with a mixture of well-thumbed books and estate folders and account books crammed the modest space. The rug on the floor was a worn example, ejected from another room a long time ago and now threadbare where his father's feet had come into constant contact with it.

The scratched leather top of the desk was evidence of his father's industry, with oak boxes filled with papers and folders. Amongst them, he knew, was one labeled "Lord Valentinian Shaw." It contained details of his inheritance and his marriage contract. Val did not rely on his expectations from the estate. He had made his own provisions for his future.

His bow was met with an impatient wave of his father's hand. "Sit. It isn't as if I didn't see you at breakfast. Your brother sends his regards. He's blissfully happy. They are anticipating a happy event early next year." He waved a letter. That must be from Val's older brother, currently resident at the country estate with his beloved wife. They had visited London for all of two weeks at the start of the season and then left for home. People designated Marcus as "the quiet one," but they didn't really know him. Very few people did, but Val was one of them. So was his father.

"I'm glad."

"Even more so because now you are under far less pressure to marry, eh?"

Reluctantly, Val nodded. "They will produce a brood of children, I'm sure of it, sir." The argument would no doubt help him. "In fact, that is what I wanted to discuss with you."

The marquess put his pen back in the stand and leaned back in the comfortable though worn chair he'd used ever since Val could remember. Val dragged a green plush upholstered chair over from where it stood against the wall and sat.

He leaned his elbows on his knees and clasped his hands. He got straight to the point. "Lady Charlotte wishes to be released from our contract." Nothing like getting the matter out in the open.

His father was just as direct. "Why?"

"She has found someone else she prefers." He hated even saying the words.

The marquess barked a laugh. "Ha! What, your much-vaunted charm and address failed you?" The marquess's smile melted away. "I cannot pretend surprise. Your manner will succeed only with those who look for amusement and a little distraction. Lady Charlotte is a woman of intelligence. She wishes for more than amusement in a husband." He grimaced. "You know she is in love with you, do you not?"

Shocked, Val raised his head. "When we first met she was infatuated with me, but that is all. She wanted to love her husband, and I am, sir, at the very least, lovable. I ensured she was disabused of that. It would not be fair to allow her to continue in her illusion."

"If she was infatuated with you, surely that was her choice?"

"I was her knight riding in on a charger to rescue her," he said dryly. "You would be the first person to contradict that I am anything of the kind."

His father regarded him steadily. "I have my doubts," he said. "I have sometimes suspected your scandals are much less than people suppose. Of late I have noticed signs that you are settling."

"Papa, I cannot settle. You know it. I've been that way since I was a child. I have grieved my mother. She's said so any number of times." The problem had troubled him until he worked out the solution—never to stay too long in one place.

"Most children cannot settle. They grow out of it. I have no reason to believe that you are not the same."

Val knew better. His restlessness consumed him, except when he was involved in a new project. Then he could engross himself completely until the next bright idea came along. "I do not think I will ever grow out of it, Father, but I have learned to live with it. However, it would be unfair to subject to someone as constant as Lady Charlotte to my pets."

"Have you not noticed your change in mood recently?" his father asked.

The question sounded casual, almost careless, but, aware of his father's perceptiveness, Val was on his guard. He had no idea what his father meant. "I cannot see any change," he said.

"Sometimes the person closest doesn't notice." The marquess flicked back his lace cuffs and reached for his pen but did not dip it in the inkwell. Instead, he toyed with the slim quill, spinning it between his hands in a way that used to fascinate Val when he was a boy. "Recently your concentration on certain projects has lengthened. Your involvement with your cousins in a little family problem never wavered." He looked up, one eyebrow arched in query.

Val had enjoyed the "little family problem." Very few families had a problem like theirs. "I had to see it through to the finish."

"Is it finished?"

Val straightened up and leaned back in his chair, assuming his customary pose, one leg crossed negligently over the other at the knee. "We believe it has finished, yes. We may never be perfectly sure, but it seems reasonable to assume so."

His father was right, in one way. He had not noticed the length of time the project had taken. His venture with his brother was taking even longer. In fact he was attending a meeting after this uncomfortable interview with his father. Had his affliction really left him, or had he learned to cope with it? He could never imagine living in the country, devoting himself to one woman, as his brother had. Marcus was cut of entirely different cloth; steady and true, he rarely deviated from his path. Val, on the other hand, was constantly distracted by the new, especially if he had never encountered before. It would not be fair to subject Charlotte to his variable moods.

However that would never happen. Charlotte had decided she was done with him, and so the matter was at an end. "To be honest, Papa, she deserves better. In a few years, I will want to move on to another love, to another mistress, and I will tear her heart out. She is constant and true."

His father took his time, playing with the quill, a frown furrowing his brow. Then he looked up, in his eyes sharply perceptive. "You do not do yourself justice, my son. You are intelligent, far more than is comfortable, and I believe that more than half of your problem is boredom. You will find constancy when you need it. But you're past the first flush of youth."

Val smiled wryly. "If you are about to say that I will grow out of it, I doubt that very much. I do not think I'm any more intelligent than most of the people I know. Darius has a quick mind, for example, and can easily beat me in certain areas."

"Darius is another such. He has his own problems and his own way of solving them. It grieves me that he has chosen this path, but I will not cease to call him my son."

That was why they all loved their father so much. While he did not understand Darius's problem, as he put it, he continued to stand by his son. Darius did not regard his preferences in bed partner as a problem, except that he was dancing with the law. Their father would never understand that, but it did not matter. He loved Darius as much as he loved his other children. Some would call him easygoing, but not the people who knew him best.

"Nevertheless," his father continued, "you have an exceptional intelligence. You pick up concepts that most people, including myself, labor long and hard over before we understand. Perhaps that is a gift you have to pay for."

Val did not want to admit how much his father's words touched him. He cleared his throat. "Thank you, sir. I will try to justify your faith in me. But the topic remains. Charlotte wishes to accept the addresses of another man. I cannot in all conscience prevent her."

"Who is this man?"

"Lord Kellett."

His father shrugged. "I'm not sure I know him."

"He is a viscount, wealthy and devoted to Charlotte. I have every expectation of him making her an excellent husband. He has intimated to her that if she were free he would make her an honest offer."

"And he has a peerage in his own right. Does that concern you at all, that you will not have one?"

Val could tell the truth about that. "Not in the least. I'm making my own way and enjoying it. I will never stop being a Shaw. That in itself will assure people I do business with. Can you imagine me in Marcus's position?" He laughed. "I would be even more trouble to you."

His father did not repress his shudder. "I have to admit that is not a prospect I regard with any enthusiasm."

"The peerage will no doubt have an effect when Charlotte discusses the matter with her father. I have to request that you begin negotiations to dissolve the contract between us."

The marquess shook his head. "I will not be the one beginning the discussions. Let the man come to me. He owns a neat little parcel of land near our estates in Yorkshire. That will prove an interesting negotiation point."

Val should have expected his father to be on point. He nodded. "I see your reasoning, but for Charlotte's sake, do not prolong the discussions, please."

"For her sake, I might do so. But for the sake of my son, a little delay is to be expected." The marquess leaned forward, resting his elbows on his desk, threatening to topple a pile of roughly stacked paper. "Think about this action, Val. I want to see you happy, as your older brother is. With Charlotte you seem happier and more settled than I have ever seen you before."

"Nobody else has seen that," Val said dryly. "Perhaps it is a figment of your imagination." But even as he assumed his air of world-weariness, he knew he had lost that particular battle.

Indeed his father had noticed more than he had. Only when the notion of losing Charlotte had arisen had he realized that he didn't want to lose her. But it was too late now, and in any case, it was all for the best. She would not withstand life with him. Few people did.

With his father apprised of the situation and his duty done, Val excused himself and made his way to his next appointment.

He did not have to go far.

Upstairs, the sound of men's voices punctuated by laughter came from the direction of the library. After straightening his coat, Val flung open the door and joined the fray.

The large table in the center of the room contained files and papers similar in appearance to the ones on his father's desk. However these belonged to him and the other two men sitting at the table.

They looked up at his entrance. "About time." Darius ostentatiously consulted his watch, flipped the lid closed, and dropped it back in his waistcoat pocket.

Darius's salmon pink velvet coat, heavily embroidered and laced with gold, hung on a peg by the door. Feeling the warmth of the day, Val removed his own of more sober dark green, with a more acceptable level of decoration, and hung it next to his brother's extravagant confection.

He tapped it with a disparaging finger. "That is hideous. Whatever made you order such a disaster?"

His twin grinned. Darius's grin was entirely his own, crooked up on the right side, giving him the impression of a demented elf. "I heard old Lord Simpson declare that one could not tell ordinary men from the perverted kind by the clothes they wore. I will show him differently when I go to White's later today."

Val groaned and clapped his hand to his heart in a mock groan. In reality he wanted to hunt Lord Simpson down and give him a pummeling he would never forget, but he had long since learned to control his protective instincts toward his brother. Darius could fight his own battles, and he would not appreciate offers of sympathy. He dealt with his detractors in his own way. "That must have cost you a pretty penny."

"We can afford it." Darius tapped the paper in front of him. He glanced at the man sitting next to him, their cousin Ivan Rowley, the third man in the venture.

Ivan, a man of forbidding appearance with thick dark brows and black hair to match, proved that he could smile as broadly as any other man. "We are well on the way to riches beyond the dreams of avarice, if we haven't reached that point already."

Casting aside his problems, Val took a seat and pulled the nearest paper toward him. "So where are we?"

"Two ships at sea, two due in port any day, and a collection of new ventures," Darius said. He flicked through the accounts book. "Word is getting around and we've received a few requests." He glanced up at Val, his brows arched. "You've been busy, brother."

Leaning back, Val smiled like a cat who'd stolen a whole pitcher of cream. "The venture is more fascinating than mere gambling. A card game is limited, which is its interest, but I have never played a game so changeable. Card games were the training for this."

Darius nodded. "They certainly were." Val haunted the fashionable areas, listening to rumors and speculation, adding his own mite. Darius had access to places the other two did not, but they made up for it in other ways. Ivan took the coffeehouses and clubs, where men spoke of serious business matters. Their tiny office in the City was his domain for the most part.

For the last two years, the three men had worked together in the terrifyingly volatile world of insurance. Shipping insurance was a growing field, and the three men had access to areas others did not. They'd used it. Val had entered it, fascinated by the numbers. The calculations that had kept him engrossed when he gambled proved even more fascinating here because there were so many more variables and the imponderables to deal with. Then he got into portfolio management, where they could insure a safe cargo at a low rate and increase it for a riskier cargo. They were investing in the cargoes from time to time, too. "We should ask for a percentage of the profits instead of a flat rate." Val tapped the accounts.

"That would mean we'd have to trust the company. Perhaps we'll take a look at their books," Ivan said.

Val nodded. "True enough, but if you keep your eyes peeled, you'll identify the right ones." He shrugged. "It was just a thought. We could scrape a few margins that way."

Darius pushed a sheet toward Val. "Here's the current situation."

Val whistled through his teeth when he saw the bottom line. A carefully scripted set of figures showed the potential profit of current ventures. "It's just as well we drew up articles of association last year. This is more than we planned."

The venture had been a sideline, a lark when they'd begun it, but now it meant much more than that for all three of them.

In fact, the two years he'd devoted to the project had not yet bored Val and showed no signs of doing so. That was because the minute he'd solved one problem, another emerged to take its place, so it was a series of linked but different problems. He traced a line of calculations down with one finger, not because it needed checking, but because his reckoning on that piece of work had given him great pleasure.

"Here." Darius pushed another paper across. "Sign. You've already read this one," he added, and presented a pen, already loaded with ink.

"I hate this part." Val had recognized the contract the moment his brother had presented it, but signing was always a trial to him. "All those promises."

Darius tipped a brow at Ivan, who chuckled. "Which is why you don't make many."

Val shook his head and scrawled his signature before he could change his mind. "That's because I always keep my promises. I never agree to something I cannot fulfill." Not many people knew that, and Val preferred it that way. His word was truly his bond.

Ivan signed next. "I can do this now because my brother is in the country happily making babies with his lovely wife." Thrusting his hands in his pockets, he took a turn around the room. "I can't tell you how much that has taken from me. I can be more than the spare heir. I can make my own life."

Val grunted. "Marcus is much the same, but our father still insists on matchmaking."

"Ah, but you have the lovely Charlotte," Ivan said after a considering glance at Darius, who would most likely remain a "committed bachelor," as society often referred to him.

"Not for much longer." Sighing, Val tucked his hands behind his head and stretched. "I've just had an interview with Papa. The lovely Charlotte has asked me to release her."

Darius snorted. "I'm not surprised, I have to say. You've kept her hanging far too long."

"That does not evoke pleasant thoughts," Val commented. "The arrangement suited both of us. It meant our father ceased to harangue me about finding a wife who would, as he charmingly put it, 'settle me down,' and Charlotte had someone to keep the hordes away."

"I saw no hordes," Ivan commented. "She is one of those women invited to make up numbers or because of her standing."

Val's hackles bristled. "She's charming."

"Indeed, you should say that, brother, and it speaks well for your loyalty. But she is hardly the kind of dashing wit you are usually drawn to. Her sensible clothes, the way she has of ducking her head when she speaks, or addressing you in a monotone can hardly be considered fetching."

Val glared at his brother. "She would be lovely, given the chance. That is none of her doing. Her father is nothing short of a tyrant."

Ivan snorted. "He is proud, for sure, and insists on the kind of old-fashioned manners more suitable for our grandparents, but tyrannical? I have never heard that."

"And yet he disowned his oldest daughter," Val pointed out. He propped his feet on the edge of the table. "Would our father do that?"

Darius frowned. "Not even if she eloped with a highwayman. True, he'd give them hell and probably try to have the marriage annulled, but he'd never cast Livia or Dru off."

If anyone had reason to know that, Darius did. He had confessed his proclivities one unforgettable day when the twins had returned from their Grand Tour. Their father, perfectly calm, had told him that if he created any scandals, he would ban Darius to the country. So Val had created the scandals for him, and Darius had quietly gone about his business.

Val couldn't pretend that he'd not enjoyed himself, setting society on its ear, but he sensed that game was coming to an end. Neither he nor his brother needed it anymore. They were moving on. The prospect excited him. Except that he would have to find something else to do.

Without Charlotte. That potentiality depressed him more than anything else. He would have to watch someone else nurturing her. The day at the dressmaker's filled him with satisfaction and amusement. He would see her in that gown if he had any say in the matter. Her pure delight had charmed him, and now he was giving her the attention that she so clearly deserved he was beginning to understand what a treasure he had cast away with his thoughtlessness.

"Charlotte has found another beau," he commented as casually as he could.

"Truly? Not a fortune hunter?" Darius watched him intently. Far too much for Val's liking.

"Indeed not. Viscount Kellett. Hervey," he added with a curl of his lip.

Silence fell, the kind that did not augur well.

"What is it?"

Darius glanced at Ivan. "It might be nothing, you understand, but I know that name. I've heard of servants using their master's names before now when they did not want to be identified."

Slamming his feet to the floor, Val sprang to his feet. "What? What do you know?" Energy coursed through him. He felt revitalized. This was the first time he had heard even a breath of scandal associated with the tedious Viscount Kellett. None of the discreet and expensive bawdy houses and gaming hells he frequented knew of him. He had asked.

Darius gazed up at his brother, his eyes reflections of Val's own. "I am not sure. To be sure I'll need to know what the man looks like. I will not speak ill of him until I have reason, but a man using that name appeared at one of Covent Garden's greatest attractions."

Knowing the establishments his brother frequented, Val rapped out, "Which one?"

Tilting his head to one side, Darius eyed him. "I think I would rather show you. It is not one that I frequent, as its special services are not what I prefer, but they are out of the ordinary."

"I'll come," Ivan said immediately. "Should I contact Julius and Tony? I know they are in town."

Immediately Darius shook his head. "There's no need to create a scene. We don't want to invade the place, merely observe it. If it is him. Perhaps we should frequent a few ballrooms and society events instead."

"Oh, no," Val said grimly. "That would mean nothing. I want to see this for myself."

"What will you do?" Darius demanded.

"Whatever I feel is appropriate. But I will undertake to control my temper. For now."

Chapter 6

The following evening, after he'd been forced to watch Charlotte dancing and laughing with her new admirer at a society ball, Val glumly reflected on the adage his father had repeated to him earlier in the day. "Sometimes you have to lose something before you appreciate its value."

His father had checked the viscount's credentials, and as far as his reports went, Kellett was a suitable potential husband for Charlotte. He was everything he had claimed. His wealth was solidly invested in land and a few judicious ventures, his reputation was almost staid, as if he'd set himself to create it.

Val recognized the markers, since he'd done much the same himself to an opposite effect. Although he enjoyed gaining the reputation he now held, he had reason for it, and he'd ensured the tales had spread. To the despair and reluctant admiration of his parents, it had to be said.

He'd dressed with his customary extravagance, in a symphony of greens and ivories, and fortunately his brother had not donned the salmon pink monstrosity. Otherwise, as he'd informed Darius earlier, he'd have planted him a facer at the very least. "At least the blood would have ruined it," he'd commented dryly.

"Thanks to our excellent work, I could order another and not miss the guineas." Darius flicked a piece of lint from his dark blue velvet coat and glanced up at his brother, smiling. Val had burst into laughter. His brother could always do that to him. That was why they had probably not got into fights more often.

"Then give me notice when you plan to wear it. I'll come and watch but never acknowledge you as my brother."

"You don't think they will notice the resemblance?" Darius waved a hand between them.

They were not identical twins, but they appeared very closely alike. Val grinned.

"I can go in disguise." Darius laughed.

Standing in the ballroom, the smell of burning beeswax from hundreds of candles stinging his nostrils, Val surveyed the scene with the world-weariness of a bored roué.

"Now I know why I don't come to these things very often," Darius murmured from behind him.

"That could be because you have no interest in what goes on here." There would be no marriage for Darius, unless forced on him, but the mamas continued to push their daughters on him. Darius's proclivities were known by many but it was old gossip, so it was possible the newcomers were not aware of it. However, since the Shaws held an exalted position in society, Val doubted that. They were just trying their luck. One mama had confessed that she knew all Darius needed was to meet the "right" woman.

Val had answered, "Only if she has a cock"—a comment so outrageous he'd changed it to something more innocuous when the woman had begged him to repeat what he said. But people standing around had heard, and the comment was repeated.

The marquess had compelled Val's betrothal to Charlotte the next day. And now here he was watching that same woman, regretting what they were about to do. He'd willfully ignored her, and now it was too late. For all that he kept telling himself that she deserved better, he still wanted her. The desire that had sprung to life when he'd kissed her remained to torture him, and the personality under the rigidly preserved society mask intrigued him. That made for a heady combination.

Perhaps he would have another chance to get to know her better. He would await tonight's events.

Charlotte had accepted his invitation to dance, but apart from that spent the evening with her family. Her Aunt Adelaide, a scatty but observant specimen of the older relative, exchanged a few words with Val. "You have made my niece very happy, sir."

"What, by severing our agreement?"

"Hush!"

Val liked the extended final syllable. He wanted to hear it again, but not, he concluded regretfully, at Charlotte's expense. "Indeed, ma'am. But it is by no means a settled matter. Negotiations lie ahead, I fear." And he had no intention of adding his newfound skills to that. He would not help, but he would not stand in her way if Kellett was the man to make her happy.

Why had he not seen her gentle prettiness before? Or the liveliness, so cleverly masked when she realized she was displaying it? He should have seen them, encouraged her. Their recent visit to the mantua-maker's had provided more questions than answers. When she spoke of her father, her whole figure stiffened, and her mood turned guarded. Talking about the duke was one sure way to make Charlotte close down.

That was how Val knew the Duke of Rochfort had arrived. Charlotte was dancing with Ivan. Val was sipping wine, talking to her aunt, watching the couples cavorting on the polished wood floor when Charlotte glanced at the entrance and visibly drooped. Her manner became stiff and wooden, and her shoulders drooped. The smile on her lips faded, before she straightened up as if someone had shoved a poker down her back. Ladies in tight-fitting stays had little choice but to keep their backs straight, but the way she jerked her head up was more like a puppet on a wire than a real person.

As Val watched, Charlotte became an automaton, one of those clockwork dolls brought to the dinner table during dessert for the amusement of the guests.

Charlotte's antics did not amuse Val. What was charming and quaint in a piece of brass and wood didn't sit so well on a flesh-and-blood person.

Now Val knew who was at the root of Charlotte's disquiet. In all the time they were together, in the few private meetings he'd had with her and the public ones, she'd never intimated that her father was anything except a strict but loving parent.

Did she not trust Val, or were spies set around her all the time?

Val had no answer, but when Ivan restored her to her aunt and Darius came back to their small group, his mien was serious, devoid of the amusement he customarily wore. "We should go now," he said. "Do you mind walking as far as the Garden?" His clipped tones expressed how Val felt.

As soon as they were out in the open air, Val demanded, "Did you see that?"

"I'm not blind," Darius answered. "I was beginning to see why you were so reluctant to let her go, but after her father came into the room, I understood how you could have missed it for so long."

Ivan, striding by their side, gave his morsel. "As a totally disinterested party, I'd say she is terrified of her father."

"I can remember times when I was terrified of our father," Darius observed, "but I would never allow him to control me to that extent."

Val pushed aside the heavy skirts of his evening coat, feeling the reassuring hilt of his sword. They had given them up for the ball, but collected them on leaving the house. If he'd been in possession of it in that ballroom, Val might well have run the Duke of Rochfort through. "Charlotte has spirit. She has demonstrated it quite clearly, but never in the presence of her father. She has always retreated."

They rounded a corner at speed and nearly collided with a footman in livery hurrying the other way. He muttered at them as Ivan stood aside, but the men took no notice. Another time they might have boxed him, trapped him into the upright box belonging to a night watchman and pushed it against the wall so he couldn't escape, but Val felt ninety tonight, way beyond youthful folly.

"When we were first betrothed," Val said, thinking aloud to two of the men he trusted as he trusted himself, "I resented Charlotte, I admit it. Papa imposed it as some kind of punishment. And I had the lovely La Venezia in keeping, but not for long. She was ruinously expensive and temperamental as…well, as an operatic soprano, so I rarely got what I was paying for." He could hardly remember what the renowned beauty he'd hooked from the opera house looked like now. "She was all I could handle at the time. I used my betrothal as an excuse to rid myself of her a month or two later. She was cruel, of course."

"You should have sent her to Rochfort," Darius commented. "That would have served him right. Of all the birds of paradise you have shown generosity to, she was the worst."

"Thank you for that." Val shrugged. "Charlotte agreed with me when I said we could use each other. She was making me respectable, and I was giving her an excuse not to accept the hand of anyone else, which at the time she said she did not want."

"Her father was talking to my father at the time," Ivan said. "Pa is a decent enough man, but I wouldn't have called him a suitable husband for Charlotte."

Val shuddered. "No indeed!" They strode down the Strand toward the sins of Covent Garden, passing grand houses and tiny, thrown-up houses, existing side by side. Before the fashionable world had moved to Mayfair, this and Piccadilly were the residential areas of choice, and a few people still lived there, in the grand houses that spoke of a different time, before the neat terraces of their generation.

The light was variable. Torchères set outside the mansions vied with the inky blackness of shop doorways and tiny alleys leading who knew where. Actually Val did know where some of them led. Interesting places, those.

"The arrangement worked for both of us until recently." He would not explain the rest, even to his brother and his friend.

Until recently, he hadn't kissed her or felt the warmth of her body, the heat of her mouth. She had not allowed him past the battlements she kept around her. He had not known about the other Charlotte—the warmer, softer, more desirable Charlotte who lay waiting for him behind the fortifications.

Were they for him? Why did she keep herself protected from the world so carefully? Everyone had some kind of facade, but not as much as Lady Charlotte Engles, and not so perfect that even her betrothed failed to notice it.

Questions thronged his mind, and it angered Val that he had no answers. He wanted more of the woman he'd begun to uncover, too late it appeared. But he was ready to go on this wild-goose chase tonight and discover if there was any truth in what his brother suspected.

As they neared the Garden area, a gust from the river let the dank smell wash over them, but they were too used to it to let it bother them. Lights became more frequent, and so did people. Groups of men wandered the narrow threading streets leading to the great open area that, as well as a magnificent church and the Opera House, contained some of the seediest, most depraved houses in London. Val should know. He'd sampled most of them in his time.

A man grew tired of such pleasures, though if anyone had said that to him five years ago, Val would have laughed them to scorn. The sound of drunken revelry drifted out from open doors, and women stood outside, touting for business, bragging about the quality of the wares within.

One stood before them, blocking their path. "Clean girls and cleaner tables, my lords! How about it? Fancy a game of piquet with a pretty girl on your lap?"

"Not tonight, Mother," Darius said.

She cocked her chin at him, artificial curls bouncing wildly. "Nor any night with you, my bully. Go on there. See if you can't find somebody to suit you at Mother Riley's."

Darius did not seem surprised that the bawd knew his preferences. Perhaps she was guessing at the truth. Mother Riley only offered young gentlemen for the delectation of the customers. "We're headed somewhere else tonight."

The men elbowed their way past her, careful not to let her hands anywhere near them. A good pickpocket could get past buttoned pockets and slide inside a man's coat, retrieving him of watch, purse and jewelry before he even noticed.

Val chuckled when he saw Ivan pat his pockets. "You weren't foolish enough to leave your watch in your outside pocket," he said.

"I'm afraid so." Ivan plucked his gold hunter repeater out of his pocket and moved it to his breeches. "No harm done." He clipped the chain to a waistcoat buttonhole.

"Humph," Darius said, glancing back.

The woman was busy accosting another potential customer.

After a final bend, the street emerged on the main square that formed Covent Garden. That last bend was put there by the architect so the viewer would get the full effect of coming from a confined area to a much larger one.

The Piazza still had remnants of its elegance, with the porticoed theater opposite and the gracious height of the buildings, erected in good red brick, but the pointing had crumbled on many of them, and the frontages were blackened with soot. The cobblestones still had remnants of the fruit and vegetable market held there every morning, the produce brought in from the market gardens outside the city, the same places where the night soil men took their noxious cargoes every night.

Val pushed a cabbage leaf aside with his toe. "So where are we going? Across the piazza? To Mother Brown's?" He wouldn't be surprised to hear that Lord Kellett frequented that place. Many wealthy men did, needing some raucous entertainment after an evening of behaving themselves.

"No." Darius had lost all semblance of humor. "Nowhere near as much fun, unless you are so inclined."

A shock that felt like an arc of sizzling lightning shot through Val's body. He knew exactly where they were going. He'd entered this establishment once and found it dreary to the edge of frightening. However, he understood why some people needed this release. Men and women came here, some heavily masked. Where they could survive most scandals, this particular choice could ruin them.

Val followed Darius into the House of Correction with a sense of dread chilling his bones, rather like entering his father's study as a boy when he'd seriously transgressed. How people could enjoy this activity beat his understanding.

The madam stood inside, flanked by two enormous bullies. She wore red. They wore black, with crisp white neckcloths. The effect was instantly memorable. Val narrowed his eyes, wondering if the look would suit him.

His momentary distraction served to help him overcome his initial repulsion in entering the place. He could smell the blood. Either that or they sprayed the stuff around to create an atmosphere.

Darius paused and spoke to him so softly only he could hear. The twins had become adept at that skill over the years and still used it. "It's not as bad as people imagine. There are variations in what they do here, and at the highest level can become an art form."

Val wasn't at all sure about that.

The madam dropped a stiff curtsy. "Welcome, my lords. How may we serve you?"

Darius stepped forward, an easy smile on his lips. "Thank you, madam. We are not interested in diversion at this time, but a little information."

Her lips tightened into a thin line. "We never reveal who comes here or what they do. That is the reason we have the reputation for complete discretion. The people who come here have particular tastes, sir, and they may not wish their practices bruited abroad."

"You are to be commended, madam. If only every house held your standards." That was Ivan. No doubt he was remembering a time when his brother's wife was severely compromised, although she had done nothing wrong. Only the combined efforts of the Emperors, together with a judicious retreat to the countryside had saved her. She made rare appearances in London these days, but by all accounts, the marriage was blissful.

The madam inclined her head graciously. She was not in the first flush of youth, but her figure was trim and her waist breathtakingly tiny. In fact, Val wondered how she managed to breathe at all. Her breasts moved enticingly under the low neckline, but Val felt no stirring of attraction.

Her skirts were shorter than the current mode and when she moved the shadows of her legs were visible beneath. The lady had a clever way of advertising the nature of her house without appearing extreme. She would draw people in with that.

And he did mean "people." The anonymity of this establishment was well known, and where ladies would ordinarily fear to tread, in this place they could arrive masked and remain so throughout their time here.

What Val did not understand was how people were drawn to this practice. He wanted to know, but not enough to put himself through an experience he might not enjoy, one that could destroy his enjoyment in bed sport. For him, intimate relations included a rich sense of fun, sharing mutual pleasure and much laughter. That was why La Venezia had not lasted long in his bed.

He doubted this house rang to the sound of laughter very often.

"Madam, what do you do here?" His question was far too abrupt, but it was out now.

"We provide complex equipment and services to people who find they need them." She spoke as if reciting a lecture, as if she weren't engrossed with disturbing bodily desires but with more abstract concerns. "Our business is in power and control. Who has it, and who uses it."

"An interesting philosophy." Those few words explained much that had puzzled Val when he thought of this house. He had never entered before, held back by a kind of superstitious dread, but perhaps he had overreacted. "So for people of power this serves as a release?"

"Sometimes. At other times it serves as a way of expressing emotions that would not be welcome elsewhere. We have a choice of weapons, and we can manufacture them to the user's specification."

The notion intrigued him. Although he was not drawn to pain and restraint as a way of expressing desire, he wondered why people would wish it, what delights they experienced.

Val bit back his next question. What if something went wrong? If the flagellation was too severe, or the person left hanging in chains too long? He could not understand why anyone would volunteer for this, but tolerance had been bred into him. He shrugged. They were here for one reason.

A scream came from above. Gritting his teeth, Val stood his ground, aware the madam was watching them closely, probably looking for potential custom. Not from him, never from him. A series of smaller screams followed, and disturbingly, Val could not tell if they were from pleasure or pain.

His stomach tightened. He would be glad to get out of this place. He glanced at Ivan who was standing completely rigidly, a frown between his thick brows. Ivan was no happier with that place than he was.

Val opened his mouth to ask his question, but his brother forestalled him.

Darius bent over the lady's hand. "I will convey our request, madam, and then leave you in peace."

He produced a purse from his pocket, which Val knew contained twenty guineas, a veritable fortune to some and a year's wages for a maidservant. They had calculated the amount to a nicety, knowing too much would evoke suspicion, scorn, and probably lies, and too little nothing at all.

He handed the purse to the woman who weighed it in her hand.

She nodded. "You may ask. Come this way. I don't want my hall thronged with people who don't intend to give their custom to me." As she led the way to a room at the back of the hall she shot a sideways glance at Darius.

Assessing and cold, it chilled Val to see his brother summed up like that.

The room she took them to was normal in appearance, a round table in the center surrounded by chairs. Several prints lined the walls, of a vaguely titillating nature, but not blatantly explicit, as if the lady did not want to scare people away. Hints of nudity and raucous scenes of people enjoying themselves confronted him. They seemed out of place here.

Darius helped the madam so sit as if she was a great lady. Val and Ivan took their seats at a gracious wave of her hand and for the first time since they'd entered the house a curl of amusement softened the tension in his belly.

"I am specifically making enquiries about a certain person," Darius began, "but I will not press you for a name. I am sure you would prefer I kept my questions hypothetical."

The lady frowned. "Go on," she said cautiously, hefting the purse.

"Let us say that a peer of the realm—a viscount, for example—availed himself of your services. How far would you go to indulge him, especially if he paid well?"

She bristled, folding her arms under her breasts, careless of the expensive triple lace ruffles at her elbow. "So far and no further. I don't like the gentleman ruining my employees for other clients, for instance."

"Striping?"

Darius asked the question so coolly Val took a moment to recognize what he meant. He had always considered himself suitably debauched, but because this perversion had never appealed to him, the cant was new to him.

"If the employee needs time to recover the client pays for the recovery time. My people are specialists in their field and not easily replaced."

"Don't they just want bodies to flog?" Val asked the question before he could bite it back.

She glared at him but gave him an answer. "Not at this level, sir. We do not encourage simple vices here." Pointedly, she turned back to Darius. "We do not encourage brutality. For that, the client must go elsewhere."

It did not surprise Val that there were places catering for the worst depravities. That was sad, that he knew it without anyone telling him. However, this house was reasonably spacious, and the rent would be high. The madam would have to provide more than average fare.

He had already presumed this was the place Darius thought he would find evidence of Lord Kellett. So far they were getting nowhere, and he was growing impatient. For two pins he'd name the man and probably be thrown out on his ear.

Forcing himself to remain quiet, he was startled when a shriek came from the upper landing, followed by thundering feet. A woman screamed as she clattered down the stairs, missing a couple on her way.

Val had never stood by when a woman was in distress. He sprang to his feet and barely beat Ivan to the door.

In the hall, a naked woman sagged in the arms of one of the bullies. Blood poured from her back and rear, the tops of her thighs cruelly striped. The demonstration of the term was vivid and cruel.

The sight gave him a vital second's pause, allowing the madam a chance to elbow her way past him.

Arms came around him from behind, holding him back. "She'll take care of it," Darius murmured in his ear. He didn't let him go until Val nodded. Then he extinguished the candles in the candelabrum that stood on the table, plunging the room into darkness.

Only just in time. Feet thundered down the stairs. Through the open door, the three men stepped back as Lord Kellett entered the scene. Val kept his hand on his sword.

"You gave me a weakling," Kellett said. "A girl totally unsuited for this house. Find me another!" He was half naked, his torso sheened in sweat, his bottom half incongruously dressed in fine gold velvet breeches and elaborately clocked stockings. Blood spattered the breeches, and Val had some satisfaction from the knowledge that the stains would not come out of a fabric that fine.

"Sir, you have treated this girl cruelly," the madam protested. "I do not allow this extent of damage."

The girl currently sobbing in the bully's arms raised her head. "Ma'am, he had me tied but I got away. He wanted to use a knife on me." She went back to weeping, her sobs increasing in volume. The madam jerked her head, and the bully hoisted the girl into his arms and carried her back up the stairs. The marks opened as she sagged in his arms. The bastard had cut her to the bone with his whip.

The viscount continued to bluster. "I come here because you can provide me with the girls I need, but the last two have been insufficient."

"No, sir, your behavior has worsened. I cannot and will not dispose of your mistakes." She sounded like a great lady.

"Is there a way upstairs?" Val murmured to Darius, who shot Val a sharp glance and nodded to the corner of the room. Of course. These houses frequently had hidden stairways for servants. This was nowhere near as large as the house he lived in, but perhaps—yes, and the door didn't even creak. Neither did the stairs when he ascended them.

He emerged onto a narrow corridor. Ignoring the sounds of pleasure mingled with the occasional slap of flesh against flesh, he headed toward the only door that lay open. This was the cause of the crash they'd heard before the girl had hurtled down the stairs. She had flung herself out of the room. Angry voices echoed up from the hallway as Val slipped inside.

The scent of blood forced him to swallow the bile that rose up his throat. Cords hung from the bedpost of the elaborate four-poster that appeared more suited to a medieval castle than a town house in London. On examination, he saw how the girl had escaped. The cords had a weak spot and the bedpost a sharp edge, probably—no, make that definitely—put there on purpose. So the madam here did have a consideration for the safety of her employees and she did not leave them completely helpless. Whether she did it for commercial reasons or for considerate ones, Val didn't know, but the knowledge eased his mind somewhat.

If she did not, she wouldn't get girls to work for her, but sometimes the wretches had no choice. They would be abducted off the streets or from coaches arriving in town from the country. Boys suffered a similar fate, only to have their lifeless bodies dumped in the Thames. The dark side of London remained secretive, although the magistrates were making some progress in preventing such atrocities.

The room contained several odd pieces of furniture to which Val paid only fleeting attention. Certainly the average normal bedroom would not contain a large wooden threaded device that opened like a pair of nutcrackers, or a piece that looked like a rack, but shorter. He left the mysteries to themselves and concentrated on what he searched for.

A blood-spattered shirt. That would do. He swept it up, and picked up the crumpled neckcloth that lay under it. The fabric was pristine, sheltered by the less fortunate shirt, but as he made to drop it, something glittering fell from it onto the floor.

He was in luck. He snatched up the item, discovering a long gold pin decorated with seed pearls and diamonds in the shape of the initials HS, with a K superimposed over them. Hervey Smithson, Viscount Kellett. For the first time since he'd entered this benighted house, Val grinned, but it was an expression of satisfaction. He shoved the pin in his pocket and bundled the shirt up into a small enough package to slip under his coat. It would have a laundry mark and embroidered initials so the maids could identify the owner. That was all he had wanted, a way of proving Kellett's presence in the house tonight. He had a vague idea of having to persuade Charlotte, but he would only use them in extreme circumstances.

The noises from the floor below abated. When the front door closed with a resounding slam, Val knew his time was up. He made good his escape, slipping noiselessly along the corridor and down the stairs to the small room where Darius and Ivan waited for him. He nodded to the men, and Darius slid the door closed, plunging them into darkness.

But not for long. The lady bustled in, seemingly unperturbed by the blackness and walked to the cold fireplace, skirts rustling. In a moment sparks flew against tinder. She lit a taper, and relit the three candles in their holder. "Very good, gentlemen, I take it you wanted to see and not be seen? Have I answered all your questions?"

As soon as the lights flickered into life, Ivan stepped before Val, half covering him from the madam's sight. "Indeed, ma'am." Coins chinked. "Please consider this a bonus. We never came here, and you do not know who we are."

She chortled. "You don't need to tell me that. But thank you." The money disappeared as if it had never been there in the first place. A flick of her wrist, and it had gone. "And you saw nothing, did you?"

"Nothing at all."

"That gentleman won't be coming back. He's ruined two of my best girls. Striping is fine, but not that deep and not that many. He was warned, and I don't care how high up he is or who he knows. Does he think I don't know them too?"

"I would wager you know more, and you know them better," Val commented.

"Nobody knows a gentleman like his whore." She nodded sagely. "You remember that, sir."

Val did. Because of that he took care to show his mistresses only what he wanted to. His wife now, she would know him much better.

Chapter 7

Charlotte could hardly believe her escapade at the dressmaker's went unremarked, but after several days passed she accepted that she had escaped notice. The gown had not arrived yet, but parcels arrived every day, and her clothes were not usually remarked upon. Her father considered the matter of clothing below him, although he had no compunction in sending her back to her room if he considered what she wore inappropriate or immodest. Which he did frequently. If she ever wore her new finery outside, she would have to use a great deal of subterfuge to escape her father's eagle eyes.

Not that she planned to.

The Monday after her visit to Cerisot's, she had another appointment to keep and another subterfuge to undertake, but this was more usual, so much that it had almost become routine. This trick seemed almost tame by comparison.

At her father's customary demand for her to outline her plans for the day, she said, "I have an appointment at the milliner's, sir. I will take Louisa, who needs a new hat. Afterward, I will return to receive your visitors for dinner. I plan to wear the dark green brocade." The color was not becoming to her, but she cared not. Tonight's dinner promised to be particularly stuffy, her father's guests consisting of several of his generation who would toady him and with any luck put him in a good mood.

"Not the green," her father said. "Wear something else."

"Yes, sir." Having finished her breakfast, she got to her feet, curtsied, and went to stand behind his chair. Although of age, her sister never breakfasted with them. She was too cheerful, and she chatted too much, he said. Of course that was not the true reason. But his comment about the gown gave her tacit permission to fulfill her earlier appointment. Louisa really did need a new hat. Her one and only straw was tattered and worn. Their father cared little for Louisa's appearance because he refused to let her into society, even though Louisa was of an age to make her debut.

However, that was not the real reason for their visit.

Half an hour later, they were on their way. Louisa liked to hold someone's hand, so Charlotte took off her glove and clasped her sister's hand warmly as they bumped over the cobbles in the family carriage. The vehicle might be grand, its embellishments lavish and the shield on the door repainted every week, but the suspension had a lot to be desired.

Louisa and Charlotte were happy enough. Louisa delightedly pointed out the sites of note as they passed, as if she had never seen them before. Charlotte marveled with her and added comments about some of the people they passed. Several bowed to the carriage. Presumably, they thought the duke was within, until they saw the inhabitants riding inside. Some gave Louisa a second look, but most accepted her presence. She was dressed so plainly that she could be a maid.

The carriage deposited them at the milliner's, but it didn't stay to wait for them. "His grace says we're to return to take him to 'Change," the footman told her regretfully. "We'll come back for you as soon as he says we may."

Charlotte couldn't blame them. They had more to lose than most. Her father would not only cast them off, he would blacken their characters so they would have difficulty finding anywhere else. The duke was very careful to uphold his reputation. A stickler, yes, too pompous for many, but not actually cruel, they'd say.

Sometimes Charlotte wished her brother was duke, which would of course mean their father had died. That was a sin—such a wicked one she forced herself not to think it. But it returned unbidden to her mind, to torture her in her quieter moments.

The route was very busy today. The milliner's shop was at the end of King Street, usually a peaceful thoroughfare. Only when the carriage had rattled off did Charlotte realize what was going on. "It's Monday."

"That's right. Monday." Her sister smiled.

Charlotte was forced to smile, too. "Clever girl! You remembered well."

"It's hat day."

Yes, it was. It was also execution day. They were on the route to Tyburn. She had forgotten the significance of the location of Mrs. Miller's shop. It was set on the corner of King Street and Tyburn Street. She glanced up the long road, for the first time noting the thickening of the traffic.

A man nearly bumped into them, a hawker with a tray full of cheaply produced prints. "'Ere, lady, I 'ave the best reports you are ever goin' ter see of the 'orrible murderers, pimps, and thieves who will meet their end today. Among 'em you will find the terrifyin' Gallows Man, the 'ighwayman 'oo robbed 'undreds of honest, 'ard-workin' people crossin' 'ampstead 'eath. Watch 'im meet 'is grisly end!"

Drat, a highwayman. The crowds loved it when one of those met his end at Tyburn Tree. People came in their hundreds, crowding around the gallows to watch the man's last performance. Highwaymen were considered the glittering stars of the underworld. To many people, they represented adventure and untold riches. Of course most people knew they lived sordid lives and rarely had much money, but the stories were so much more appealing.

People were making their way toward the corner of Hyde Park, and the scene of today's drama. Most likely Charlotte would know some people there, as they would hire balconies and drink to the health of the condemned.

Charlotte's father had taken them once. Charlotte would never forget it, nor the way Louise had shrunk into her and wept, shaking in terror. Their father had shown his disgust and forced a glass of brandy down Louisa's throat. At least that had put her to sleep, despite the screaming crowds, the delight ending in a roar when the platform fell away and the prisoners swung free. People had rushed to them, relatives or hired men, to hang on the feet and end their suffering sooner. Men who had ten minutes before laughed and joked with their audience now urinated on them, as the strangulation had its inevitable effect.

Charlotte had sworn never to go again, but she'd done it quietly, ensuring she always had something else to do, rather than defying her father directly, a battle she was doomed to lose, one way or another.

How had today's significance eluded her?

She had been too busy on her own life. That was it. So taken up with Hervey's increased attentions and her troubling reaction to Val's increased interest, she had not noticed the significance of the day. Their lives took on their usual course, but even attending church yesterday morning had not jogged her memory.

And she had to bring Louisa here. They could get a hackney and go home, but their father would most likely scold them severely for that transgression. Only common people got hackneys. Charlotte wouldn't dare try sedan chairs, not with her sister in the excitable mood she was.

"Where are they going, Lottie? Can we go?"

The crowds heading up the road had a cheerful aspect. Some carried baskets of provisions, as if visiting the countryside for the day. Perhaps watching someone worse off added to their enjoyment. The idea of public executions was to set an example to law-abiding folk, but the event had become a spectacle, as eagerly anticipated as Garrick's new play, but cheaper.

"Come," she said now, slipping her arm through her sister's and tugging gently. "We're getting you a pretty new hat today."

Her sister was easily distracted and smiled happily as Charlotte led her in the direction of Mrs. Miller's hat shop. The bell clanged as they entered, and the lady sprang up from her chair to greet them. The familiar smell of damp straw and beeswax greeted them, and Charlotte's mood eased. She was safe here, as if she'd reached sanctuary.

Although at one time Mrs. Miller had been a fashionable hatmaker, these days she was seen as démodé, but she had her regular customers and they remained loyal. Mostly the older generation. But she was a friend, and Charlotte trusted Mrs. Miller with much more than she would a fashionable milliner.

The shop was dark after the bright sunlight outside and far too warm for the day. Mrs. Miller felt the cold, she said, so her customers put up with it. Mrs. Miller greeted them with a brief curtsy and a smile and then addressed her assistant. "Could you get some tea for myself and Lady Charlotte, and a chocolate drink for Lady Louisa?"

The assistant hurried off. Mrs. Miller lost no time, thrusting her hand in her pocket and coming out with a letter, one that gladdened Charlotte's heart. While she opened and scanned the sheet anxiously, Mrs. Miller led Louisa to a nearby table with a mirror hung on the wall behind it. "Let's try on some pretty hats," she said. "I have been saving some for you, dear."

Charlotte spared a moment to check that Louisa was happy, but she need not have worried. Louisa liked Mrs. Miller. She felt safe with her, and safety was something Louisa had in short supply, especially when their father was in an ill temper. The chocolate was a treat, something Louisa had all too rarely. The rich scent filled the air as Charlotte turned to her letter.

Two years ago, her sister Sarah had eloped with the man she'd fallen in love with. Sarah was never mentioned at home. According to their father, she had ceased to exist.

Sarah was well, and Charlotte's niece thriving, she read. The pain Charlotte felt when she read about the way her niece was developing was nothing compared to the knowledge that without Mrs. Miller, she would know nothing at all. As it was, she could not risk taking the letters home. Her father or one of the servants would be bound to find them, however well Charlotte hid them.

At the back of the shop stood a small writing desk. Charlotte would make use of it to draft a quick reply. Then she'd spend five minutes choosing a new hat, give Mrs. Miller the postage money and a vail, and they would take the carriage back to the joyless house.

She read the rest of the letter and exclaimed in delight.

Sarah had fallen in love with a man of respectable birth but no fortune. He earned his living as a writer, composing novels, poems, articles for journals, anything he could receive payment for. Recently he'd found a lucrative line in sermons, writing them for clerics too busy to compose their own. They had found a small house in Oxfordshire, and Charlotte had wondered if at last she could accept her sister's hospitality and leave their father for good.

However this news was even better. Sarah's husband had unexpectedly inherited a small estate in the north. His great-uncle had passed away childless. The change for Sarah would be immense, and at last—at last!— Charlotte and Louisa could find sanctuary, if they wanted it. If she could persuade their father to let Louisa go.

Charlotte longed to leave. Sarah had asked her many times, but Charlotte could not leave her youngest sister behind, and she had no means of getting her away.

But now she had Hervey to look to. He had sworn he would provide a home for Louisa, and he would care for her as if she were his own sister.

When Louise laughed, Charlotte looked over to her and smiled, just as the bell chimed once more as someone else entered the shop. Hastily Charlotte thrust the letter in her pocket.

Of all the people who frequented the ladies' hatmaker, she had not expected her erstwhile betrothed to arrive there. He bowed to her and then drew closer. "I called on you, and they told me where you were. When they gave the address, I was alarmed. Had you forgotten the day?"

"I had until we arrived and the carriage left. It will come back for us." Someone banged on the window and startled her enough to make her snatch a breath. Outside, the crowd had thickened.

Mrs. Miller looked up from where she and Louisa were trying feather trims and tutted. "I shall have to close the shutters soon if it gets worse. People are not as considerate as they were in my youth." Glancing at Charlotte, she made her curtsy to Val. "Sir."

"Lord Valentinian Shaw," he said, as if that explained everything. In a way, it did. In the eyes of the world he was still her betrothed. "Delighted to make your acquaintance, ma'am. Pray do not let me disturb you."

But Louisa had been distracted. Scrambling down from the chair, she scurried to where they stood and dropped an untidy curtsy. "Is this the man, Lottie?"

"Yes, Lou, this is my…betrothed." Truthfully she didn't know what to call him, but Louisa liked consistency. She would have a hard time understanding. She would be happier without Val. Every time he was by, she lost her reasoning and her hard-won calm exterior threatened to crack. "Lord Shaw, this is my sister Louisa."

He glanced at her and then down at Louisa. He had to look farther down, because Louisa was diminutive. She had not yet achieved five feet and seemed likely never to do so. "I'm pleased to make your acquaintance, Louisa."

But when he reached for her hand, Louisa snatched it back and put her arms behind her back.

"Louisa does not like being touched," Charlotte explained.

Val accepted the stricture without a blink, as if it were normal. "Then I will merely bow, my lady."

When he followed action to words, Louisa giggled. As he rose to his full height, Val was grinning.

The assistant chose that moment to enter with a tray of refreshments. The chocolate, brown and frothy, was set before Louisa, while she set the tea tray on a side table. "I'll get another cup," she said, before hurrying away.

Val regarded Charlotte carefully. "Lottie?"

"Ah, yes." Heat rose to her cheeks. "Lou has difficulty with long names. She called me Lottie when she was a child, and she is happier with that."

"I think I would be. It suits you better than Charlotte. Charlotte is for someone far more stately."

"Oh!" Charlotte had always considered herself as reasonably stately.

"When I have you to myself, you are far more than that. Lottie makes you sound like a woman who laughs. I shall make it my duty to make you laugh more, when we are married."

"But we will not be married—" Charlotte snapped her mouth shut.

"Just so." He shot a meaningful glance at the couple in the corner. "Meantime, won't you sit and pour me some tea?"

The assistant returned with an extra cup, which she placed on the tray. At a glance from Val, she retreated to the back of the store.

"I will escort you home," Val said. "I have my carriage outside, with two stout footmen as well as the coachman and groom. You cannot stay here much longer. I came to have private words with you."

"Oh." He had made progress with the cancellation of the betrothal contract? It could not be anything else. Unaccountably, Charlotte's heart sank. But after all, she had requested this outcome, and her choice was a sensible one. "Yes, of course."

By the time they'd finished their tea, the crowds outside had diminished. Presumably they were congregating at the gallows, which meant the first executions would happen soon. The carts containing the principals of the show would be driving up, and they'd make their last speeches, if they wanted to.

Val got to his feet, in a graceful movement he probably wasn't even aware of. "We should probably set out now. Is your sister ready?"

Louisa wore an extravagantly decorated bergère that their father would probably condemn, but which gave her a great deal of pleasure.

"I believe so," Charlotte said, smiling at her sister's pleasure.

"Where is your chaperone this morning?"

"With my father. I assured her we would be fine."

If she hadn't been watching him closely, she would have missed the swift glance he threw at her pocket, where the letter from her sister remained. Yes that was the reason. Aunt Adelaide could be trusted only so far, since she was under her father's thrall and had been for a long time. Hastily she drew it out and smoothed the crumpled paper, leaving it on the table. Mrs. Miller would put it away for her. She put a crown on top of it, all she could afford today.

Val did not comment. Indeed, how could he, since he was about to relinquish any claim he had on her? This could be the last time they could meet privately with any semblance of propriety. She would miss his quick mind and his ready understanding that meant she did not have to explain things to him. And his friendship. She would miss that most of all.

At least she thought she would. But what of that single kiss, the way he'd woken her senses?

She had shared a kiss with Hervey, but she had not been tempted to repeat it. The kiss had not repeated itself in her dreams. When she woke up with phantom hands holding her, they were never Hervey's. But he had other attractions. He wanted her, and he would devote himself to her. She could learn to love him.

"It's time to go," she told her sister.

Fortunately, Louisa had been put in a sunny mood by Mrs. Miller's overindulging her in an extravagantly decorated hat.

"Louisa loves pretty things," Charlotte murmured to Val as she joined him.

"I can see that. She's a very pretty girl," he answered, loudly enough for her to hear. "How old are you, Louisa?"

Her sister shuddered and turned away.

"Call her Lou," Charlotte said. "Only our father calls her Louisa."

"Ah." He sounded as if he understood. Perhaps he did. "Lou, how old are you?"

The change in her mood was instant and startling to someone who didn't know her. She turned a beaming smile to Val. "Seventeen, although my eighteenth birthday is in two months."

Val turned to Charlotte, absolute bewilderment clouding his eyes. "Why have I never met her before? Why is she not in society?"

Charlotte glanced at Louisa, reassuring herself that her sister was not upset by Val's change in tone. "She prefers it." That was not the complete truth, but it would do for now.

After thanking Mrs. Miller, they left the shop. As if by magic, Val's splendid equipage drew up outside the door, so they were not discommoded at the least. A great roar of many voices swept into the ordinary sounds of horses, carriages, and street-hawkers.

The first executions were underway.

Swallowing, Charlotte allowed him to hand her into the carriage, and then her sister. The heraldic shield on the door proclaimed it to be the property of the Marquess of Strenshall, but it was both smaller and less carefully touched up than the one on her father's carriage.

Inside was a completely different prospect. The worn brown leather of her father's carriage stood in sharp comparison to Val's dark blue plush. When the coachman set the vehicle in motion she discovered the suspension was far superior, also.

Louisa smoothed her hand over the fine fabric, making a sound of appreciation. "I like this."

"It's good to touch," Charlotte said.

Louisa smiled broadly. She would be easier to handle when they got home. Perhaps her father would bear that in mind when she needed to visit Mrs. Miller again, although Charlotte doubted it.

"Do you like traveling, Lady Lou?"

She nodded vigorously, a powdered curl escaping her coiffure. "Very much."

The relatively short journey was achieved with stilted conversation. Charlotte's stomach tightened as they approached her front door. Her father might take umbrage that Val had brought them back and not waited for his carriage, but Val explained that easily as they drew up outside. "I came here first, but they told me you were at the milliner's. When they gave me the address, I agreed to bring you back before the crowds grew too raucous."

"Thank you."

He handed them down.

After ordering tea, she led him upstairs to the small parlor she used in the afternoons. The furniture was old-fashioned but serviceable. Her father preferred the styles of a generation ago—William Kent rather than Chippendale, stateliness over grace.

He did not remark on the furniture or the gray day outside. Rain dripped on to the windowsill and over the strictly neat and tidy but cheerless garden. Like everything else here, it was arranged as the duke pleased, and he never consulted anyone else on his decisions.

"I suppose you have worked out why Lou isn't in society." Her words dropped into the silence.

Val thrust his hands in his pockets and made a circuit of the room, behind the heavy sofa, around the front of it, and behind the big armchair. That brought him back to face her. "Yes, damn it, I do."

She didn't comment on the inappropriate word. Gentlemen tended not to use it in a lady's presence, although several showed no compunction. Strangely, the roué and shockingly scandalous Lord Valentinian Shaw had not done so.

Even if their association was about to end, she might find a friend in him, one who could help her in her little conspiracies. "Lou will probably always have a child's mind." She kept his gaze, needing to see his reactions. "She was born with the features you see, not unpleasing, but certainly different." Louisa's eyes were smaller than the norm, and her face rounder. "As time went by, we noted disturbing traits. She finds difficulty speaking sometimes. Her studies did not progress. Our father does not demand a great deal of education, but ladies must be able to sew, to keep a set of housekeeping books, and to play a keyboard instrument. She must curtsy gracefully and converse with politeness and deference. Most of all, she must obey." Charlotte firmed her jaw, waiting for his response.

"That sounds deadly dull." His mouth quirked in a flash of a smile that disappeared into nothing. "Have you been trying for that all this time?"

"We all did," she said. "We have little choice. But Lou failed. She could never do it, and the more she tried, the worse it got. Father could not stand the sight of her. We did our best, my brother, my older sister, and I, but it was never enough. He wants to commit her."

His head jerked back as if she'd slapped him. "Is she dangerous?"

"Not at all. She is gentle and shy. She dislikes crowds. At one point we considered introducing her to society, but it would not do. She could not bear all those strangers looking at her, and she went into strong hysterics the one time we tried. That would have played into my father's hands.

Louisa suffers from delicate health, and our father has used this to excuse her absence, when people asked after her."

"Oh, my dear." Dragging his hands out of his pockets, he reached for hers.

His warm hold gave her the strength to continue. Recalling that time hurt. Only two years ago they had tried to introduce Lou, choosing a dinner party as the best way. Lou didn't even get that far. In the drawing room, before they'd gone to eat, she'd started screaming, clapping her hands over her ears. Gripping his hands tightly, Charlotte continued. "Lou prefers a quiet life, but his grace gives us no quarter. Where he goes, we go. We assume he wishes to catch Lou in enough wrongdoing to send her to an institution for the insane. When I—" No, that was going too far. She could not tell him of her father's threats.

"That is how he keeps you in line, is it not?"

She tried to laugh off his suggestion but failed miserably. He had plunged straight to the heart of the matter. "Partly. He sent George abroad on the Grand Tour, and Sarah ran away. Eloped." She cleared her throat. "One day she will return, but until recently she has been ill, following the birth of their first child." A smile broke through. "She is almost recovered. Her husband would not hear of her undergoing more strain."

"She eloped with Sir Samuel Heath, did she not?"

"Did you know him?" she said eagerly.

Regretfully he shook his head. "Not well. I met him no more than twice, but the elopement was the talk of the town."

She nodded. "Father took us into the country."

His perceptive gaze scanned her. "I will ask more, but not now."

He dropped her hands as the maid came in with a tray of tea. She gave him a glare before she left. The duke would get to know about this, she was sure. So she said, "Could you inform my aunt that his lordship has arrived and I am in need of her chaperonage?"

The maid dropped a sullen curtsy and left.

"She won't come," Charlotte assured him. "She's out with my father."

He nodded and watched her cross the room to pour the tea. She felt his gaze burning her back, but she kept her hands steady. "Do sit down."

"If you join me."

She did so, bringing the filled tea dishes over to the table before the sofa. Taking her time spreading her skirts, she folded her hands neatly in her lap, preparing herself for the ordeal ahead. After all, she had asked for their association broken. She was still convinced she had taken the right path. In Hervey's presence she never faltered or felt too conscious of who she was and what she was doing.

Hervey never touched her hand and tugged, drawing her close. He never leaned over her and cupped her cheek with one hand, gazing at her as if he could see into her soul.

The one kiss they'd shared had been dry and chaste. Not like this one.

The moment Val touched his lips to hers, she leaned into him, lifting her hand to rest it on his shoulder. Even under the layers of cloth coat, waistcoat, and shirt she felt his muscles shift and flex. He pulled her closer, urged her without speaking to rest her head on his shoulder while he plundered her mouth, sliding his tongue inside to claim and possess.

Wildness surged through her, taking her into a place that terrified and excited her. She hardly knew herself. Where had this wanton creature come from? This was wrong. She should not, could not continue to do this.

He had the potential to make her his slave, and Charlotte was done with slavery. She yearned for an equal relationship, one born of rationality.

Rationality was the last thing she was thinking of now. She could not continue in this way. While he stroked her, urging her to do more, to give him more, she had no choice. He seduced her, body, soul and mind. She was his.

The front door slamming and the sound of her father's voice booming, filling every part of the house, broke the spell and made her shudder. Hastily, she dragged herself away. Or rather, she tried to, but his arms firmed around her.

He gazed down into her face. "I'm not ending our betrothal," he said.

Chapter 8

Regret seared Val as the lovely woman in his arms turned into the straitlaced, horrified Lady Charlotte Engles. He wanted her to accept him, but obviously that would not happen any time soon.

When she pulled away, this time he let her go, although his senses screamed at him to keep her, to continue what they had started.

Why this woman and why now? The idea of marrying anyone at all had always sent him running before. Even his betrothal to Charlotte had the aim of avoiding betrothal to anyone else. At the time several mamas had come too close, and his parents making encouraging noises for him to propose to one or the other. His choice of Charlotte had shocked them, but the solution had struck him as audacious and expeditious.

Now it appeared anything but, and the notion of a marriage of convenience laughably distant. He had tripped himself up with his own cleverness. Maybe it served him right. Because he wanted Charlotte with a desperation he barely recognized in himself.

"Why are you doing this?" she demanded. "Why?" Her voice rose into despair.

He could not tell her the truth. Charlotte was an innocent; he could not tell her of the depths of depravity her suitor had sunk into. But perhaps he could modify what he'd learned, make it more suitable for a lady's ears. "I have my doubts about Lord Kellett. I won't release you to him while there is any doubt about his character."

"Doubt?" Her voice remained shrill. "He's a perfect gentleman. He has never treated me with anything but respect. How dare you insinuate anything else? Do you mean to ruin his character?"

There was no need for that. Val had already decided to collect more evidence, and he'd begun to send rumors around the clubs. The sight of the girl at the House of Correction and the red-faced furious Kellett brandishing a whip would never leave him. That was not a perfect gentleman. But he was much worse than that. Kellett was a savage brute, one he would never allow near his sweet Charlotte.

Charlotte looked anything but sweet now, her features pale and trembling. "You would ruin me?"

"Anything but ruin you."

"But associating with you will ruin me for sure. My father will never allow it!"

As if conjured up by magic, the door opened to reveal the Duke of Rochfort. "What will I not allow? I will not allow you to speak for me, madam. That is certain."

Val was forced to make his bow. Despite her agitation, Charlotte dropped a curtsy. When she rose, she had donned the face Val was beginning to hate—smooth, untroubled and cold. The only sign of the inner Charlotte was the slight trembling of her hands when she poured tea for her father.

The duke bade Val sit, much as a king would address a beggar boy. He avoided looking Val in the eye, because Val, as a younger son, was not worth his regard. Val would change that, he vowed. The duke would bow to him before he was done.

Angry at the duke's unwanted entrance into a scene he was beginning to understand, Val turned his fury on to him, especially when Charlotte placed the tea carefully before her father and then went to stand by the side of the chair he sat in.

With his new knowledge, Val understood what was happening here. Charlotte would not leave her sister, and he could not blame her, but until she reached the age of twenty-one, Louisa was a minor and under her father's control. Val would do everything he could to get her away from him. Perhaps he could contact their older sister, but he didn't know if she could do anything, either.

He hardly recognized the carefree, debauched Lord Valentinian Shaw anymore. But he would not walk away from this, as he usually did when situations became difficult. He would never forgive himself if he did that, and he would be right.

The duke did not care to make polite conversation. He sipped his tea, slurping it before replacing the dish in the wide saucer. "Do you have any requests for me, sir?"

"I collected your daughters from the milliner's since the crowd was growing rowdy and insulting."

"Crowd?" The duke narrowed his eyes.

"It is execution day at Tyburn, sir. I judged it appropriate to remove your daughters from the scene."

The duke regarded him for a minute. Presumably he was employing a technique that intimidated his womenfolk, but he had no threats that would hold with Val. He would fight this man, if need be. He'd send the entire force his family could unleash on to him. His mother had been a Vernon, and he was a Shaw, the combined power of their families more than this man could handle. If Rochfort wanted a battle, he could have one.

Eventually the duke spoke. "I dare say since you were there, it was not an inconvenience to you. I trust my youngest girl behaved correctly?"

The thought of the sweet, innocent Louisa in this man's control hurt Val. Louisa needed a far less restrictive atmosphere. Encouraged to be herself, she might flourish. Here, in this cold, strictly run household, she would wither away. "Perfectly, your grace."

Although she didn't move a muscle, he felt Charlotte's relief. Did she really think he would betray her? The notion sent a shot of anger through him, but Val suppressed it. "I came to inform your daughter that I do not wish to release her from our arrangement."

"You do not? Are you then the vacillating kind of youth who appears all too frequently in today's society? You have no backbone, sir. I would remind you that my daughter has been approached by a gentleman much more agreeable to me."

If he told Rochfort what he had seen, would the man step back?

He doubted it. He would be more likely to ask Val what he was doing in the House of Correction. Val doubted the duke knew about Kellett's less savory activities.

The duke dug in his pocket and brought out an elaborately gilded snuffbox. He opened it and helped himself to a generous pinch. Without being asked, Charlotte handed him a white handkerchief, which he proceeded to despoil.

He did not offer the box to Val.

"Have you created yet another scandal, Lord Shaw?"

"Not to my knowledge." Val's words were clipped, and regretfully he made a note not to allow his temper out. Not yet. Not until he was sure Charlotte was out of that man's clutches. At least her father kept her safe, although in his eyes she was more of an investment to be made judiciously than a flesh-and-blood person. But he valued her.

If what Val had seen in Covent Garden was typical of Kellett's private life, he would kill Charlotte in a year. Val would not allow that to happen. The mask had been torn from Kellett's face, and Val had seen the ugly truth beneath.

"I would appreciate a private word with you, sir."

At a curt nod from her father, Charlotte left, her head down, her manner servile enough to infuriate Val.

He wasted no time getting to the point. He explained what he had seen in terse, unadorned sentences. The duke listened in silence.

"I cannot believe you will wish for your daughter to marry a man who engages in such matters."

The duke cleared his throat. His expression had changed, his already florid complexion redder, his eyes narrowed. "I cannot condone your interference in what is no longer your business," he said. "Sir, I will thank you to leave. Your association with my daughter is at an end."

Val's mouth tightened. "Not if my father does not agree. The contract is signed, sir. We will not hesitate to sue you if you try to break it without our agreement." And he would never agree to break it while Kellett was in the picture. "Do you have no concern for your daughter's safety?"

The duke lifted a massive shoulder. "Kellett is evidently ridding himself of his baser instincts in an acceptable way. If Charlotte is amenable and obedient, she need never fear him."

Anyone who behaved as Kellett had did not have enough control to be certain of that. Val had been making enquiries. He had discovered men who preferred the House of Correction and received enough information that indicated Kellett's behavior was, as the madam had said, unacceptable and well out of the ordinary. How could Rochfort condone that? How could he even consider leaving his own flesh and blood in the care of such a man?

The duke refused to discuss the matter any longer, apart from forbidding him to tell Charlotte anything of what he had learned. Val refused to give his promise. He would do his best to keep such painful knowledge from her, but he would not put it out of consideration.

He would not stay here any longer. The negotiations between his father and the duke would take a different turn. He was still willing to release Charlotte, even though the thought of relinquishing her made him despair, but not to Kellett. Not to that madman. The duke had formed an opinion on the character of the man and refused to budge from it.

Not only stubborn, but stupid.

* * * *

Val hated leaving Charlotte in that house. Her father would castigate and humiliate her and force her to apologize for something that was not her fault. The duke was a monster. The way she had stood by his chair infuriated Val. Nobody should make his children do that. But he could not take her today, so he reluctantly behaved politely to the duke, appeared to agree with his strictures without making definite promises, and left.

He entered the London town house intent on finding his father and stopping any negotiations to cancel the marriage contract, but he was distracted by a call from his brother. "Val—come in here."

Obligingly, he went into the room at the front of the house, a small parlor the family often used to meet privately. The furniture was comfortable but not showy, the atmosphere completely informal. His sisters often spent time reading or sewing here, in preference to their own bedrooms or the grander state rooms.

He was not surprised to find Ivan Rowley there, but Ivan's solemn expression gave him pause. "What's wrong? What's happened?" Val demanded.

Darius closed the door quietly and leaned against it, folding his arms over his dark green coat and plain buff waistcoat. The clock on the mantelpiece struck the hour, and he waited for the chimes to stop until he made his announcement. "Janey died an hour ago."

Val took a minute to identify Janey. Then he had it, and realization slammed into him. "The girl from the House of Correction?"

Darius nodded.

"Where is her body? Will the madam report the crime?"

Ivan gave a hollow laugh. "What do you think? It was only because Darius returned to check on the girl that we know."

Darius heaved a sigh. "Her wounds were deep. The madam called a doctor, who cleaned and dressed the wounds, but she took an infection. The end came mercifully fast for her. It could not have been pleasant."

Janey would never get her stripes bonus. As soon as he thought it, Val experienced a wash of shame and nausea. The girl had suffered greatly because of Kellett. He would pay for that. "I am on my way to find Papa. I'm not canceling the marriage contract with Charlotte. I told her father what kind of man Kellett was, but he refused to reconsider betrothing her to him."

"I would not trust Kellett not to fight for her. He might offer the duke more inducements."

"That's why I'm talking to Papa." Val would call on every weapon in his armory to defeat this monster. "He'll take my word that I have proof."

"And do you?" Ivan asked. "Have proof, I mean?"

"I have Kellett's pin with his initials from it and his bloodstained shirt."

Darius shook his head. "There was no crime, not officially. It has not been reported. Where there is no crime, there is no punishment."

Briefly, Val thought of the executions at Tyburn. A shame he could not send Kellett there, but his brother and cousin were right. "We could compel the madam to testify."

Darius laughed, but there was no humor in it. "You have as much chance doing that as seeing pigs fly. Nobody at her house will go anywhere near a court of law unless they are compelled to do so. Fielding of Bow Street has a particular hatred of women of pleasure, and he will condemn any who go to him."

Val shrugged. "He's surrounded by them. He's a reformer, so there may be some chance there, but with such little evidence it's doubtful we can do much in the courts." He paused and met Darius's gaze directly. "There are other ways of punishing him. I will not release Charlotte from our contract for her to marry him."

"Would you if she met someone else?"

Darius's question gave Val pause. After the delicious hints he'd received that Charlotte could be much more rewarding between the sheets than he'd previously supposed, perhaps not. "I would consider it." He turned to stare out the window, but he saw nothing but Charlotte's sweet face. Why not marry her? She would make an excellent spouse, and he would treat her as she deserved. "I will use the weapons I have. Kellett will know where he lost his pin and the shirt. I'd have taken the neckcloth too, but it lay under the shirt and was unmarked."

"There are identification markings on the shirt?" Darius asked.

Val gave a terse nod. "A monogram embroidered at the base and a laundry mark. It's enough. I have it safe, and my valet and the maids know not to touch it."

"If you are willing to marry Charlotte," Ivan said quietly, "why not do it now and put an end to the matter?"

Val shook his head. "I would have done so, but there is another problem."

Half an hour later he was explaining the problem to his father in the study upstairs. He told him Kellett was a villain but went into few details. The less his father knew about Val's plans in that direction, the better. The marquess would no doubt curtail his son's plans for that man, since it might involve some less than legal action.

He went on to the other difficulties he had learned that day. "Charlotte has a sister."

"She has two sisters," the marquess said. He folded his hands before him on the table, the lace at his cuffs providing an arresting contrast to his strong, worn hands.

"Yes, but one is beyond their father's jurisdiction." And the better for it. He would not tell his father that Charlotte had been in clandestine correspondence with Sarah. That would be breaking a confidence.

"Charlotte is of age. You do not need her father's permission to marry her."

Val's lips curled in a smile. "I am aware of that, sir. Are you suggesting that I elope with her?"

He received a corresponding smile in return. "I would never do that. But we could force the issue. And you know we will care for her until you are able to do so."

Val shook his head regretfully. "That would put the burden on Charlotte's younger sister." He paused. "Louisa is a natural, sir. Her understanding is well below what it should be. She is of delicate health and afraid of crowds."

The marquess shot his brows up widened his eyes. "I never knew that."

"He takes pains to ensure it isn't widely known, from what I understand." Val's mouth flattened. "But he will use her to make Charlotte do his will. And if Charlotte leaves the house, he could make Louisa's lot much worse."

"If she dislikes crowds, what is the girl doing in town?"

"I assume her father likes to keep her close, the better to force Charlotte to his will." He closed his eyes. "How could I have got everything so wrong?" He'd assumed Charlotte was sweet and biddable, that she had no spirit. He could not have been further from the truth. Below that smooth surface, Charlotte had passion and intelligence. He would not allow that treasure to be crushed by someone as villainous as Kellett.

"My son, you were not looking properly." The marquess grunted. "Neither was I, I must admit. Charlotte seemed the person to calm you, to ensure you did not run completely wild. When the duke approached me with a suggestion, it was a way of cementing a business deal. I knew he wanted access to our family, and this was one way he could do it. His involvement was useful, if not particularly convivial." He paused. "So what do you want to do? Not the immediate outcome. We are agreed on that. The marriage contract is signed, and unless all parties agree to it, it will not be broken. That is easily done. But do you mean to make her wait another two years?"

Val didn't need to think about that. He shook his head. "No, sir. I will marry her as soon as possible, unless someone she prefers appears. I will do my best to take Louisa into my household. I have procrastinated long enough. I cannot in all conscience, do it for longer."

A gentle smile curved the marquess's lips. "I believe at last, at long last, you are growing up. I trust you will make her happy."

"I will do my best, sir."

* * * *

Charlotte could not remember ever being so angry before. She stalked her room, trying to calm herself down before it was time to dress for dinner. Not when her sister left, nor when her father had forbidden her to take Louisa into the country had she felt this level of ire before. She had continued and done her best with the paltry weapons she had.

But to have Val calmly inform her that he was not ending the engagement—that filled her with righteous fury. How dare he vacillate and change his mind from one minute to the next? She had considered her future settled, that in a few weeks she would be married to a man of her father's approval and hers, a comfortable arrangement she could happily bring her young sister into. Hervey had agreed to petition her father to allow Louisa to go to one of his estates. She would live happily there.

Val had ripped that future from her hands. He'd taken her unborn children and her only chance at happiness. For he would not marry her, she was sure of that. As far as she knew, he had never stuck with one decision in his life. He was fickle with his mistresses, with his friends, and his affections. His recent kindness to Charlotte was all of a piece with the rest. Tomorrow he would treat her with careless affection again.

That attitude was no longer enough. Charlotte had no choice. She had to take her future into her own hands. If she did not, she would find herself alone and helpless.

Why had she ever signed that wretched contract? At the time, it had appeared like a way out, of escape. After her older sister left, Charlotte had known despair. She never wanted to feel that helpless again or so unhappy. Ever since she had done her best to appease her father on Louisa's behalf.

The devil of it was, she could not leave Louisa behind. She had no illusions. Her father would lock Louisa away if she became a nuisance, and without Charlotte to intervene, he would doubtless do so. Louisa was harmless, lovely, gentle, and she would not last a year in an asylum for the insane.

She had heard of families doing that before—sending their unwanted members to asylums, to live out their days in fear and despair. That would not happen to Louisa.

After a tap at the door, Hunter entered, bearing a box. "This came for you, my lady. Is there a mistake? It is from Cerisot, and you do not patronize her. I will send it back."

Charlotte rushed across the room. "No. It is no mistake. I ordered a gown at Lord Shaw's request." Recalling that time, a flush of heat ran up the back of her neck. All her emotions returned in a great flood. The recollection of the kisses Val had given her, no doubt in a moment of playfulness. She could not think any more of it. She must not. No doubt they meant far more to her than they did to him. He had probably forgotten them already. Something she would never do.

But she had this, for a time, at least. Eventually she would return it to him, but now, eager to see what Cerisot had done, she picked up the scissors from her dressing table and set to slicing the string that secured the parcel.

She opened the box breathlessly and plunged her hands into the layers of silver tissue, tearing them apart in her anxiety to get to the contents.

The petticoat came first. She had not been aware that the petticoat was ordered, but here it was. She breathed softly, afraid she would spoil the miraculously thin silk. A deep ruffle adorned the hem, and twisting pink floss flowers were embroidered over the join.

She laid the fabric on her bedcover. The dark brown of her cover was easily discernible through both layers of the fine ivory silk. With a glance at its loveliness, Charlotte plunged deeper into the box.

She drew out the gown. It rustled expensively, caressing her hands.

After a moment of savoring the silky loveliness of the garment, she shook it out. She had never owned anything so beautiful. The gown was a deep, rich, gorgeous blue. The robings at the front were decorated with twining vines, interspersed by the pink flowers, with brilliants forming their centers, catching the light with a flash as she turned it. The deep pleats at the back were sewn down to the waist, flaring out in an extravagant mass of skirts. And the whole was lined with ivory satin, the same shade as the petticoat but of a more substantial fabric.

Charlotte had no idea she could fall in love with a gown, but she did.

"Where am I going tonight?" she demanded.

Hunter coughed and then cleared her throat. "Lady Butler's, ma'am."

A grand ball, she recalled. Perfect. "I will wear this."

"But his grace, ma'am. He has not seen this garment. You cannot—"

Charlotte was tired of being told what she could and couldn't do, especially by the servants. "I can, Hunter. Another word, and you are dismissed. You may help me to wash my hair."

"Of course, ma'am."

"If I find this gown moved or despoiled in any way, I will hold you personally responsible. It is a gift from my betrothed, and I will wear it tonight to please him."

Excitement built in her gut. She would do this. She would really do this. How could she not? The gown had arrived as an answer to her prayers. She had no idea if her father would attend, but she guessed he would, because Lady Butler's ball was a high spot of every season.

Fighting Hunter proved tiring but at the same time exhilarating. Charlotte left off the hair powder, which took a great deal of argument, but she refused to allow Hunter to leave the room. If she had, she would have raced downstairs to inform the duke.

However, she allowed Hunter to swathe her in petticoats, so the ivory one was rendered opaque, and to tuck a kerchief around the low neckline, to render it more respectable. Such subterfuges appeared ridiculous in an evening gown. She even allowed her maid to pin her gown nearly closed at the front, covering all but a tiny strip of skin at her throat. However, she insisted on wearing her finest ruffles, triple Mechlin lace inherited from her mother, tacked carefully onto her shift at the elbows. The row of pink bows that decorated the front of her gown was deliberately crowded together, further disguising the woman beneath.

A sapphire pendant, also from her mother, and a matching bracelet and pair of earrings, modest and old-fashioned, finished her appearance.

To her relief, her father barely noticed her new finery. He was paying attention to their dinner guests, as exalted as he was and just as unbearably pompous. Charlotte bore their patronizing smiles and barely concealed smirks when they spoke about their children's brilliant matches. Not even the taunts about her long betrothal period touched her as she ate sparingly and agreed with everything everyone said.

Her aunt sat at the foot of the table, appointed her father's hostess, probably so the guests could prove their superior taste and knowledge over her.

Charlotte kept her temper, barely, and endured the long dinner and then the even longer hours after, when the daughters of the guests proved their ability to play an elaborate melody on the keyboards with no emotion whatsoever. Charlotte should know these women better, but they were as sheltered as she was, and they felt no desire to associate with each other.

She watched the new Lady Drysden agree tonelessly with whatever her husband said, glancing at him for his approval every time she ventured an opinion. Even in her marriage, Marie had not escaped the total domination of her personality and her very self. Her father, another like the Duke of Rochfort, had commanded her marriage to one of his friends, and she had done so. What had made her do that? Did she have a younger vulnerable sister too, or did her parents threaten to cut her off without a penny? Or maybe she never learned to rebel.

If Charlotte did nothing else notable in her life, she would have tonight. She absolutely refused to lie down without a fight, to allow her father to ride roughshod over her and her sister any longer. She did not yet know what she would do, and she had spent all her money on the gown she wore tonight, but she would do something.

She included Val in the list of people she wanted to thwart tonight. His capriciousness had brought her to this point. Tonight she would bring him to the point.

Chapter 9

Lady Butler and her family lived in a large house on Grosvenor Square. Tonight the doors were thrown open and light blazed from every window on the first floor. People thronged outside, some attending the ball, some there to gawp at the guests. Charlotte would give them something to gawp at. Although her father had complained about the unsuitability of her hair, Charlotte had pointed out that it was too late to powder it and apologized humbly, even though the words stuck in her throat. But if she had not, he could have forbidden her presence. Then he asked her about the gown, and she repeated what she'd told Hunter, that Val had sent it to her. "I believe he means it as a parting gift, your grace. We do not want him to take one of his pets, do we?"

However, when he said, "I wish you to be at the very least respectable. That gown is far too extravagant. I do not like it. When you remove it tonight, send it to me. We will burn it together," rebellion, fiery and shockingly sudden, burst into full flame inside her.

She had thought of telling him she had a cut on her head and the powder irritated it, or that she had simply run out of hair powder, but she had eventually decided that such tactics were below her. Instead, she informed him that her natural color enhanced her gown more than powder did and left him thinking of a suitable response.

Then she went upstairs and in a frenzy of anger, altered her appearance. Wrapping a heavy cloak around her, she went downstairs to the waiting carriage.

He spent the whole of the journey here scolding her and threatening to send her home, despite the presence in the coach of two of the guests from dinner. They listened largely in appreciative silence, only agreeing with the wisdom of the duke and admiring his manner of taking no nonsense from his children.

Tonight he would take all the nonsense she could put his way.

Despite the warmth of the evening, Charlotte had worn her heaviest cloak because it was the only one that covered her gown adequately, but the journey was a short one, and she was not too badly discommoded.

She did not loosen the ties, or let go holding the front together until they had entered the house and her father had doffed his hat, leaving his guests and his daughter to follow meekly behind him. Her heart in her mouth, Charlotte asked for the ladies' room.

There, she found a maid to take her cloak and hat, and then she put the final touches to her appearance.

The fichu had gone. Once she'd torn it off, she revealed the low neckline of her gown, enhanced only by a narrow frill of lace which drew attention to the bare flesh rather than concealing it. Studying her reflection, Charlotte smiled when a lady glancing over at her gasped. She didn't care if she never saw that kerchief again. Instead of the full white cap with lappets, she had reduced her head wear to a mere scrap of lace. And her petticoats were gone, all but the one that came with the gown. She'd hastily stepped out of them just before she'd left her room to get into the carriage. All she had under her finery was her shift, and she'd pulled that up and tucked it under her stays until she was barely decent. Most of her legs were on blatant display, shadowed by the gown, but unmistakable in bright light. She wore a little face paint, where her complexion was usually bare.

Anything more different from the scraped-back hair and boringly modest gowns of her usual attire was hard to imagine.

Sucking in a breath, she watched her bosom swell enticingly above the tight-fitting gown. Her temper still simmered under all that silk, adding fire to her eyes and a snap to her stance. She would use every weapon she had at her command tonight. She knew exactly what she wanted to achieve.

Her anger with Val and her father's threat to destroy such a lovely thing had combined to make a combustible forest fire, and now it was fully ablaze. Years of oppression, of forcing herself into molds that did not suit her, that hurt to maintain, gave her the impetus for this one night of rebellion.

So the Marquess and Marchioness of Strenshall wanted a sensible, biddable woman for their son, did they? She was about to show them that she was nothing of the kind and never meant to be.

She had not expected her father to wait to escort her into the ballroom, so she was not disappointed when she entered the room alone. The Butlers were possessed of a fine suite of rooms on the first floor of their grand

London mansion, and they had enhanced the grandeur with a multiplicity of candles and enough flowers for a state funeral, with some left over. They must have stripped every greenhouse and garden on their estate to obtain this amount of roses, lilies, and Lord knew whatever else flowers. All, interestingly, in white and pink.

Their hosts must have commandeered every white and pink flower in the whole of Covent Garden market for a week or more. Heady scent filled the room, chokingly sweet. Or maybe that was just her. She was definitely feeling queasy. As her nervousness increased and her temper subsided, her stomach made its presence felt.

Reality sank in. Her temper had led her into this. After years of suppression, it had broken free into one fiery act of defiance, and now it was declining just as quickly. She should go home, claim sickness, and retire. But even when she thought it, defiance returned to challenge her. If she left here, she would never trust her own judgment again. She had no choice but to go on.

Lifting her chin and forcing an expression of calm on to her face, she entered the packed ballroom.

Any expectation she had of passing unnoticed melted the moment she met the startled gaze of Lord Ivan Rowley. His darkly handsome eyes widened slightly before he bowed. "My lady, I am delighted to see you looking so well. Won't you allow me to take you onto the dance floor?"

That suited her perfectly. She did not particularly want to converse. Not yet, at any rate. Not until she'd regained some of her usual level bearing. She had not felt like this in public for a long time, if ever. From childhood on, her father had trained his children to bear the still and unfeeling exterior of a statue. It had become second nature to her. Appearing in this way made her feel vulnerable as never before.

As Lord Rowley took her into the center of the polished wooden floor, several pairs of eyes tracked her progress. Her vulnerability was overlaid by a sense of triumph, newfound confidence giving her a new and different kind of shield. Attracting attention drew its own kind of protection; she had never realized that before.

His lordship drew her around, and she concentrated on getting her pose correct. Not only correct, but graceful, turning her hand elegantly as she had seen other ladies do but rarely attempted herself. The gesture was easy. Her confidence building, her pleasure rose. She knew this dance, a country dance that meant she would change partners during its course. She did not have to concentrate on the steps, so she could refine them. She enjoyed that, but her father probably would not. She did not seek him out but replied to a remark her current partner made with a brilliant smile. She didn't have an inkling what he'd said, but it didn't matter.

People stared at her, or rather, they did the polite equivalent—glancing at her, glancing away, and then back when they thought she wasn't looking. Charlotte pretended she didn't care. When the dance was half over, she truly did not care. A sense of exhilaration took her.

When the dance concluded, she knew she had made an impression. Her work here was done, but she did not want to leave. She had never enjoyed herself at a ball like this before, never felt this sense of freedom. It was new to her, and she reveled in it. Before tonight she'd been too busy doing the right thing, behaving the right way, but she had nothing to lose now. The evening might have dire consequences, but she would deal with them when they happened.

If her father sent her sister away, she would fight his decision, work to prove that Louisa was no more mad than she was. He would not punish her as he used to, either. And she would not allow people to decide her life for her. True, she might have to obey him until she married, but Hervey, gentle, kind and considerate, would treat her with respect. He had pledged himself to her, gone down on his knees to do so. All she had to do was persuade Val to let her go, and she would have the life she wanted.

Wouldn't she?

Hervey waited for her at the edge of the dance floor, but to her surprise, Lord Rowley stayed with her. She would have expected him to relinquish her to her next partner, but he did not do so. When she tried to remove her hand, he merely tightened his hold on her. She didn't even know Lord Rowley very well. Why would he suddenly behave so possessively? She could not believe that a change in hairstyle and a new gown would have such an effect on him. But he was obviously refusing to leave her, even though Hervey tapped his foot impatiently.

The next set had already begun so they could not excuse themselves and join it.

"I trust I find you well, sir?" She offered Hervey her hand.

Hervey glanced at Rowley, his glare challenging the man to stay a moment longer. His opponent did not appear the least disconcerted.

Hervey bowed over her hand, dropping a light kiss on to the back. "All the better for seeing you."

Perhaps not the most original of comments, but she appreciated it. That was, until his eyes widened and he took in her complete appearance. "Has your father decided on a change in style?"

"No, I did."

"Charming, the effect a new gown can make," Lord Rowley commented. He took an enamel snuffbox from his pocket and helped himself to a pinch, accomplishing the feat far more elegantly than her father could. He snapped the box closed and returned it to his pocket without offering it to Hervey, a studied insult.

Hervey did not deserve that treatment. Charlotte glared at Lord Rowley, who gave her a sweet smile in return.

Hervey's second perusal of her appearance was decidedly less approving than his first. His fine blue eyes narrowed and his mouth turned down at the corners. Hervey had probably seen the shadows of her legs behind the fine fabric of her petticoat when she'd shifted slightly.

Inside, she groaned. Why had she done that? Added to the sheer effect of her petticoat, every time she breathed, her bosom rose from the tight lacing of her bodice, the upper slopes bare except for the teasing frill of lace. She must appear an absolute wanton. Hervey didn't like it, and now she was not sure she did either.

The pleasure she'd taken earlier that evening faded away under Hervey's sharp and disapproving glare. She didn't like his assumption that her father had imposed the changes.

"I would ask you to dance, but perhaps you would prefer to accompany me into the supper room," Hervey said gently. In the supper room he could find her a table to sit at and hide her shame.

No doubt he could feast his eyes on her swelling bosom. Breathing shallowly did not help, either. It merely made her breathe faster. Why, oh, why had she done this?

Her father would never allow her to wear this gown again. As well as its scandalous appearance, it was far too fashionable to meet with his approval. She had seen his disapproving glares over dinner, and that was before she'd rid herself of the kerchief and petticoats.

A movement caught her attention. Her father was heading in her direction, a grim expression on his face. He would have no compunction in manhandling her out of the ballroom and home, now he'd seen her. If he could catch her, that was.

Forcing a smile, aware she needed to do something to get away, she reached out to Hervey again. "I would love to dance with you," she said simply.

He could hardly withdraw his offer, although he tried. "You are sure you don't wish to take supper?"

She lifted a shoulder and shook her head. "It is far too early for supper, sir. I would much rather dance."

If she had not made Hunter lash her into her stays with a firm hand, she would not have risked herself to the jolly bouncing country dance that the quartet was striking up. However, if she did not move, her father would reach her.

Hervey blinked and smiled back. His gaze turned speculative. What he was thinking she had no idea, but at last he took her hand and led her on the floor. The dance commenced, and they moved around the floor with increasing vigor as the country dance went for its climax.

Charlotte had never entered into the spirit of the dance so thoroughly. She lifted her skirts to point her toes, hopped, skipped, and capered along with everyone else, garnering more than a few admiring gazes, mostly from gentlemen. She even began to enjoy herself. Nobody had told her how heartening collecting such admiring glances could be. It built her confidence so she almost forgot her state of near-undress. Not quite, though, especially when she glanced down to see her breasts almost bursting from her bodice. But not quite. They would not leave the confines. At least she did not think so.

Then another partner whirled her back into the dance by his quirky smile and his touch on her hand. It only took that one touch to realize that her betrothed had joined the dance. He let his gaze drop. It washed over her half-naked breasts.

His attention had the effect that none of the others had. Heat flowed over her. Shame, pride, and defiance, in a confusing combination, mingled so she could not tell which was dominant and which she should suppress.

They came together briefly, and he said something, but she couldn't hear what it was before she passed on to her next partner.

Moderating her movements, aware as she had not been before, she smiled and danced and responded to her other partners until the circle was done and she returned to Hervey. He should be a steadying presence, as he had been in the last few weeks, but somehow he joined with the others—an admirer, a man with hot eyes and a loose mouth.

Where was Val? If she had not felt that thrill when he touched her she would have thought she'd imagined him. The room was so full she could not see him in the throng of gaily dressed, loudly chattering people. Colors mingled, clashing and harmonizing, a combination of exquisite fabrics and breathtaking jewels. The world she had grown up in was full of extravagance and excess, so much that she hardly noticed, except at times like this when she was looking for one person in particular.

She had spent too much time standing against the wall with the older ladies and the unmarriageable. Whatever happened next, she would not do that again.

Hervey had her arm and was almost dragging her toward the supper room. Charlotte was not ready to go. He would probably hustle her out of the building and home, if the set of his mouth and the gleam in his eyes were any judge. She dug in her heels, bringing him to an abrupt stop. The people gathered around, exchanging polite conversation stared. Some giggled.

"What are you doing?"

He turned to face her, exasperation pressing a frown between his brows. "Charlotte, my love, you may not know this, but your gown is not…suitable for a young lady such as yourself. You should not allow people to ogle you so blatantly."

Charlotte flicked out her fan and did her best to give a roguish look over the top of it to a beau who was blatantly examining her through a quizzing glass. "I am no more unsuitably dressed than many of the women here."

He groaned. "But you are not them," he said through his teeth, forcing a smile, probably for the sake of the spectators. "You are a sweet, well-brought-up young lady, and you demean yourself by stooping to their level."

"I rather enjoy it," she confessed. The feelings washing over her were not all pleasant, but most were. "Why should I not act my age instead of someone twenty years older?"

"Your father—"

She caught her breath, but after swiftly glancing around she could not see him. "What about him? He is here somewhere."

"Do you wish to betray him by this unseemly display? Truly, if I were not so totally devoted to you, I would wonder at your conduct tonight. No doubt reports of your behavior will be all over London tomorrow. How can you wish for that? You are a goddess, far above the other women here."

"Is that why I usually spend every ball bored to tears, propping up the wall and discussing politics and embroidery with the other rejected spinsters?" She shook her head, her curls bouncing silkily against her neck. She loved the feeling, much more than the sensation the heavy greased and powdered locks gave. She'd had to pull down a few curls herself and do her best with her fingers to turn them into ringlets, since Hunter had tried to pull her mistress's hair back into its usual tight unforgiving knot.

"It is better to set a good example than a bad one."

"Is that so?"

The voice breaking into their conversation had all the timbre and throbbing intensity Charlotte wanted. Even though Val's behavior since she'd asked him to break their engagement confused and angered her, his presence still held the magic it always had. Her body responded as if trained to the task, softening and opening for him in a way that made her yearn to lean into him, to feel his body surrounding hers.

Arrant nonsense, she told herself roundly. She would not succumb to the wiles of any man tonight, least of all Val Shaw. She turned so the men faced each other and she stood between. "You have rushed over here just for the pleasure of dancing with me? How flattering."

"Something of that nature. I should have known you would be here, and I should have arrived earlier, but I was detained."

"By your mistress?" The smile she gave him was as sweet and sugary as she could make it. Several people standing by them gasped. Ladies were not supposed to mention such matters, at least not in mixed company.

He returned her smile in full measure and added a swift lowering of his eyelids. "Not at all. I gave my last mistress her congé a long time ago." Catching her hand, he lifted it to his lips. "I devote myself entirely to you, my love."

Hearing that endearment on his tongue drove her back into anger. "How pleasant. Perhaps you will become bored with me before long."

"How could I ever do that? You are a fountain of invention. You surprise me more every day." Stepping back as far as he could, which was not much because of the crush, he surveyed her, taking a leisurely perusal of her appearance. "I have never seen you so fine before." He released her hand as she snatched it back and she nearly overbalanced.

"Do you recognize the gown?"

His smile broadened, which she would not have considered possible a moment ago. "Indeed. It is the Cerisot, is it not? I told you her creations would do you justice. Indeed, I wonder you will go anywhere else. You appear to great advantage, my dear."

They were peppering their words with endearments, but Charlotte did not fool herself that they were anything to do with her. Battle was joined.

"You hold on to Lady Charlotte as if she is a prize to be won," Hervey remarked. "I would treat her as a woman to be cherished."

"As do I," Val agreed smoothly. When he turned his head the light from above glinted on his beautifully dressed dark hair in vivid contrast to the powdered heads around him. "I will do my best to cherish her in the years to come."

"A word, sir," Hervey said. "In private, if you please."

Val raised a brow. "I would not be so churlish as to leave my betrothed alone here."

"I will restore her to her father."

"Is he here?" Val made a great play of turning around, searching for him. There he was, ploughing through the fashionable crowd as if it were not there. He would be on them in a moment.

Val grabbed Charlotte's hand and towed her away. She had not realized Lord Rowley and Val's twin were standing nearby, but as Val dragged her in the direction of the nearest exit, they folded in, neatly preventing Hervey and her father pursuing her. Her protested "Val!" went unheeded, unless it served to quicken his pace.

She was almost breathless when he dragged her into the hallway and then across to the private part of the house. The grand rooms were opened for the ball and, so it appeared, were some of the lesser rooms on this floor. Open doors indicated where people were sitting around tables playing cards or where a group of women stood around chatting. Val did not stop but opened a different door and tugged her inside, closing it behind them. He turned, pushing her against the paneled wood. "I love the gown, but maybe it would be better with a little more padding," he said.

She sucked in air, breathless after his breakneck rush to get here. "I am tired of criticism. If the gown survives the evening, you will find it on your doorstep tomorrow."

He leaned over her, planting his hands either side of her head. He glanced down. "I love the way you blush," he said softly.

The heat in her cheeks was not all from the temperature of the room and her breathlessness, then. "You shouldn't make personal remarks."

"Why not? Plenty of other people seem to be doing so." His eyes glittered as he lifted his gaze to her face.

"Some people have the right." Even as she said the words she wondered at them. Did anyone have that right? Only if she gave it to them, which she decidedly did not. She would dress as she chose. "Dash it, I will go to Cerisot in the morning and demand that she takes the gown back. I am a duke's daughter. She will not deny me."

"No, she will not." He spoke so softly, his breath trickling over her body like a caress. "She will not because I have told her not to. I want to see you in more of these."

"I will wear what I please." She did her best impression of a haughty princess, calling on all her prowess. But with this man, her mask seemed to have gone. She could not muster the stiff expression she habitually wore however hard she tried. "I will not dress as you order." Emboldened, she met his gaze. "And I will marry whom I please. That is not you, Lord Shaw."

"Oh, is it not?" His voice softened. Cupping her chin with one hand, he moved closer.

When his tongue flicked out to moisten his lips, she gasped, a tiny sound but he would be close enough to hear it. His expression turned fierce, and he turned her into jelly. His concentration on her was absolute, as was hers on him.

He lowered his head at the same time as she stood on tiptoe to meet him. She could not go another minute without his kiss.

He took her with the promise in his eyes, and the power of his desire. She flung out her arms, finding his shoulders, her fan falling to the floor with a clatter they both ignored. They were too busy devouring each other.

Sensation poured over Charlotte, a rich cascade of pure exhilaration, rising to swamp her and float her out of control.

She let him take her with him, guide her to a new place. He touched her bare shoulder and slid his fingers under her sleeve, gliding them down and tucking them under her stomacher and stays. Nobody had touched her there before. Nobody had wanted to, but the small groan he released told her that he did.

In the confines of her bodice, he worked wonders. Shuddering, she pushed her breast into his hand, trying to help him any way she could. She wanted more of this. More than that, she needed it.

He had three fingers in there now, and when he tugged, he half pulled her breast from its confines. His lips left hers, barely, and he glanced down. The heat in his eyes when he looked back at her face was almost unbearable. She felt helpless, unable to say anything or fathom where they were going. But every cell in her body pleaded for more.

He ran his thumb over the flesh he'd exposed. She shivered, and her mouth fell open as the most uncivilized sound fell from her. He responded to her long groan by kissing her again. Responding to him, she curved her hand over her waist, seeking an opening. She ached to touch bare skin, needed his warmth, the intimacy of him with nothing between them.

His kiss turned lascivious, openmouthed, and his breath came in short, choppy gasps as he pressed his mouth to her cheek, her throat and farther down to her shoulder. Although the bones of her stays dug into her painfully, she wanted more. The pain was a delicious counter to the caresses he was pressing on her, sending contrasting thrills and driving her out of her mind.

"You're the most passionate, responsive creature I have ever met," he muttered as he touched her skin with his mouth, as if trying to kiss every part of her he could. "And to think I nearly let you go."

His words made her head spin. That was, until the realization slammed into her. He let her go? Yes, he did. And she didn't want him, this man who would take her and wreck her. She had no skills, she could not hold someone as brilliant, as passionate as he was.

Her back was against the door so she had nowhere to go, but she jerked sideways. As he followed her, intent on more, she held up her hands.

"No, Val. No."

With a sudden movement, he straightened. Tipping his head back, he sucked in two noisy breaths before he spoke, his chest expanding. "I'm sorry," he said to the ceiling. Then he lowered his head and gazed at her, a laugh forcing itself out. Gently, he brushed her hands aside and took over the task of restoring her breast to its proper place. "Dear God, Charlotte. What were we thinking?"

"Val, I..." She tried again. The tide of passion was receding, or at least getting into controllable levels.

He caught her hands once they were free, raising one to his lips and then the other. "No, it was my fault. I should know better than that. I have no excuse, except..." He bit his lip. "No, it would be cowardly to blame this on you."

She ploughed on. "Val, I need you to let me go."

His eyes widened. "Even now, with this passion lying between us?"

At least she'd succeeded in knocking him off-balance, too. He'd unnerved her, which was one reason she needed to talk to him. "Yes, with this." She made a fuss of shaking out her skirts. "Because of this." Nothing but work but the truth, but she had not realized that articulating it would be so difficult. Lifting her head, she folded her hands before her in her usual gesture. Neatly, quietly, without fuss. Assuming her normal posture gave her strength, drew power into her. It wouldn't be so bad. He'd understand. "It's too much, Val. If you do this to me, I will become your slave. As I became my father's slave. With him I had no choice. He is my father. He may rule my life until I marry."

"Yes, until you marry. Are you comparing me with him? The Dignified Duke?" He laughed harshly as he pronounced the derogatory name society had labeled her father. "Do you think I would make you stand in my presence?"

"No. I think you will enslave me in a different way. This is more dangerous because I'm compliant with it. I'll go willingly. I can do nothing else. Your experience, your confidence, your passion—it all goes to making me obedient. Submissive."

A wild look sparked his eyes to life but was gone immediately. What had she said?

"You will learn. I know passion can make a person helpless, unable to break away, but that will pass, I swear."

"That's exactly the point, Val. You will move on. I will not."

"No, no."

She would not let him speak. He would persuade her, and then she'd be lost. "It's the truth, Val. Since when have you stayed with a woman for more than a year? Six months? Your affairs are notorious. I can't live like that, wondering who is next and where I stand in your list. You are a philanderer and worse. Only your family has kept you from serious scandal."

His face suddenly blanked of expression. She blinked. Was he as good at hiding his emotions as she was? But no, a glimmer remained, and he sighed, shaking his head. Like everything else about him, that did not last long. "That is true. But I learned that I am not as wild as some. Not as depraved, I might say."

She would not allow him to distract her. "Maybe, but I am not betrothed to them. Let me go, Val. Unless you want to ruin me, let me go."

His lips firmed. "Not to Kellett."

"Yes. He is my choice. He is gentle, kind, and true."

Val laughed harshly and his eyes flashed. "You think so? Let me tell you something about Lord Kellett."

"No!" She refused to listen. He would only blacken Hervey's character, and Hervey did not deserve that. "Let me go."

"If he'll take you after this." He prowled closer.

She held up her hands, warding him off. "After what?"

"After the scandal we created tonight."

She faced him defiantly. "I set out to create a scandal. I wanted to become as notorious as you are. Then my father will work harder to release me from the contract. Your parents wanted me for you because they thought I would be a steadying influence on you. So what if I become as wild as you?"

If she hadn't been a lady she'd have damned him to hell when he threw his head back and laughed.

"One evening dressed in a mildly scandalous manner will not accomplish that, my lady. You'll have to work harder than that. Perhaps you already have."

"Perhaps I have."

"Not in the way you might want. How many people saw us come in here? It only takes one, and she murmurs it to her friend, and they go about the room, increasing their story exponentially. Some leeway is allowed to us because of our betrothal but not this much."

Shock arced through her with the force of pain, a slash of recognition. He was right. She had no idea how long they had been in here. Half an hour, perhaps? As if to mock her, the clock in the corner chimed the half hour. "I will not marry you," she said, gasping the words as she turned and wrenched open the door, bursting out of the room before fear overtook her again.

Her father was waiting outside. He grabbed her arm roughly. "We are leaving," he said, before dragging her away.

Chapter 10

After he'd put himself to rights, Val left the room, feeling foolish and angry. There was a lot of anger around tonight. He'd heard her father's voice and was not surprised to hear from the gossips that the duke had hauled his daughter away. He could do nothing about that, not yet, but he would.

He'd heard enough. The duke was a tyrant. Now he had met Charlotte's sister, much became clear. Louisa was eighteen, under the age of consent and probably the trump card the duke held to keep Charlotte in check. He would do his best and encourage his father to help him get her away, though there was little he could do about it if the duke chose to keep his youngest daughter for another three years.

All he had was the signed marriage contract, and he would not let that go easily. At the moment it was his only weapon, his only way of striking back against the man who aimed to take Charlotte and make her into God knew what.

The news about Janey had crystallized what he felt and what he knew he must do. Even if she did not want him when he was done, he had to give Kellett the right-about. Val could not allow the man anywhere near her.

As he left the room he met the stares boldly, but for the first time he felt shame at what he did. He truly had not intended to make her situation worse. He strode through to the ballroom, intent on finding Kellett. He would make his position clear before he left, and the man would listen to him.

Darius came up to him. "He's in the card room. He was waiting for her to emerge, but her father got there first."

Val studied his brother in silence until he regained the sangfroid he was famous for.

Darius jerked a brief nod. "You'll do."

Val had never deceived his twin before, not as thoroughly nor as completely. He surprised himself with the ease he used putting on his society mask. Perhaps Charlotte had inspired him. He'd seen when she'd tried to assume her usual mien and privately rejoiced when she was unable to do so with him. He was breaking through to her.

His course was set. Kellett would never have her if he had anything to do with the matter.

"Did you tell her about Janey?" Darius said quietly.

His every sense revolted. "How could I? How do you tell a respectable woman that? She would likely refuse to believe me in any case." Then she would believe he was a liar as well as fickle.

"She should be warned."

Val shook his head and moved on, leaving the ballroom in favor of hunting his quarry.

Ivan was already in the card room. Groups of people were sitting around half a dozen small tables. Some were laughing and enjoying their friendly game. Others were playing in earnest. The seasoned players had a way about them. Man or woman, they affected carelessness, but their gazes were sharply intent. Either that or clouded with drink. Some only played when they were intoxicated, but they won all the same. Recklessness could lead to riches. Or of course, it could lead to ruin.

Val helped himself to a glass of rich ruby-red wine from one of the bottles standing on the sideboard. The company had made their way through quite a few already, even though the well-trained staff were busy clearing away the spent bottles.

He took his time observing the company, waiting until his mind was once more coolly analytical. He would not undertake his plan until his head had cleared. The familiar sounds of clinking coins, soft conversation, and cards being dealt entered his senses.

His quarry was sitting at a table with four others, a few coins on the table indicating their state of play. One gentleman glanced up, nodded at Ivan, and left the table. Nicephorus, Viscount Westwood, was taller than most gentlemen in the room. He even topped Darius and Val by an inch or two. He did not stop for a word, but passed through the other door in the direction of the ballroom after nodding to his cousins.

"Reinforcements?" Val queried.

"He happened to be here. I happened to mention that we would appreciate his help." Darius nodded to the empty chair. "Off you go. Ruin him."

Trust Darius to know exactly what was in his twin's mind.

Val's proficiency at the card table was well known, but these days he only played moderately. Before they had begun the insurance business, he had taken his playing to extremes. Known for playing deep and recklessly, he'd won and lost a great deal, but he appreciated the better odds and deeper stakes in his business venture and saved his acumen for that.

Not tonight. "Good evening, gentlemen." He took his place at the table.

Kellett looked up sharply, an arrested expression on his face. He met Val's eyes. If he rose and left, the Emperors would take that as an insult. He did not need Val to tell him that. If he stayed and played a hand or two he might survive the evening, but Val had plans to stop him leaving once he began to play too deep. He put his hand in his pocket and drew out some gold, dropping it in the cup carved into the wood by his place at the table.

A gentleman glanced at him and then at Kellett. Word about Val's disagreement with Kellett had obviously flown around the ball, as he presumed it would. He had not planned it that way but had taken her into that room in a whirlwind of anger and concern. However, he wasn't above using it, if he had to.

After murmuring excuses the two other gentlemen left the table. Val hardly saw them go. The tension in the room rose, and a few people filtered in. They were expecting a show. He intended to give it to them.

Darius and Ivan took the other two places at the table and bade everyone a genial good evening.

As Kellett pushed back his chair, Val dropped an item on the green baize. Diamond chips glinted as the article rolled over and settled.

The cut steel buttons on Kellett's waistcoat glittered as he heaved a breath. His dark eyes met Val's. If his were any reflection of his brother's, they were as hard as the stones in the tie pin he had just dropped.

Val leaned back and crossed his legs at the ankles, but he never relented in his perusal of his adversary.

Kellett reached for the pin, but with seeming leisure, Val put his hand over it. "It's a pretty piece, is it not? You have to play for it if you've taken a fancy to it."

"I believe my initials are on it."

Val picked up the pin and made a play of examining it. "So they are." Flicking a glance at Kellett, he raised a brow. "Is it a coincidence, or are you laying claim to it? I came by it in the most unusual place."

Kellett shrugged. "It could have been lost anywhere."

"In Covent Garden?" Val twirled the long pin between his fingers, drawing attention to the item.

Kellett stiffened. "I go to the theater regularly."

"And to the other side of the piazza?" Val wasn't talking geographically. The shock in his opponent's eyes told him that he knew that. "Not every house there is as salubrious as the theater."

Darius and Ivan remained very still.

"I see." Kellett lowered his gaze. "I will play you for it, sir."

Val had just told him several things, and he did not believe Kellett had missed one of them. He knew about Janey, and he had evidence of Kellett's transgressions. Except that this pin was strictly evidence of nothing, unless Kellett laid claim to it. "So is it yours, sir?"

"I may have owned one like it once."

Val had made a note of the hallmarking on the piece and made a rough sketch. He could identify it and the jeweler it had come from. But no court of law would accept it as evidence of murder, unless Kellett lay claim to it as his.

He did not hold out any expectation of that, or of bringing a murder charge since no body was forthcoming. Nevertheless, Kellett would pay, in one way or another. If Val could not bring true justice, he would get it another way.

"An aberration," Kellett said, tracing a pattern on the table.

His finger was not entirely steady, Val noted with satisfaction.

"Every man tries something a little different from time to time, do you not agree?" His gaze went from Val to Darius.

Ah. The threat did not have to be any more blatant. He was implying that he would expose Darius. He was not giving up without a fight. Val shrugged, although his heart missed a beat. Darius could be hanged for what came to him naturally.

Val knew how to protect his own, and he would give his life for his brother. He picked up a wrapped pack of cards and broke the seal. "Whist?"

They agreed, and he dealt. Casually he picked up the pin and secured it on his coat, where Kellett could feast his eyes on it.

The first rubbers passed as the stakes slowly grew and the men threw guineas into the table as if they were pennies. Kellett had enough money to keep up with the trio. They would not beat him that way.

Gentle murmuring from the onlookers did not interrupt them. People at the other tables continued to play. The chink of coins and gentle conversation was punctuated by the terse declaration of bets and a few desultory exchanges of conversation.

"You have made quite a splash this season, sir." Darius growled the words, obviously, at least to his twin, affected by Kellett's threat. He was not talking about water.

"Indeed." Kellett dropped a two of spades. Hearts were trumps, but nobody used one.

Darius won the play and placed a ten on the table.

"I intend to continue. I have come to town to seek a wife."

Why? Did he want someone to torture, or someone to cover his torture of others? "There are many lovely young women making their debut this season."

"One in particular."

Val gathered the hand he had won and added to the small heap of coins in the center of the table. "Indeed. I fear she is spoken for."

"Not for much longer."

The man had a nerve. He knew Val was aware of his murdering ways, and yet he dared to threaten him?

Or was he merely trying to anger his opponent? Val refused to be veered off course. He would not support his brother at the expense of his betrothed. He would win them both.

"A contract is signed."

"It will be broken."

Val would rather kill him. Instead, he took the next rubber. By that time he was breathing steadily again, but anger simmered steadily inside him.

Kellett paused in the act of gathering the cards for his deal. The emerald on the ring on his hand glinted like the eye of a snake. "I will have the lady, sir. I have the assets she requires. Her father is amenable to my suggestions, and I expect to be victorious soon."

Val raised a brow. "Interesting. How do you propose to achieve that?"

"By asking."

"And what if I object?" Val bared his teeth.

Kellett shrugged. "You will not, sir. You will be too busy elsewhere." His sly glance at Darius explained his meaning.

Fear streaked through Val. Had the bastard collected information about Darius? Would he lay that before a magistrate? Fielding of Bow Street had the reputation for incorruptibility. If Darius were caught in an illegal act in his jurisdiction, he would find himself in Newgate.

Anger followed. Val would do more than win Charlotte from this evil specimen of humanity. He would destroy him. Nobody threatened the people he loved and walked away free and clear. Cold determination drove him now.

Darius glanced his way but said nothing. He would have recognized his twin's mood enough to know he could do nothing about it. Darius was always the more easygoing twin, despite Val's usual casual manner. "I believe I can find time for both tasks."

Kellett shook his head sorrowfully. "A man's time is always restricted. I believe you will be busy enough with your family's concerns. I will remove one of those from your shoulders when I marry your betrothed."

The murmurs from the onlookers increased and Charlotte's name was clearly mentioned.

Ignoring everyone else, Val uncrossed his legs and leaned forward, his elbows on the table. He plucked the pin from his coat. Sweeping at the coins aside, he dropped the pin in their place. "We will play for her. If you win, I will agree to break the contract. If you lose, you will step back."

If he won this play, he would free Charlotte from any obligation she had with him. She would have a free choice, as long as she did not choose the man before him. He would do that much for her. He knew, better than anyone, that he did not deserve her. But he would do his best to earn her regard and perhaps even her love.

Brave words. His act would be the first self-sacrificing thing he had ever done in his adult life.

"I believe Lady Charlotte has already made her choice. This would merely ratify it."

The ruffian had the impudence to name her. Playing cards for a lady's hand would make Charlotte notorious. She could be ruined. Kellett had done it on purpose. Once ruined, she would have little choice but to marry whoever asked for her and retire in disgrace. Val had no intention of that happening. Her endearing efforts this evening to make herself notorious were now eclipsed by this genuine scandal. Her carefully cultivated reputation for quiet respectability had shattered when Kellett used her name.

Val would have his head for that.

He picked up two packs of cards and broke the seals. "Piquet." He glanced up to receive his opponent's assent before he set his fingers to work. Val would call all his talents to use now. Never had he needed his skills more.

Piquet was a two-hander and required only the seven and up of each suit. Val took barely five minutes to sort through the two packs, shuffle, and deal the required hands and the talon, the reserve cards each player could call on.

As Val had dealt, he had the first use of the talon. He duly won the first set of six, known as a partie, but not by a great number of points, taking his time to learn his opponent's style. Piquet was one of the few card games where skill could make a difference.

He had Kellett's measure after the second partie. He was a steady player, with no attempt at reckless play. His gains were sound but not spectacular.

For the next few parties, the honors remained even. While they were playing for an ultimate prize of Charlotte's hand, they still used gold to mark the play. At the end of each partie, they tallied the points and handed over the money. Then Val lost heavily, and what was more, he lost when he dealt, which by the odds of the game should not happen. Kellett's pile overflowed the cup carved into the wood of the table, the smooth bowl completely hidden by the glint of gold. Notes of hand replaced coin as the stakes rose.

Ivan was keeping score, announcing the tallies after each hand in a toneless voice. Darius checked the numbers. Kellett must be keeping it in his own mind, because he nodded tersely when Ivan declared the points.

The room was tense now, the silence overwhelming. People gathered around the table, watching the play. Nobody was making the polite conversation usually heard in these situations. It could be said that the ball had turned into a gaming hell.

When Val lost again, the gasp from the spectators was almost palpable. He had lost ten thousand guineas, the stakes having risen with each partie, but he kept his expression blank and his smile fixed firmly in place. This time his loss was not so bad.

"I will send you an invitation to the wedding," Kellett purred.

Val growled softly. "I will *not* send you one." He shrugged. "Shall we make this the last game?"

Kellett smirked. "Are you losing your nerve?"

Val won the next partie, but only by a narrow margin. Not that he cared. He had calculated to a nicety what he needed to win. He assessed the risk and found it high, but not too much for him to overcome.

A little manipulation was in order. Leaning back, he held his cards negligently, as if they would drop at any moment, and crossed his feet once more. Nodding to a servant, he touched his glass and received another drink.

When Kellett made a play, Val immediately put his card on top, as if he weren't thinking about his game. He had a reputation for growing bored easily. He might as well use it.

While Kellett pondered, Val took snuff and gave his box to his brother to note the exquisite enamel. "A new shop has opened in 'Change. Remind me to take you next week. I fear this week might become somewhat crowded with regard to engagements."

Darius did not need any more hints. He had played this game before. "Do you intend to use the box at the theater tomorrow night?"

Val shrugged. "I don't think so. I know the world admires Garrick, but occasionally I find his antics tedious. I may take my betrothed to Ranelagh."

Kellett growled low in his throat. He bent over his cards, studying them as if his life depended on it.

Val had allowed society to see him lose his temper earlier this evening, so he had ground to make up. During the declaration part of the hand, he claimed an outrageous number of bids, which Kellett, having won the previous two parties, riposted with high claims of his own.

They played. Val won. His winnings covered his losses that evening, and five thousand more.

A ripple of applause ran through the crowd when people realized what he had done and how audaciously he had done it. By letting Kellett win, he had led him into over-declaring his hand later on, believing himself the superior player. Val could not have used that tactic at the start of the play. He'd risked a huge amount of money to assess his opponent's mettle. But he had never risked Charlotte. Even if he had gained a reputation for cheating, he would not allow Kellett to have her.

But he did not. He had won the lady and five thousand guineas on top of that. After accepting the note of hand the man scribbled, he picked up the gold pin and restored it to his pocket. "I believe our business here is done," he said mildly.

"Expect to hear more from me, sir." Pale-faced, Kellett stood and strode from the room.

Val did not feel like a winner. The battle was not yet over.

Chapter 11

Charlotte's father had refused to speak to her all the way home from the ball. Their theater visit was, of course, curtailed. She went straight to her room, where Hunter undressed her in silence.

He'd made a mistake, leaving her to her own devices for an evening. Instead of haranguing her as he usually did, he'd left her to think, and by the early hours of the morning, she had a plan.

They would throw themselves on Hervey's mercy. He had promised to make a home for her and Louisa, and he had enough money and influence to help her deny her unwanted suitor. She would take Louisa and they would leave today.

Having made her decision, Charlotte turned over, tucked her hand under her pillow to cover the spare key to her room, and fell into a dreamless sleep.

The duke sent her a note the next day, tersely instructing her to remain in her room until he summoned her.

With the knowledge that with the day, a new life dawned for Louisa and herself, Charlotte felt emboldened. She dressed as she preferred, refusing hair powder and dismissing her maid as soon as Hunter had laced her into her stays and put her hair up. She could manage the rest herself. Hunter would rush down to tell the duke, via his valet. What she didn't know was that Charlotte had loosened the stranglehold of her fichu and pulled her hair out of the scalp-tightening bun and done her own, softer, one once her maid had left. Then she had added a smaller prettier lace cap rather than the plain, all enveloping linen one that had made her look like a Puritan maid. She wore the slate blue gown, plain but serviceable. Even that looked better with her new looser style.

She had come this far. She might as well continue along her road to perdition.

Her decision did not help her tenseness as the morning wore on and still her father had not called for her. She could leave now, collect Louisa and just go. She would have sent a note to Hervey, but her father might stop anyone leaving the house with it, and then she would have effectively forewarned him. Her frustration served to deliver a churning stomach and tight throat, a distinct sense of nausea making her glad she was not summoned downstairs for breakfast.

What remained of her savings weighed down her pocket. She dared not leave it behind. On her father's orders, Hunter could search her room and find her last vestige of independence there. If she had to leave her father's study and walk out the door, then she would do it. But not without Louisa. They might have to fight a court battle, if the duke sued them for the return of Louisa, but better out in the open than hidden behind closed doors. Louisa was not mad.

She turned her mind to the coming interview.

The most likely outcome was that which would separate her from anyone who might help her. That meant a sojourn in one of the smaller of her father's houses where she could be efficiently confined. He would want to ensure that she obeyed his bidding, even after her marriage. She would never be free of him if she gave in to his wishes now. Her one night of freedom carried a huge cost, but she would bear the consequences the best way she knew and fight for her freedom.

She would not go quietly or willingly. This time, whatever it cost her, she would fight back. Nobody could help her now, not Val nor Hervey. Her defiance had been absolute.

Worse than that was what the duke might do to Louisa. His most diabolical trait of making one child the scapegoat for another's transgressions made Charlotte determined to persuade him to allow her to take all the punishment. If he beat her, so be it. It wouldn't be the first time.

She strode up and down the worn carpet laid in her room, waiting for the summons.

A tap on the door broke into her agitated thoughts. Then that someone tried the door, rattling it as if he didn't believe it was locked.

"My lady." Her voice was muffled but Charlotte recognized her maid. "Your father requests your presence in his study immediately."

In this house, "request" meant an order.

Assuming her mask of calm, Charlotte unlocked the door and gave her maid her best blank stare. "You are dismissed," she said, meaning for good, not for now.

As she expected, Hunter took no notice but followed her downstairs, more like a guard than a servant. Their feet echoed on the highly polished floorboards. The quiet of the house was absolute, but it was not a comfortable silence. It was fraught with tension. Upstairs servants would be attending to the bedrooms, their steps as soft as they could make them. The door to the downstairs area was thicker than usual because the duke preferred it.

Outside, wheels grated against cobbles and people went about their everyday business, but in here, all was hushed, reverent silence.

Charlotte hated this house, where the public rooms and those her father used were furnished luxuriously, but all others had the bare minimum they needed, and the furniture was scuffed and old. The place contained in its own bubble of tense silence, every being inside waiting for the will of the master.

After today, if her plans went well, she need never see it again.

A footman in full livery stood outside the study. He flung open the door and announced her, as if she were a visitor rather than a member of the family. "Lady Charlotte Engles, your grace!"

As usual, Charlotte dropped a deep curtsy and rose in one smooth motion, keeping her head bowed.

"Do you dare to come before me in undress, madam?"

She did not look up. "The hair powder irritates my skin, your grace." Normally she would have assured him that she would attend to the matter immediately, but she was in no mood for that.

He shot her a hard glare. "You have displeased me greatly. After we left last night, two of the guests—I will not call them gentlemen—played piquet for your favors." Without warning, he slammed his clenched hand on his desk. Everything arranged neatly on the surface rose a full inch before crashing down again. His crystal ink pot bounced but remained in one piece, and his pot of quills shattered, spilling the pens everywhere. Piles of papers split apart, tumbling on to the floor.

Charlotte leaped along with the items, as if all his possessions were jumping to his will. Her heart leaped too, pounding against her ribs and making her breathless.

She knew these responses. She recognized them so she did not panic as another person unused to this treatment might have done. Knowing the way to recover, she concentrated on her breathing and keeping her expression calm.

Her father roared his anger. "I will not have my house brought into disrepute. You alone have created the biggest scandal in my family that I have ever experienced. I had no idea I was harboring a wanton, madam. Your appearance shocked everyone who spoke to me last night. You are a disgrace, and you must learn to behave."

He drew a breath and watched her. Charlotte remained, her hands folded before her and her face clear. She said nothing. There was nothing she could say, for he would attack every word she uttered and every word she did not. Why should she waste her time?

"You will leave for the country this very day. Your maid will pack what is suitable, and you will stay at the manor of Conset in Devonshire until you learn correct behavior. I will cancel the marriage contract with Lord Shaw, and you will not be allowed to see Lord Kellett again."

Shock arced through her. "Father!"

He stared at her, even his jowls unmoving. She knew what he was waiting for. He wanted her to use his title and beg for mercy. From previous experience, she knew she would obtain none. "Sir," she said, "why would you do this?" To her shame, her voice quivered. Tears were imminent and she could do nothing about them. Either she stopped and controlled herself, or she let the tears fall. "Those two gentlemen are my only expectation of marriage." By the time he allowed her back to town she would be an old maid, truly on the shelf.

"They were the gentlemen wagering over you last night. They brought your reputation into disrepute, madam, as if you had not done enough in that direction already. Society is gossiping about you. Gossiping! You will prepare for your departure."

They'd cared enough to do that? Despite her terror, a thread of warmth crept through Charlotte's being.

"Your sister," he went on relentlessly, "will go where she was always meant to be. I have found a house to take her."

That only meant one thing. "You're committing her?"

"It is time." He sounded as if he were talking about someone else, someone he knew only tangentially.

"She is not insane! She's your daughter!" Now terror had her in its grip. If she did not know where Louisa had gone, how could she rescue her? She'd be under guard at cold, charmless Conset, unable to do anything to help her sweet sister.

He met her gaze coldly. "So are you." Slowly, he got to his feet and his fist came down on the desk again, crashing in time to his words. "You have let me down. You have disgraced this house and the family name. You will make amends for your transgression if it is the last thing you ever do!"

She was breathing too fast. Concentrating, she tried to slow it down. He was sending Louisa to a place that would surely kill her. There was nothing wrong with Louisa, but he would drive her mad. Without her helper, her family, and her familiar possessions, she would fall ill and waste away, if her delicate health did not get her first. "You cannot do this. You would not be so cruel!"

The front door slammed, and her father's concentration broke for a brief instant. Voices sounded in the hall, and he grimaced. "Go to your room and dress for your journey."

Charlotte couldn't do it. For her sister as much as for herself, she stood her ground. "No," she said. "I will not go to Conset." She even stamped her foot.

His head snapped around to regard her with a dead snakelike stare. He had probably assumed she was finished business, such was his arrogance. "I don't think I heard you properly."

"Yes, you did." She clamped her teeth together to stop her jaw trembling. She had to do this, or she was lost, a creature instead of a person.

"Go." He flicked his fingers as if getting rid of a fly. He glanced at her sharply. "You will be whipped. I will instruct Hunter to do so."

At her age? He had not done that for years. She would not allow it. "No."

The duke's face reddened, and his eyes narrowed, the gleam needle-sharp. Turning, he picked up the switch that he kept behind his desk. "I will inflict your punishment myself. Turn around and lift your skirts."

The voices outside came closer. None that she recognized, at least—shock turned her rigid. A female voice mixed in with the protestations and shouted instructions. Charlotte knew that voice.

Whirling around, she flung open the door to the study and flew to the arms of the woman she wanted most to see. Her sister, still in bonnet and cloak held her arms wide. Tears poured down their cheeks, as they shared their first embrace in two years.

Charlotte did not have much time before they would be separated. Servants were converging on them, and they would not hesitate to pull them apart. "He's sending me to Devonshire and locking up Louisa!" she cried in between gulps as she fought to control her emotions. Sensations heaped on her and over her, as if bombarding her with everything she had denied in the past few years. The rose fragrance she remembered so well swept over her, bringing back a wave of memories to add to her already overloaded system.

Sarah's arms tightened around her. "I will fight him," she said. "I have allies now." She spoke over Charlotte's head to their father. "You, sir, should be ashamed of yourself. I know your game, and I will not let you make another play."

Charlotte swallowed, forcing calm on herself. She could not reach her handkerchief, so she grabbed her fichu and pulled. It came free, and she pressed the linen against her face, drying her tears and blowing her nose. Sarah put her arm around Charlotte's shoulders. "Come, my dear." Over her shoulder, she snapped out instructions. "Bring tea to the drawing room, and something to eat, too."

"Why did you come?"

Her sister hushed Charlotte and led her to the drawing room. Charlotte stumbled, but kept her footing until they were inside.

The usual chill greeted them, but Sarah dissipated that. "How can it be so warm outside and so cold in here? I had never noticed it before." She spoke as if entering a house on an ordinary visit.

Her tone went some way toward calming Charlotte. Sarah pressed her into a chair and then stood to face their father.

"You will eject this strange woman," the duke ordered.

"I have brought servants of my own," Sarah said. "If you want to engage in a battle royal, go ahead and have your servants try to manhandle me. My servants will take that amiss, I can assure you. It is, of course, your choice, but when I leave, my sisters are leaving with me. I will not let them suffer any longer now I have the means to save them."

Charlotte peeped around her sister's skirts. Her father was all but breathing fire. He resembled nothing so much as an enraged bull. In a moment he would start to paw the ground. "Leave. I will have nothing to do with you. My daughters are my concern. Have you forgotten that Louisa is underage?"

"Unfortunately, she is," Sarah admitted. "However, I will create a scandal such as you have never seen before if you keep her from me."

"Oh, Charlotte has already created one." The duke smirked, but it appeared more like a grimace. "No man will take her now."

Sarah stuck her clenched fists on her hips. "And that is exactly what you wanted, is it not? You refused to let me go when I received half a dozen respectable offers for my hand. Then I met my dear Sam, and I knew you would treat him the same way. I made my plans, because with you as a father, I needed to. You never had any intention of letting any of us go, did you? You want all three of us dancing attendance upon you until the day you die."

"Madam!" His jowls were certainly shaking now. Every part of their father trembled with rage. "I will say it one more time. Leave my house."

"When my business is done."

A bump sounded from the floor above. What was happening? Nobody took any notice but Charlotte, as Sarah continued in her tirade. "The contract with Lord Valentinian Shaw suited you well. You never had any intention of that contract coming to fruition, and you knew Lord Valentinian was happy with that."

"Who are you?" he said cruelly. "The wife of an impoverished journalist. What influence do you have? You have no right to take my daughters away."

"Matters have developed since you spoke to me last. I am the wife of a new Member of Parliament in possession of the fortune he inherited from his great-uncle who has connections in all the right quarters. So here *we* are, and here *you* are." Her voice hardened.

Charlotte recognized the sound. Sarah had often used that tone when she had come up against their father. She had defied him and taken the punishment meant for her younger sisters, until she had left. Her elopement had been the talk of society, but not for long. Something else, someone else had taken its place, as it always did. Sarah had thrown herself away on a poor hack who could offer her nothing. But her fortunes had changed.

This heated argument would be the talk of the highest in the land. Their pictures would appear in the cartoon shops in the morning. Sarah must know that. She'd left the door open to let everyone in the house witness the scene. Even her father could not stop the servants talking. Some would hurry down to Grub Street and sell what they knew to the hacks who lived and worked there.

Charlotte could hear the rustle of speculation, sense the news passing down the street outside and rippling toward the print machines.

One thing her sister said resonated with her and put everything she had experienced into its rightful place. Her father never intended for her to marry.

He wanted to keep them close, dancing attendance on the only man that mattered—the Duke of Rochfort. He had opposed the men who had proposed to Sarah, finding fault with them all until Sarah had fallen in love and eloped. Charlotte's betrothal to Val had suited the duke because he never meant the marriage to happen. He might have ended the contract and then made it impossible for Hervey to claim her. She was a fool for not noticing, but she had been too busy fighting the little battles to discern the big one.

"I have been cursed." The duke's voice cut through the cacophony and chaos.

Two of his footmen faced two very large servants Sarah had brought with her, obviously expecting more than a verbal fight.

"I am cursed with females. Get out of my house, all three of you. Get out now. From today I have no daughters, only a son. That is all I need for my name to continue and the dignity of the title to endure. You have an hour. Then be gone."

He turned around and left.

Charlotte let out the breath she hadn't been aware she was holding. Air whooshed into the room, as if life had returned to a room mired in limbo.

Sarah nodded to one of her men. "Go with Lady Charlotte and assist her. We had best make haste."

"What about Louisa?"

A smile spread across Sarah's lips, growing slowly. "While I created a distraction, Aunt Adelaide got her outside and into the carriage."

Charlotte's strength returned quickly, and she raced upstairs, no longer trying to be quiet and decorous, intent on taking only what she wanted. She would have left her father with the clothes on her back if she'd had to, so an hour was a bonus.

She hurled items into an open traveling trunk. Hunter was nowhere in sight. That was just as well because Charlotte had no intention of taking her, wherever they were going. She didn't care. She was leaving this hellhole for good, probably penniless, without a portion, and with the prospect of having to earn her own living. None of that mattered because Sarah had come, and they were free to go.

When she threw her new gown into the trunk, she paused and let her fingers linger on the silk. Last night seemed so long ago now. Only one event remained powerfully in her mind—Val's kiss. The memory of it lingered, all she had left to remember him. He would not marry her now. The Marquess and Marchioness of Strenshall would not allow a penniless nobody to marry their son.

Would Hervey take her? She felt sure he would. He had always told her he wanted her for her sweet self, not for her position or her status in society. He'd said it with such sincerity she could not help but believe him. They would go with Sarah now, and she would have a message sent to him, where he could collect her.

She tossed items into the trunk until she had filled it. The man standing by the door came forward at her nod and fastened and locked it for her. She had left behind all the linen caps, the plain woolen stockings that itched her legs, the worn-out shifts and pairs of stays, and the thick linen fichus. The clothes she took were admittedly dowdy and dull, but she had to have something to wear, and she would not be able to buy new.

The servant hoisted the trunk onto one shoulder as if it weighed nothing. Charlotte took one last look around her room, sad that she would miss nothing about it. She had no private items, no letters from her youth, no toys either, since her father had them disposed of as soon as she'd left the schoolroom. Her dressing case stood waiting, so she picked it up and left.

Charlotte did not hesitate until she was inside the traveling coach outside. She did not look back as they drove away.

Chapter 12

Breakfast at the house of the Marquess of Strenshall was a noisy affair, even with a member of the family missing. Last night, while Val had been cavorting with his betrothed and teasing Lord Kellett half to death, his oldest brother had arrived from the country with his wife.

Viola was an old friend. She had been the daughter of the steward to the estate, and more besides. In a breakneck adventure last year, Val's older brother Marcus had saved her, been happily compromised, and married her. Viola's presence at the table seemed as if it was meant to be.

Claudia, the missing member of the family, was in the country with her husband. Claudia's twin, Livia, missed her terribly, but she was holding up, and it wasn't as if her sister weren't blissfully happy.

Val strolled into the breakfast parlor wearing a brilliant purple banyan, one of his collection of the soft garments that took the place of the formal coat indoors. He had floor-length ones too and took great pleasure in seeking out the brightest he could find. They made a wonderful contrast to the pale man with red-rimmed eyes who was suffering from the effects of the night before.

Not today though. Today he was stone-cold sober.

After greeting Marcus, he took his seat and reached for the coffee. His mother had long ago instituted an informal meal at noon to which all the family were summoned. Servants only entered when she rang the bell at her elbow. They were alone and they could speak frankly, sometimes brutally.

His mother's sigh alerted Val to the fact that he was not in her best books this morning. Such a small sigh, but so full of meaning.

He rubbed his chin, the stubble rasping his palm. "You are about to comment on last night's events," he prompted her. Better to get it over with, and then he could eat his breakfast in peace.

"Fill your plate first, my son. You're going to need it."

Damn. Rising from the table, Val sauntered to the sideboard and did as she bade him. The usual delicious array of chops, kidneys, bacon, eggs, fried potatoes, and the other viands her ladyship deemed necessary for her family's start to the day lay in silver warming plates over spirit lamps, keeping sizzling hot. Val helped himself, but he only took a modest amount. He could still see the floral pattern on his plate when he had done.

Returning to the table, he took his place. He would far rather visit his father in his study than face trial by family. "Let battle commence." He picked up his knife and fork and cut into his chop.

"Val, you have a positive gift for getting into trouble," his mother complained. "Your little drama last night was enacted in front of half of London. The other half is reading about it this morning. They are now speculating about the bad blood between the Emperors and the Smithsons. We have only just settled our differences with the Dankworths. We are hardly looking for another fight."

"I'm not so sure about that," Marcus muttered. He had his own reasons for holding the Dankworth family in contempt. Val felt for him.

"We have to," the marquess put in. "Let's call it an uneasy truce."

"Yes, let's," Marcus said morosely. He touched his wife's hand, and she gave him a bright smile. Too bright. Marcus lifted Viola's hand and pressed a kiss to the palm.

"Love at the breakfast table," Darius said thoughtfully. "Too rich a dish for me."

Marcus glared at him, but Darius only gave him a bland smile and turned to his own food. Marcus's happiness had been hard-won, and he deserved every bit of it. Moreover, the event had changed Marcus from a humorless dullard into a man unafraid to voice his needs and opinions.

"What are you doing now, Val?" His mother sounded resigned, but her tone did not fool her second son.

"Opposing the vile comments made about my betrothed wife."

"Charlotte? I heard you were playing piquet for her hand. Were you playing to win or to lose?"

Val shot a glance at his father, who shook his head infinitesimally. He had not told her of Lord Kellett's proclivities, then. Morosely, he silently thanked his father for that. He would have to tell her himself. And the rest of his family, it appeared. "Kellett is a miserable specimen of mankind.

Charlotte favored him, but she is not aware of the full extent of his activities. Neither would I tell her. They are not fit for a respectable female's ears."

His mother snorted with derision. "Are you telling me that women do not know these things?"

Val shook his head. "But I would rather eat my breakfast without thinking about it. The man turns my stomach."

"And so you picked a dispute with him."

His appetite restored, Val forked up a piece of kidney. "He picked one with me. Charlotte is still my betrothed, and it is my responsibility to defend her against unwarranted attacks."

"Is that what he did?" His mother poured coffee and pushed it over. He smiled his thanks and finished his mouthful.

"Not precisely, but he did mention her name in an inappropriate place. So I defended her."

"And won five thousand guineas," Darius pointed out.

"That as well." He would devote the whole amount to Charlotte. She had earned it.

"I cannot be but pleased, however, that you are ending your arrangement," his mother said. "You might have to wait a week or two, but Lady Charlotte appears to be having a change of heart. She seems determined to make herself notorious."

Val opened his mouth to reply, but as he did, his father cleared his throat and picked up his magnifying glass to focus on an article. "I believe your scandal may be joined by another. I went out early this morning, and they are talking of nothing else in the coffeehouses."

"Do not keep us waiting, John." The marchioness tapped her spoon on the table. "What is it?"

The marquess glanced up at her. "There are some indelicate parts." He nodded meaningfully at his unmarried daughters.

"Hah!" Livia joined the conversation. "I am studying such indelicate matters. I wish to learn, so that I might help." Livia had recently taken an interest in charitable work. Her twin's recent marriage had dispirited her, making her look at alternatives to marriage. She seemed to be convinced that she had missed her opportunities, and it was true. She had never attracted the attention some of her contemporaries enjoyed, but she should not give up just yet. Unless she wanted to, but from the occasional wistful glance she cast at her married acquaintances, Val guessed she did not. Perhaps she would have a favorable outcome, too.

The family had quieted, and everyone stared expectantly at its head. The marquess sighed and picked up the journal. "It says here, 'The esteemed

Mr. John Fielding, magistrate at Bow Street, had a violent awakening from his slumbers yesterday morn. On rising, his servants informed him of the sad parcel of humanity left at his front door. Mr. Fielding, being a compassionate man, ordered the female brought indoors, but it was discovered that she was past saving. The girl was cut over her back, so deeply as to show the bone.'" He broke off, appealing to his wife, but his children insisted he continue. Val sat frozen to his seat. He remembered vividly one girl cut to the bone. With a whip.

"'The girl had a note pinned to the remnants of her gown which indicated she was Jane Trotter. On enquiries, Mr. Fielding discovered that she was the unfortunate daughter of a button-maker in the City. On being informed of his daughter's fate, the father broke into wails of distress, claiming he had not seen the girl this past twelvemonth, when she had left his house after a dispute. He identified the unfortunate victim as his beloved daughter. The marks on her body were severe and prolonged. They showed old scars as well as the ones that killed the girl. Such wickedness cannot be allowed to go unpunished, and Mr. Fielding has pledged to discover the person or persons who committed this terrible crime.'"

Sighing, he put the paper down. "This is a sad occurrence, but it is fast becoming the first in gossip."

Although his heart sank to his feet, Val became aware of a slight sense of relief. Taking his admittedly poor behavior from last night out of the public eye was good news, although he wished heartily it had not been because of poor Janey. The news that she had died had hit him hard and had led to the loss of his control when confronted with her murderer.

Did the authorities have any idea where she had come from or who was involved?

When breakfast ended, he lost no time visiting his brother's chamber. He even tapped on the door, something he did not always remember to do.

Darius was at his dressing table, putting the final touches to his appearance. He tended to dress plainly, and Val guessed he would be out of the house long before he had prepared for his daily London round. His brother caught Val's entrance and lifted a finger. His valet disappeared through the jib door.

"He will not listen," Darius said.

Val nodded. He trusted his brother to know his own servants. Darius had his dressing table at the side of his room. Val leaned against the wall and folded his arms. "So, Janey. Janey Trotter."

Darius rubbed his nose and grimaced. "Yes." He stared at his reflection and then turned back to Val. "I persuaded the madam to give me the poor girl after she died. I did not like the idea of disposing of her body as if it meant nothing. I felt sure it would mean something to someone. So I left her outside Fielding's house."

"Who else knows?"

"Me, and now you. The madam didn't know what I intended to do with her. I could have dropped her in the Thames for all she cared, as long as I got the girl out of the house."

Val frowned. "How in God's name did you get her from Covent Garden up to Bow Street without anyone seeing you?"

Darius shrugged. "I dressed her in a cloak and carried her there with my arm around her waist. To all intents and purposes, the girl was drunk. Then I dropped her at the house door. People watching would think she was dead drunk. I was masked. Nobody recognized me."

The matter of fact way he described his act minimized several important factors. First, however small and thin the girl was, it took a tremendous feat of strength to carry her with one arm for that distance. And the act indicated how much Darius hated injustice. The killing of Janey Trotter was an enormous one.

"You know Janey's killer will probably never be brought to justice for the crime." Val pointed out gently. "The madam will never lay evidence against the man." Even though his brother had assured him that his valet had left, Val still took care not to name the man. Once that rumor started, there would be no stopping it, and Val wanted to keep the information to himself a while yet.

Darius dropped the buffer and picked up his nail-paring knife. He played with it, twirling it deftly between his fingers, watching the flash of the small but delicate razor-sharp blade. "I know. The least I could do was to give her family surcease."

He had done that. "Did you know she had a family?"

"I guessed. The few words I heard from her lips were in a London accent, relatively refined at that. While she could have come from a rookery, or an orphanage, I wanted to give them the chance. And to leave her at Fielding's door seemed like a kind of justice. The man is incorruptible, so they say."

"They do." Val had yet to believe any magistrate incorruptible. Money was a big persuader, he had found. However, Fielding was the nearest they had, and he had taken the fate of the women who occupied the houses around his court and Newgate gaol seriously. He utterly refused to send women to Bridewell, the prison specializing in females, because he accused it of being an academy. Such outlandish ideas had raised the anger of others, but there was no doubt he was sincere in his actions.

"He probably told the journalists," Darius said. "I thought he would."

"Will you take her cause?"

Darius shook his head. "I have done all I can. The girl is restored to her family. We know who did it, and you have the matter in hand."

Val kicked away from the wall. "The man is insufferable. He has already insulted Charlotte beyond bearing. I owe him, Darius."

"You plan to marry Charlotte then?" Darius raised his brows, surprise evident. "I thought you intended to let her go once the scandal of last night had blown over."

"Yes, I'll marry her," he said firmly. "I cannot leave her to what she may expect without me. I know more than you about her situation, Darius, and it is not the most pleasant. Her father is a despot behind doors as well as a disciplinarian in public. He is more than proud, more than arrogant. He is tyrannical."

Darius met his brother's gaze directly, his blue eyes frank. "Is he unkind to her?"

"I believe so. I blame myself for not noticing before. Oh, I knew he was strict, but not downright cruel. Did you know that the youngest sister is simple?" At Darius's arrested stare, he continued. "He uses the youngest one as a lever to persuade Charlotte to do his bidding. Unfortunately, Louisa is underage, but I am working on ways to extricate her as well as Charlotte. I do not think she will marry me and leave her sister to endure alone."

Darius gave a low whistle. "So that is why she would not push the match. I wondered about that."

Val choked out a laugh. "I never did. I was too busy getting into trouble and starting our venture. Only when we have established the business did I notice anything amiss with a two-year betrothal. It suited me, and thoughtlessly I assumed it suited her. I have amends to make."

"Don't marry her to try to make it up to her. You will fail, and you will make both of you unhappy."

"You speak from experience?"

Darius nodded stiffly. "You know Mama has tried to push women onto me. I naturally avoided the ones who gazed at me starry-eyed. I could never fulfill their expectations. But I seriously considered others. If I found someone who agreed to let me be, who would have me go my own way, then how much easier would my life be?"

Val swallowed. He had not thought of that. He had not thought properly about anything recently. Too engrossed with his own concerns to think too deeply about anyone else's. Oh, he would give help when his relatives requested it, but out of loyalty, not because their cause concerned him at more than an intellectual level.

"I will never fail you." Simple words, but he meant them down to his soul.

Darius covered Val's hand with his own. "I know. You feel and think more than you give yourself credit for. Now go and claim your bride, if you are sure."

Val nodded. "Yes, I'm sure."

* * * *

An hour and a half later, dressed in his careful best, a vision in crimson velvet and gold brocade, Val presented himself at the door of the Duke of Rochfort. The butler opened the door himself and the eerie quiet of the house reached out to take him in. The silence was anything but peaceful, however, and it was soon broken when the duke came downstairs, dressed for going out. He spared Val a glance while he allowed a footman to reverently place a hat on top of his beautifully curled wig. "Sir?"

Val noted that while he insisted on everyone, including his daughters, referring to him by his title, he had no such compunction when speaking to anyone else.

"I called in the expectation of an interview with Charlotte," he said.

"I know no one of that name."

Val's heart missed a beat. Oh God, what had he done? Val stepped into the hall, feeling like the fly entering a spider's web. The door closed behind him, so quietly that only the absence of street traffic sounds alerted him to the fact. "Your daughter, Lady Charlotte Engles."

The duke regarded him through hooded eyes. "I see. I sent another in her direction not an hour since. You should know, my lord, that if you marry her, you take her with nothing. I am done with my thankless daughters."

Did he still control the youngest? Charlotte would not thank him if he did not enquire after Louisa. For that matter, he would not forgive himself if he omitted to press the issue. "All three of them?"

"All of them. They have been a sad disappointment to me. However, my lord, if you wish to take her, we will talk further."

No they would not. If he had tossed her out of doors, Val and his family were done with the insufferably proud man. "Indeed? Where have they gone?"

The duke shrugged. "I know not. They are safe, however. They went with their older sibling. I am on my way to the club. Do you care to accompany me?"

At that moment Val felt sure the duke was mad. That was the only explanation for his behavior. Caring not who overheard, he spoke his mind. "I would not accompany you to heaven, sir, although I feel sure you are headed the other way. You let your daughters leave without knowing their destination?"

The duke sighed, as if Val had put a weight on his shoulders. Or that he was slow to understand. "They went with their older sister. They will be perfectly safe." That was the first time he had even mentioned her safety.

"What happened?"

He didn't expect an answer, but to his shock, he received one.

"Charlotte has run mad. I expect her to regain her senses before long, although I will not welcome her back without a husband. She has ruined herself. You walked away last night, once you saw her condition, and I do not blame you for it. She turned wanton, and I informed her of that fact. I will not have such a one in my household. A woman like that is beyond redemption. Her lack of respect to her father and her insolence compounded her sin. I have done my best to bring my daughters up without the benefit of a helpmeet by my side, and I expect gratitude. I have reared them to the highest standards, but they have all defied me. My oldest is beyond my help. She married so far below her I cannot accept her as fit for my company. Charlotte disgraced herself and Louisa—" He held out his hands helplessly. Or not, because the butler took that as a sign to ease him gently into his gloves. "The only way they will return here is respectably married. You, sir, have shown no sign of redemption, although your father assured me you were not as rackety as you appeared. That was his word, rackety. I would choose something bolder and more descriptive." He lowered his now-gloved hands. "You may well have aided in her downfall. I have sent a steadier, more respectable man after her. I will thank you to stay away. If he takes her, he will make her the woman she should be. He has assured me of the fact."

Val did not have to hear the man's name. He knew who the duke had sent. He probably considered the deed a gracious one.

"The man you sent is purely evil. He will beat her and destroy her spirit."

"She needs to be broken. Only then will she become a good and obedient wife and daughter. He has my blessing." He swept Val with one last, contemptuous look. "I will pray for them."

As if they had sinned past forgiveness.

Val would not forgive them, because they had done nothing wrong. There was no need for forgiveness on Rochfort's part. Only on theirs.

Where had they gone?

When he asked, the duke ignored him. If he had not held his hands carefully by his sides, he would have struck the man. But there was no sense distancing him yet. Later, when he had done with him.

Before he swept from the house, the duke turned to him. "You do not have my blessing, sir. I no longer wish her to ally herself to you."

Val couldn't resist one last dig. "Our marriage contract is still in force. Either you have nothing to do with her, or you do not. If you continue in this way, I will sue you for breach of promise."

"Not after I have laid my case before your father."

That was where he was going, not his club at all. Val would pay good money to see the confrontation between his father and Charlotte's, but he had other business to pursue. The duke had virtually thrown Kellett at her.

"I sign my own contracts, sir. You will have to persuade me to agree."

Where had she gone? He would get no more from this arrogant fool, even if he held a naked blade to his throat. He would see what a little judicious gold would do in the right pockets.

As soon as the front door had closed reverently behind the duke as he left, a woman clattered down the stairs. Val took a minute, shading his eyes from the sun streaming through the lunette over the front door. An older lady, carrying a bulging canvas bag. Ah, he had it. This was the chaperone, the duke's sister.

"Lady Adelaide." He put on his most charming smile and bowed with a flourish. Here was his best chance of finding Charlotte. "Well met."

"Not at all." The lady pushed back a wayward lock of dark hair, shoving it impatiently under her straw bergère hat. "Pray, sir, do you intend to stand there all day?"

He had considered Lady Adelaide completely under the duke's thumb. Distasteful though it might be, necessity drove him and he had prepared to intimidate the lady if he had to. He would bear the guilt. Better that, than the guilt of driving Charlotte into the arms of a murderer. "I would prefer to be of any assistance to you that I may."

"That poor girl will be lost without me."

"Lady Charlotte?"

"No, you dolt, Louisa!"

"Do you know where they are?"

"Yes, but they won't be there for long." Without ceremony, Lady Adelaide shoved the bag into his hand. "Come on." She glanced at the butler, who was standing openmouthed by the front door. "Have our belongings packed and sent on." Not waiting for the servant's response, she turned back to Val. "I had to return for some precious things of Louisa's that we forgot."

Goodness, this was a Lady Adelaide Val did not recognize at all, but he was glad that finally, she had found her courage.

Outside, she looked around. "Where is your equipage?"

"I walked," he said, shamefaced. "I wanted people to see."

"Ah." She eyed his garb. "I see. That coat is quite dazzling in the sunshine, is it not?"

"Also hot," he confessed. Velvet was not the most forgiving fabric in the world but he'd selected it for its color. He wanted to be noticed, walking into the duke's house to claim the hand of his daughter.

"We'll need a hack." She marched off toward the edge of the square.

Val lifted his hand and nodded to the disreputable vehicle loitering at the other side of the street. The driver turned his horse with little regard for the other traffic, earning himself curses aplenty, but he got the job done and drew up by Val and Lady Adelaide.

They climbed aboard, Val giving his grand attire scant notice. Lady Adelaide gave the direction and they set off for one of the busiest coaching inns in the City.

While they traveled, Val engaged Lady Adelaide by requesting an explanation of exactly what had happened that morning. They were nearly at their destination by the time she had finished, even though Val did not find the need to interpolate questions very often. In fact, Lady Adelaide proved an intelligent and perceptive woman, yet another bullied by the duke into submission.

And she was devoted to Lady Louisa. Val would make it his mission to find a comfortable and happy place for them both. As well as saving Charlotte from the machinations of a man not fit to lick her dainty feet.

As the idea flashed through his mind, a twinge of discomfort hit his groin. Even the thought of touching her did that to him these days. He couldn't account for it, but there it was; after two years of tolerating the woman, his mind had woken. He had so nearly lost her. He might lose her yet.

No, that thought was unbearable. He could not let that happen.

They had arrived. The inn was in its usual state of partially organized chaos. Ostlers raced in and out, attending to the horses of the coaches that swept through the arch into the yard. No stables were in sight, because they were underground, an ingenious way of stabling dozens of animals. People ran in and out, travelers with food and baskets in their hands, hurrying to the coach, anxiously checking with each other that they were on the right one. The air was filled with the cacophony of many people talking all at once, together with the whinnying and neighing of horses and the clatter of shod hooves on the cobblestones.

After a glance around the yard, Val led Lady Adelaide indoors.

Here the great tables and benches were packed with people, many of them leaving, but some with trunks and bags, having just arrived.

Lady Adelaide sighed. "Louisa will be in a pet." She patted the bag Val was carrying for her. "We left without Louisa's favorite toys, and without them she will not be happy. I went straight back to the house for them."

"So you brought them? You brought nothing of your own?"

She shrugged. "I have a few necessities. These are far more important. Louisa is easily distressed. If she is happy she is one of the most lovable people alive, but she will not like this disturbance."

A cry attracted Val's attention. He had only heard it once or twice before, but it was engraved on his brain.

Changing direction, he headed for the rooms at the rear of the inn; the private parlors. He did not hear the sound again, but nothing daunted he flung open the doors one by one, leaving Lady Adelaide to smooth over any disturbances he might create.

Then at the end, he found her. The last door burst open to reveal Charlotte in a man's arms being soundly kissed. But the way she held her hands against his shoulders, beating at them, did not indicate her willingness. Val did not wait for any more. With a shout, he sprang forward and delivered a hard flat-handed blow to the man's shoulder. That was enough to break his hold. Charlotte staggered back, wiping the back of her hand over her mouth. "I said no, sir, and I meant it. You will not touch me."

"I have your father's permission to touch you whenever I like," he growled. He glanced at Val, his stare one of pure contempt. "You will leave my betrothed and myself."

"You are sadly mistaken, sir," Val said, at his haughtiest. "Lady Charlotte is my affianced wife. What makes you think you are good enough to touch her?"

Lord Kellett opened his coat and tucked his hand in his pocket, but Val took little notice. He was more concerned for Charlotte.

Her sleeve was half torn away, and a bruise was already forming on her upper arm. Her hair was partly down, and red marks marred her throat, the signs of brutal handling. When he saw the trickle of blood emerge from the corner of her mouth, he was no longer calm, no longer thinking logically.

Knocking the paper out of Kellett's hand, Val plucked the token of his fury from his coat pocket and brandished it before tossing it contemptuously to the floor. "Name your seconds." His low, throbbing voice filled the room, as Lady Adelaide entered it.

Kellett was white. "You cannot do this."

"You have given me little choice."

"There is no need for this. Read the letter the duke gave to me."

Val was as cold and stiff as an icicle in the middle of winter. His anger had gone beyond heat, passing through to a cold need for revenge faster than he had ever experienced before. He knocked the note from the man's hand. "I care not. The lady is mine, by any definition of the word."

"Then perhaps you should have ensured she did not stray." Kellett had recovered from his initial shock, and a sneer curled his thin lips.

"I did not see any willing compliance when I entered the room."

"I'll be witness to that." Lady Adelaide stood with her back to the closed door, her arms folded. Behind Val, Charlotte gasped. "You were forcing yourself upon her." She turned her attention to Val. "You don't have to call him out. He should be begging you to forgive him."

"No, he should be begging her." When Charlotte moved forward, he touched her arm, and she started. "You will leave now."

Kellett stayed in his place. "Tomorrow on the Heath, with pistols."

Damn, the man meant to kill him. Swords would mean first blood, unless the accused stated otherwise.

"Dueling is illegal," said Lady Adelaide.

"Shooting practice," Val said shortly. He turned his back on Kellett, displaying his contempt for the man.

Caring little for who was in the room, he held his arms wide. With a choked sob, she came to him.

He closed his arms around her. "Marry me," he said. "Today."

Chapter 13

Charlotte's head spun. She had expected Hervey to sympathize with her, to offer to help. Instead he'd brought her into this private room and despite her stated wishes, he'd forced an embrace on her. At first he'd smothered her face and neck with wet, unpleasant kisses, but she did not yet understand what he meant.

When Val's arms held her, she could relax. She trusted him as she did nobody else, not even her sisters. "He tried to r-r-rape me. He said once the deed was done I was spoiled goods, and I would have nowhere to run." Tears poured down her cheeks, but she ignored them. "I had not thought he would do anything like that. I wouldn't have come with him had I thought that. He said he had a note from my father. I thought he had decided to give in."

"Where is your sister?" He spoke calmly and quietly, doing much to soothe her agitated spirits.

"Upstairs with Louisa, who is having a tantrum."

"Excuse me," Aunt Adelaide said. "Are you content to remain here and let his lordship look after you?"

Her forehead buried against his shoulder, she nodded.

The door closed quietly as her aunt left. She should not, but they had gone way beyond propriety here. Val guided her to the padded settee set against one wall and sat her down, curving his arms around her. She rested her head on his shoulder and fought her tears. Producing a handkerchief, he gently wiped the evidence of her distress away. "He is not worth crying over."

The events of the last ten minutes still settling in her mind, one event stood out. "He's not worth fighting over."

"I can't back out, even if I wanted to. He has to be stopped."

"He has stopped," she pointed out. "He won't do it again."

"No," Val said. "He will not." He stroked his finger under her chin and smiled down at her. "But the events have made our marriage somewhat expedient. Marry me, Charlotte."

He'd said that before. "Why?" She meant a million things with that word, but he only answered one.

"Because if you do not, your reputation will be damaged beyond repair. Word will get out. People will know. If I am protecting my wife, that will act as your shield. Especially if I do not come back from the Heath."

He watched her steadily. "No!" Her revulsion was immediate and absolute. "You must come back. I won't let you go." If they were married, could she keep him busy? Her knowledge of bedroom behavior was, admittedly, vague, but surely if he wanted her so much she could persuade him to stay? Desperation filled her. "I can't marry you only to lose you."

A steady blue gaze was all she received. Then he kissed her, fierce and brief, a kiss of claiming. "Marry me," he said.

"Don't we have to post banns?"

He shook his head. "I have a special license in my pocket."

"Why?"

"Because I want you. You opened my eyes that night in the garden, and although I swore I would do the right thing and let you go, I couldn't forget you." He kissed her again, gentler this time. "Say yes."

"What if I say no?" One man had tried to force her into a situation she did not want already today. She had stood up to him, and she would do this now if she had to.

"Then we will find a way."

She swallowed, refusing to allow tears to fall. "My father told us to leave. He has disowned me. My sister Sarah came for us. Without her I'd be without a home."

"That will never happen. My family will ensure that. Your father will acknowledge you again, although you do not need to go anywhere near him."

He hugged her when she shook her head. "I don't want to come to you with nothing."

"You bring me your sweet self. Anything else we will arrange another time, if you wish it. I wish for nothing other than you."

Taking the handkerchief from him, she finished wiping her eyes. His gentle cleaning was all very well, but she needed firmer pressure. But she snuggled closer, because that felt better than anything. "Aren't you hot in that coat?"

"Humph, maybe. I wore it to impress you."

"Consider me impressed." She sat up to allow him to remove the heavy item of clothing, although when he was done he tugged her back.

"One more kiss, and then we'll find a cleric. It shouldn't be too hard."

"Wait." Her mind was working again, thank goodness, and she had come to at least one conclusion. If he had a license, they could marry when they wished, but he wanted to do it now. Because if he died tomorrow morning, he would die knowing she was not the subject of scandal again.

She would not be a martyr's widow. She utterly refused to let him go to his death thinking that he was at peace with the world.

Putting her hand on his chest, feeling his heart pound under her palm, she made her decision. "I'll marry you tomorrow."

His eyes flared. "Before my appointment with Kellett?"

"Afterward." Sitting up, she blew her nose. "You will have to come back to me then, will you not?"

He watched her, fascinated, a slight smile on his lips. "You, my lady, do not play fair."

"If I did, I'd soon bore you, wouldn't I?"

Laughing, he caught her close and delivered a smacking kiss. "You could never bore me. How could I ever have imagined you were staid and proper?"

"I can be." Recalling her years under her father's yoke, Charlotte still could not imagine how she had gotten this far. Either she had spent most of her life in a dream, or the stars had finally come into alignment. "If you kill him, will we go abroad?"

He smiled down at her. "I have no intention of killing him. Why would I want to be brought to trial for such a miserable specimen of humanity? No, I will teach him a lesson."

"Are you good with pistols?"

"Tolerably."

Her mind still spun, trying to accept everything. "How do your parents feel about you marrying me?"

He hesitated.

She nudged him. "Tell me."

"They are not in favor of it." He touched her chin, tilting it up so she had to meet his gaze. She had never seen those blue eyes so tender before. For her? "I don't care. We'll bring them around. They know you, and once I tell them what I know about your father, they will approve even more."

Alarmed, she tried to sit up, but he urged her back, murmuring softly. "What will you tell them?"

"That he is a worse tyrant in private than he is in public, and that he controlled you through your sister."

"He could do that still."

"Not once you're an Emperor."

If she became an Emperor.

* * * *

Despite Val's urging, Charlotte utterly refused to marry him that day.

However, she understood that she had to do it soon. Tomorrow she would be the subject of scandal once more, and this time would be worse. If people knew Val and Hervey were fighting over her, her name would be trampled into the dirt. Half of society had heard them discuss her. People would make the assumption. Besides, they already knew about the card game.

Although she kept a brave smile firmly in place, Charlotte cared deeply for the loss of her reputation. The scandal made her vulnerable, and she doubted that her father had finished trying to bring her under his control. He would certainly try to separate them from their brother and hurt them that way. She would write to George as soon as she could. Perhaps tonight. That would take her mind off the ordeal ahead.

If she married Val, she would become an Emperor, a member of the most valued family in the country. Their influence covered the land in breadth and depth. They had fingers in every pie, from property to mining to shipping. Val's mother was one of five children to the old Duke of Kirkburton, and they had all married well. That made for roots that ran deep and wide. Her father would not want to be left out of those connections.

Val accompanied her upstairs to the two rooms Sarah had bespoken. When they had realized Louisa had left her toys behind, Aunt Adelaide rushed back to the house while they waited here before leaving on their long journey north. Although they were cramped, and the furnishings more practical than fashionable, nobody cared, because they were to leave first thing in the morning. The bare floorboards had gaps big enough to push pennies through, and the beds were so solid the horsehair mattresses made little difference to their rigidity.

Louisa, presented with her favorite doll, was caressing its tousled hair and holding it tightly, as if daring anyone to take it from her. Nobody here would.

Sarah's husband was there, too. Sarah had favored him for years, thinking their father would relent. Sam Heath was a strongly built man with eyes that at the moment were more harassed than displaying his habitual kindness. He had not witnessed Louisa's tantrums before, and when she'd flung herself headlong into one, she had woken the baby, who had started to scream.

Charlotte had been glad to accompany Hervey downstairs to a private parlor when he'd appeared requesting a private interview. She'd thought he had only come out of the goodness of his heart. Even when she'd informed him that the previous contract was still in place, he assured her that was merely a formality, and then he had truly frightened her.

She had realized she was vulnerable in this room, with the sound of the inn drowning out any cries for help and no chaperone anywhere close by. But she had not expected such a forceful attempt to make her bend to his will. He had torn her gown in his efforts to get to bare skin, telling her roughly, "Hold still, damn you!"

Val took one look at the rooms allotted to the party and shook his head. "This will never do. I'd like to escort you to my parents' house. We have much more room there, and it is more appropriate for you."

Sarah shook her head. "Charlotte is a single lady, sir. Her reputation has been compromised enough."

"No matter," Val said. "My brother Darius and I will sleep at our club. Charlotte has done me the great honor of agreeing to marry me tomorrow, so we will not be in such a precarious situation after that. Allow me to send a note ahead of our arrival, if you please, and we may gather your belongings."

Sarah's broad smile told Charlotte what that meant. "Sir, I am delighted by your news. That you would support my sister despite her troubles speaks a great deal for your character."

Val took Charlotte's hand and squeezed it. "I never thought of doing anything else."

Although Sarah and Sam protested the move, Val was firm. "Lady Louisa will be much happier in a room of her own with her belongings around her. Do it for her sake."

Reluctantly, they were brought to agree. Val scrawled a quick note on the uneven paper with the sooty, gritty ink that was all the inn provided and sent one of the potboys from the inn to deliver it.

Packing did not take long. However, Val asked Sarah to accompany Charlotte and himself to his home, promising to send the family carriage back for the others. His control of the situation was nothing short of masterful. Charlotte had never seen him like this, calmly in control, forgetting no detail.

The little rooms were horribly stuffy. If they opened the windows, the racket going on outside and the unmistakable odor of life lived in close quarters, coupled with the aroma of horses close by were added to the atmosphere. A night spent here would have been difficult, but Charlotte, relieved of her father's strictures, would have endured it gladly. Sarah and Sam had traveled post, so they had no carriage of their own to concern them.

Charlotte was still trying to control her emotions and assess what had happened here.

They arrived at the Shaws' London house to find everything miraculously ready for them. The marchioness welcomed them as if they were honored guests, while Val had a private conversation with his father, all smiles.

Charlotte found the new situation bewildering and confusing, but she was determined to see him and try to bring him to his senses.

After unpacking her meager belongings and changing her clothes, they went down to dinner. Charlotte blinked at the way the family accepted the situation. Even the marquess barely blinked at the extra covers laid for dinner and engaged Sam in deep conversation about Mr. Pitt's intentions for war.

Louisa and their relative remained upstairs, Aunt Adelaide having declared the girl had enough excitement for one day.

The Shaw family was a daunting collection of people, but their behavior at dinner shocked Charlotte. Never in her life had she attended a less formal meal. The members of the family sat where they pleased, with the marquess and his wife at the top and bottom of the long mahogany table. They chattered, instead of asking permission to speak, or answering a question. Their enthusiasms were many and varied, except once the marchioness frowned when Livia brought up the subject of a particularly gruesome murder, whose perpetrator had just met her deserved end at Tyburn.

That was the day Val had rescued her from the milliner's shop. Charlotte should send the kind lady a note, telling her she would not require her generous help anymore. When Val pressed her hand briefly before replenishing her water glass, Charlotte knew she was not the only person to remember that day.

How would she cope with this man in her life? Her lurking fear, that he would tire of her and move on, still haunted her but she had no choice now. She had to go forward and learn to live with what she had. There was no way back, even if she wished for it. And living with Sarah? To become a respectable, modest spinster living in the countryside? Once that was a dream she cherished, but now, she wanted more.

Just before Lady Strenshall rose to lead the ladies to the drawing room, Val cleared his throat, and clasped her hand. "Charlotte and I are to marry tomorrow," he said calmly.

Only Darius appeared unmoved, watching his brother from his seat across the table, his gaze hooded.

After a silence, Lady Strenshall sat and said quietly, "Why the haste?" Her voice was completely steady and calm, but tension underlay it. Charlotte, used to noting and responding to changes in mood, felt the air change.

"Lord Kellett appears intent on creating trouble. Although Darius and I are leaving the house after dinner, he will no doubt claim impropriety." He paused, and under the table, his grip on her hand tightened, as if he were refusing to let her go. She did not try. She had already made her choice.

"Why?" That was his father, rapping out the question.

"Because he wants her. He will stoop to any level to have her."

To her shock, the marquess addressed Charlotte next. "And is this what you want, my dear? We can create an alternative for you. It would not be amiss if you were to visit us outside London and we have more than one estate, you know. You are welcome to stay as long as you wish."

Charlotte was tired of the delays. Either she did this or she went forward to an uncertain future. "My father favors Lord Kellett, but I do not. I would rather have Val." She ended her words on a gasp when she realized she'd used his first name instead of his title. To her knowledge, she had never done it in public before.

"Then you shall have him, my dear." The marchioness sounded completely in control now. "It will be thought odd not to have a wedding breakfast, but if you do not object, we shall say that you are ill. A severe cold will serve. That does mean you cannot appear in society for a week or so."

Val smiled at her. "That will serve us very well."

The thought of facing society so soon after her wedding made Charlotte quail in fear. She would need time before she did that. Although weddings tended to be private affairs, the wedding breakfast could be a large society arrangement. But an illness would work.

If she ever married at all. Neither Val nor Darius had spoken of the fateful event scheduled for dawn. If she had agreed to marry him today, she could be a widow tomorrow.

The marquess sighed. "I would like one of my children to marry in the conventional way, after a decisive courtship, a wooing and a marriage contract. No delays followed by a hasty marriage, no runaway marriages we have to explain away." He glared at his oldest son. "But as the matches are turning out to be unusually successful, I daresay I have to learn to live with my children doing as they please when they please."

Charlotte's father would have made a speech, probably an hour long, and refused to allow anyone else to speak. He would most probably have made his children stand for the rest of the meal. The marquess, on the other hand, used a great deal of resigned amusement when he spoke. He actually expected his children to have opinions of their own.

Could she join this world? Would she ever feel as these people did, become one of them?

The marchioness stood once more. "I believe we should all strive to get an early night. Tomorrow looks to be a surprisingly busy day. Ladies, we have work to do."

When Charlotte stood, Val stood with her. "I would like a short interview with my bride-to-be."

The marchioness rolled her eyes. "Ten minutes, and then I expect to see Charlotte in the drawing room."

Val led Charlotte to a small but exquisitely furnished room. He closed the door and watched her taking in the treasures lined up in the glass cabinets that formed the room's main furnishings. "This is my mother's treasure room. She calls it her toy room." He followed her to where she stood in front of a case containing a collection of jeweled and enameled boxes, some with tiny paintings on their lids. The flickering candlelight from the branch Val had collected from a servant on their way in made the stones glitter and dance. "These are astonishingly lovely."

He slid his arms around her waist. "So are you."

Whatever else had happened today, she had not changed in appearance. "I am ordinary. I pass muster, Val. I have eyes."

"My eyes tell me something that yours do not. If I call you lovely, you are." Pushing a curl aside, he kissed her neck softly.

She turned around, but he did not move back. "I want honesty," she said.

"You shall have it." He watched her gravely.

"Tomorrow you will not kill him, will you?"

"I will do my best not to. I have no desire to be hanged for killing that man or forced to flee abroad. But he needs to be stopped. He needs to know he cannot run roughshod over everyone he meets."

"You mean me."

He hesitated slightly before he said, "Yes, of course. You."

He lowered his head to kiss her but she was not done yet. "And you will not let him hurt you."

"I will not." He sounded sure, but she could not be certain he would comply with that particular request. "How well does he shoot?"

Val shrugged. "I don't know. We'll find out." This time he did kiss her, and he made the embrace sweet. She went on tiptoe, trying to make the kiss more passionate, but laughing, he urged her back down. "No, sweetheart, this is difficult enough. I had expected to be a married man by now."

She touched his lips, tracing the lines with one finger. "Come back to me safe, and then I will marry you."

"In that case, it is certain. I will come back. I'll send word to you as soon as I return to town. Sooner."

"I'll be waiting."

Chapter 14

Val and Darius elected to walk to the club, since the evening was fine. The sun was sinking toward the horizon, orange-pink tones tinting the clouds with incipient fire. Val stuck his hands in his breeches' pockets. "I have a request."

"Another one?" Darius did not sound surprised, but he would be in a moment. "I have contacted your opponent's seconds, and all is arranged. We've agreed on the weapons, and the exact spot. The usual one."

Val nodded. "I know, and thank you. I know I ask a lot of you, but I want you to care for Charlotte if I should die tomorrow."

"What makes you think you'll die?"

"Kellett is an excellent shot." He had made enquiries of his own. Fellow guests at house parties had mentioned how well Kellett shot on hunting parties, rarely missing his quarry. Would he hold his nerve tomorrow? He could shoot a target or a pheasant, but could he do the same to a human being?

"I see." They walked in silence until they reached the next corner. Darius sighed. "You could renege."

"I could not."

"I know." Darius paused. "Of course I'll look after Charlotte. If you are no longer available, I'll persuade her to marry me."

Val halted and turned to face his brother. He did not attempt to hide his shock. "You don't have to go that far."

"Of course I do. Do you think Kellett would leave her alone once he knew you were dead?" His eyes flickered away and then back, the only sign Darius gave of the stress Val must have put him under. "She needs our protection. Besides, if I have a wife, society will leave me alone. You know our parents have discussed that and tried to persuade me to take a bride. The French call it a white wedding, where the couple marry but remain friends. Whatever her answer, I will care for her. You have my word on it. She will not marry that monster."

They continued to walk. A watchman, sitting by his box, his only shelter in inclement weather, touched his hat and they nodded back. Val had changed from the red coat and waistcoat, but his garb was still fine, if somber. No point giving Kellett an easy target tomorrow. "You will ensure that the man doesn't come within a foot of her."

"I will."

"You're a good brother."

"I know."

* * * *

To his surprise, Val actually managed a few hours' sleep that night. They did not sleep at the club, but at a house Darius owned that the family were not aware of. A modest though elegantly fashionable abode, Darius used it for his private trysts, although he assured his brother he had not planned any for that night. Situated in the City in a street more associated with merchants than the aristocracy, it was a comfortable place.

Reaching for his watch, Val discovered the time was four. They should make haste. Someone was moving around downstairs. Probably Darius. They had not exchanged many more words last night. They did not have to. They understood each other instinctively, a bond that Val was not sure would end with their deaths. If Darius died before he did, which admittedly appeared unlikely today, Val couldn't conceive of living without his presence near to him.

He touched the document laid on the nightstand. His will. His betrothed would be quite shocked to discover how wealthy Val's death would make her. With luck and a good following wind, she wouldn't discover that for some time to come.

He had not discussed the ramifications of the Duke of Rochfort's refusal to acknowledge his daughter. Presumably he would deny the terms of the contract. Val would have to sue him for restitution, a task he was not anticipating with any pleasure. If he survived the encounter, he would have to bestir himself. He would become more respectable than he had ever anticipated being.

Flinging the covers back, he climbed out of bed and checked outside his door. Sure enough, although the hour was early, a can of hot water stood there. Darius kept only one live-in servant here, but she must be a good one. Hot water was welcome. He made shift to shave himself, and get ready. Although his extravagant London clothes usually necessitated a servant, he was perfectly capable of preparing himself for the day.

He'd chosen a waistcoat and breeches of dark green, and a coat of deep brown cloth, fine but not outstanding. However, he would not forgo his neckcloth and white shirt. That would be the action of a coward.

His stomach fluttered. A man who went to his death without a qualm would be strange indeed, but Val refused to allow his fear to control him. He could control it. He had better, because his aim had to be true today. He meant it when he said he would try not to kill Kellett, but blood would be drawn.

Before he could let his second and third thoughts overwhelm him, he went downstairs. His brother was up, sitting in the quiet room at the back of the house, eating a hearty breakfast. The scent of bacon made Val's stomach turn, but a good meal would help him this morning.

"I actually slept," Darius told Val as he filled his plate.

"It's not every day you kill a man in the morning and marry in the afternoon."

Val's hand did not waver as he spooned scrambled egg. "If I kill him, I won't be marrying."

"I think you should. Face what is to come as a married man."

Turning around, Val knew fury. "And drag her right back to the scandal that terrifies her?" He took his place at the small round table. "I will do no such thing."

"If you kill him, we'll call it an accident during a friendly shooting contest."

"I won't drag Charlotte or the family into disgrace." He chewed his way through a mouthful of succulent ham. It tasted like ashes.

Darius had the effrontery to laugh. "Don't flatter yourself. And don't assume they will let you go, either."

Val still intended to travel abroad if the worst happened. No, the second worst. He would not marry Charlotte either. He would leave immediately and send word later. Although he would be hard put to deceive all the Emperors, he knew that.

Life wouldn't be as enjoyable without problems.

Although they had talked last night, they still hadn't discussed the matter of the murder. Val leaned back and picked up a mug of small beer, lifting it to his lips and taking a healthy draught before he spoke. "You know where the shirt is."

Darius did not have to be told which shirt. "You told me."

"If I am unable, and he is still alive, you must prosecute him. Stop him coming anywhere near Charlotte."

Darius finished the beer in his own mug. "And any other woman. He will pay for what he did."

"Peers are not usually found guilty of murder." If the matter came to a trial, Kellett would be tried in the House of Lords, but probably found guilty of a lesser charge, or found not guilty, if he could influence enough people.

"It doesn't matter. He's ruined either way."

"But alive," Val said glumly. He would much prefer the man to be wiped off the face of the earth.

Darius pushed his plate aside. "There have been others."

Val jerked his head up to meet his brother's compassionate gaze. "Other women?"

"And boys. The man isn't particular. His pleasure is to inflict pain on an unwilling victim. He is not satisfied with the tame pleasures offered by the House of Correction. I made enquiries. Some he left badly scarred, and others disappeared."

"Janey would have gone the same way, were it not for you."

Darius nodded. "He cannot be allowed to continue."

Val asked no more. He didn't need to ask how Darius had discovered the information. Darius had connections in the darkest circles of London life, where very few people dared venture.

Half an hour later, they were on their way.

They traveled to Hampstead Heath in an unremarkable black carriage, a two-seater post chaise that Val intended to commandeer if matters went awry. A fast journey to the docks, and he would contrive to disappear before Darius could muster assistance to prevent him. He would not bring trouble down on his family's head. More trouble, that was.

He watched the city pass as they rattled through the streets. Even at this hour the place was busy, the markets open, selling the fresh food that he could expect to be on his plate before half a day had passed. Carts laden with goods rocked precariously. A flower cart passed, the heady fragrance of the blooms lingering on the air, finding its way through the open windows of the carriage to fill it with a mocking reminder of the funeral service.

Darkness was giving way to light, heralding dawn that was yet half an hour away. The gray sky was lightening and it was not raining. "It's a pleasant morning for dying," he said, only realizing he'd said it aloud when he heard the exasperated growl next to him.

"You had better not die. I will be sacrificing myself if you do. If she'll have me."

"Believe me, I have no intention of dying, but I have to let the man have his shot."

Darius growled again. "Damned man insisting on pistols. First blood with swords would have been better. He probably knows how good you are."

Val shrugged. He enjoyed exercising at the Bond Street fencing salon, but as a result, his prowess was well known. A less cowardly man would have chosen swords anyway. Not many knew how good he was with a pistol. Perhaps they would after today.

When the houses began to thin out, the gate to Hampstead Heath loomed before them. They were open, although strictly a toll was due. As they passed through, a white face appeared at a window of the inn that guarded the way, but nobody challenged them. The seconds to the duel had cleared the way.

If asked, the gatekeeper would say he must have left the gates open by accident, and he saw nothing.

The broad greensward spread out either side of the path, fresh dew glinting on the uncropped blades of grass. That would make the footing slippery. Val must take care to firmly plant his feet. He'd worn his favorite riding boots this morning, well worn, the leather molded to his calves. Leaning back, he crossed his legs, taking a lounging pose. No doubt this duel would be seen as another of his antics, once it became known.

As they approached the great oak, he felt certain it would become known. Quite a crowd gathered there, at least fifty men, murmuring and laughing as the carriage drew to a halt and Val waited for the footman to open the door.

He leaped down, pausing until his brother stood by his side, holding a box that held a pair of pistols. They would use a neutral pair, but there was no harm in bringing one's own. His other second, Ivan, fell into step on his other side. Ivan's job was to ensure a surgeon stood by and the course was untampered with. "I was here early, but his seconds were earlier," he commented. "However, I changed the course a little, and all is well." It would not be unknown for an opponent to drop a trail of oil on the intended path they would take.

A smattering of applause shocked him. The gentlemen crowding around the intended arena had probably decided to go for a stroll at five in the morning, and fortunately they'd brought their purses. The glint of gold betrayed them. They reached the table where the adjudicator stood. Val was surprised to see one. Usually seconds were sufficient, but when he saw the seconds Kellett had chosen, he understood. Lord William Dankworth, for one. Although the Emperors' feud with the Dankworths was officially over, very few of them would voluntarily spend time with Lord William, who had stooped to the vilest subterfuges in order to win their fight.

However, there had been no trouble recently, and Dankworth favored Val and his seconds with a curt nod. "Gentlemen, good morning." He lowered his voice. "I'm in no mind to provide entertainment for the masses. What say you we finish this and leave?"

"That suits me," Val said. "I'm marrying later today." That would give Kellett pause.

Kellett turned his gaze on to Val. "If you survive." His eyes burned with rage.

Val kept his demeanor cool. "Oh, I think I will."

Kellett had dressed in black. A black shirt and stock, with a waistcoat so dark blue it might as well be black. He had finished his attire with black breeches, boots and a coat. Even his shoe buckles were black.

"I'm sorry for your loss," Val murmured. "Would you prefer a postponement, so you may attend to your mourning?"

Kellett's gaze passed over Val's ordinary-looking clothes. "I am not in mourning."

The only touch of color about him was the gold pin fastening his neckcloth, the one Val had found on the floor of the death chamber at the House of Correction, the one he'd thrown in Kellett's face in lieu of a gauntlet. "I see you have your lucky pin."

"It was my father's before me. I am glad to have it back."

"I was glad to oblige you." Val paused. The combatants were not supposed to speak before their encounter, but that seemed to be another tradition they had trounced that morning. "It is not the only souvenir I possess, though. I have a shirt with interesting stains."

Kellett's eyes opened a fraction wider. Val saw it because he was looking for the response. The exaggerated sneer curling Kellett's mouth was not so telling, since it was deliberately added. "A shirt is a shirt."

"Especially when it is monogrammed and it has laundry marks." Val turned away, attending to his business here.

He decided not to kick off his boots. Some duelists might do that, but dew lay heavy on the ground and his boots had better grip than his stockinged feet. Besides, he had never appreciated having wet feet. But he did remove his coat and hand it to his brother, then tuck his linen ruffles away, folding his cuffs over them. Darius took his hat, and then Val loosened his neckcloth a small amount. He was ready.

When he turned, he noted Kellett's careful preparations. He did not wear ruffles, and he'd removed his boots, neckcloth, coat, and waistcoat. He opened his mouth, but Val turned away. He was done talking.

The adjudicator, Lord Walton, a gentleman of nearly fifty and a veteran of such encounters, opened the box holding the pistols. Darius and Lord Dankworth took them, weighed them in their hands, and exchanged weapons before they set about loading them.

The crowd hushed, watching the preparations. Darius completed his task first, and handed the pistol to Val. He hefted it in his hand, getting the feel of it, letting the handle slide against his skin before he tightened his grip. "Acceptable," he said.

Kellett nodded. Val was pleased to note that his face had blanched stark white, in startling contrast to his clothes. He would be a good candidate for a haunting.

Dawn sent its rosy glow over the scene. They would pace north to south, with the rising sun to Val's right. The great oak tree, silent witness to who knew how many encounters stood on the other side, its leaves rustling in the spring breeze that sprang up from nowhere.

Val had done with speculation, or melancholy thoughts. He knew what he wanted to do here, and then he would leave and await the consequences. If he did what he wanted to, he'd walk away with honor satisfied. That would serve, for now. Perhaps he should not have warned Kellett that he had the shirt, but that little nugget of information had done its work; he'd angered Kellett, which would put off his aim.

He had seen death in Kellett's eyes—his death, to be precise. Val had to rely on Kellett not being a good enough shot, but with twenty paces separating them he would not have to be that good.

"Ten paces in opposite directions," Darius said. "Then turn and fire in your own time. Are we clear, gentlemen?"

"Perfectly," Val said. Darius mumbled something. They held their weapons up in the approved position, and stood back-to-back.

"One," Lord Walton said.

The crowd grew completely silent. The sudden quiet enhanced the dawn chorus; the birds heralding the coming of the new day. Val breathed deeply once, twice, but then changed his breathing to normal. His hand remained completely steady as he took his first step.

He paced in time to the steady counting. On five he nearly hit a hole in the ground, something caused by an animal, not deep enough for a burrow. If he'd stumbled, he'd have gone down like a rock. He avoided turning his ankle and continued.

"Nine."

He had lifted his foot to take another step when a shot whistled past his ear, sending a thread of fire along the rim. Val's senses flashed into life, but he waited for the end of the word "Ten!" before he turned around.

Pivoting on one heel, he turned to face his opponent.

Kellett held his weapon pointing to the ground, its barrel smoking, the butt steaming in the damp May warmth. The stink of black powder tainted the air. As Val turned, Kellett stood to the side, making himself a narrower target. That white face was all Val needed.

Anger simmered deep, but he breathed it away. The last thing he wanted was emotion coloring his shot. He could *delope*, of course, but why should he? The man would probably apologize profusely, but the damage was done. He had not allowed the count to finish before he fired. Now he had to take whatever Val decided to give him. What honor the man had left depended on that.

Val took careful aim, as he'd always planned to do, but Kellett had made his task more difficult. He waited a moment but if he paused much longer the weight of the weapon would put him off his stride. He owned a pair of pistols very like this pair, probably from the same maker. It would be ironic if they belonged to Dankworth, but they were good weapons.

Putting all other thoughts out of his head, Val did what he did best; he pushed every thought out of his head except for the current task. What was happening now, this minute, mattered more than anything else in the world. He'd lived his life by that creed, and it came to his aid now.

Nothing mattered except the white face and dark clothes beneath. He aimed at the body, cursing his target when he shifted a little, and then settling again. Damn, but that improved matters. He wasn't quite so side-on now.

Cold resolution took Val as he aimed and fired.

All hell broke loose. The surgeon leaped forward before Kellett hit the ground.

Dankworth strode forward, and Val handed the pistol to him with a word of thanks. "As you can see, I'm unharmed." He touched his ear. It was warm, but not bleeding. "The man's aim must be execrable."

"Do you wish to press charges?"

Val shook his head. "Not particularly. No harm was done. I'm sure he only preempted because he was nervous." That would probably anger Kellett more. If he was alive. The surgeon stood, his hands bloody, but he searched out Val and nodded. Then he returned to his task.

"If you will excuse me, gentlemen, I have a wedding to attend."

Val didn't wait. He headed for the carriage. The footman hurried to open the door, stumbling in his haste.

The world rushed back to him, sounds pouring into his senses, the glow of the sun behind a bank of clouds warming him, the first time he was properly warm that morning. He turned before he climbed in.

By the time he'd taken his seat in the carriage, a fine tremor had suffused him. Darius joined him, took one glance, and sat next to Val, handing him his hat and coat. He rapped sharply on the roof of the vehicle, and the coachman gave the horses the office. Unless ordered otherwise, they would return to town. They left the scene of carnage behind them.

"How bad?" Val said quietly.

"You have time to get married," Darius said. He leaned back in the corner, folded his arms and watched his brother struggle into his coat. "Probably time to have a couple of children, too. You winged him."

Relief swamped Val. "There was a lot of blood. I thought he might be taken home so he could die in peace. Because of his damned clothing, I couldn't be sure. He was standing directly in front of a tree, which didn't help when it came to taking aim."

"I put a hundred guineas on you being the victor. I didn't specify if you would kill your man or not."

"Damn you," Val said without heat. "Isn't a second supposed to remain impartial?"

"Whatever gave you that ridiculous idea?"

The brothers burst into laughter.

Chapter 15

Charlotte rose on the morning of her wedding, not knowing if the groom would arrive. But since the clock chimed seven when she opened her eyes, startled from a nightmare, the ordeal was over, one way or another.

Surely if he had perished, someone would have been here before this to tell them? Or maybe not. Maybe he had fled after killing Hervey. That would be murder, and the authorities would want to speak to him. Most duelists got away with the contest, but sometimes, especially with a death, the killer would have to be brought to justice.

She remembered that day at Tyburn and the way the crowd had howled for blood. Would they howl for Val?

Lying against the incredibly soft sheets on the feather bed, Charlotte cursed it. She'd meant to rise early. She always rose early to ensure the servants prepared her father's breakfast the way he liked it.

Her father did not belong in her life any longer. He had ejected her from it. She had her sisters back, though. Hearing from Sarah, learning how happy she was had soothed her. Before, she'd had her suspicions. Sarah's letters might have been her sister putting a brave face on her affairs. After all, once Sarah left home, she'd had little choice but to marry her suitor and make a life for herself. But Sarah was truly happy with her Sam. She could not have feigned the way they moved together, talked, and held their accord.

Would she have that with Val? She doubted it. Where Sam was kind and generous, Val was careless, kind when he remembered to be, and generous when he recalled his responsibilities, of which she would be one.

If he was alive. If he came back to her in one piece. He could be badly wounded, lying in a bed somewhere bleeding to death, or crippled. She would love him anyway.

A jolt made her sit up. Charlotte drew her knees up and wrapped her arms around her legs. She stared at the portrait on the opposite wall. The painting showed a brown-haired woman with bright blue eyes, dressed in the costume of the cavalier era. From the shape of her face and the shade of her eyes, she was an ancestor of Val's. But it wasn't the portrait that roused her. The word, used unthinkingly, did that. Love. She loved him.

It had happened, that event she'd fought so hard to prevent, and she'd had no say in the way it had crept up on her. Or had she loved him from the first minute she set eyes on him? Her father had coolly informed her of the match, and she had accepted it, because she had no option to do anything else.

Then she'd seen him and her nightmare had begun. Of course she had fallen, but she'd put it down to Val's good looks and his address. He'd charmed her, devastated her senses and moved on. That was when she'd tried to put him at a distance, but every time they spent time together, he unknowingly swept her concerns aside. After their betrothal, he treated her as he would his sisters, or perhaps a more distant relative. His careless affection became dangerous, because she longed for it and wanted more. He would be kind to her, the only kindness she knew in her life, and she craved him.

She had assumed that was the nature of the hold he had on her—that she wanted more affection, and the minute she received it from someone else, the magic would fade.

Charlotte buried her face in the quilt covering her knees. Nothing had faded. She'd wanted Val with increasing desperation but hidden it because of her fear that she would be in thrall to another man, this time of her own free will.

Hervey did not have that effect on her. She liked him, but her feelings for him were far more controllable. He was handsome, thoughtful, and kind. Or she'd thought he was until he'd lost his temper and tried to hurt her. Before that, he'd appeared as her savior, a man she could share her life with but not become overwhelmed by.

Now her path was set and because of her, either Hervey or Val could be lying dead on the cold ground.

She could not know. She had to go ahead as if this were her wedding day and she was joyfully awaiting the event.

Sweeping the covers back, Charlotte got out of bed and went to the door of her chamber. The silk oriental rugs caressed her feet, a sharp contrast to the cold boards of her own chamber or the ragged rug that covered it. In the winter she'd kept her outdoor shoes close to the bed so she could wear them when she rose, although they were often cold, too. Her father didn't believe in fires in any bedroom but his own. She'd woken up some mornings with ice on the inside of her window.

At the moment there was no need for fires or of shoes, especially with the rugs, so she padded to the door and opened it, wondering if she'd have to wash in cold water. She did not. A can with a lid stood there, the steam rising from it testament to the hot water within. She picked it up but almost dropped it when a maid scurried toward her. "Oh, ma'am, my lady, I meant to be here much earlier. I had no idea you had woken! Let me help you. Her ladyship wants to know if you will take something to eat in your bedchamber."

"Shouldn't I fast?" She had never attended a wedding before, much less one that involved a special license. She knew she would be marrying in the drawing room here because the terms of the license allowed for that, but this was a sacrament, and shouldn't she fast for that?

"Her ladyship wondered if you would think that. She says to tell you that she refuses to allow the bride to faint from lack of sustenance in her house."

"Ah." But she was not hungry. She couldn't think of anything but Val and his fate.

Downstairs, a door slammed, the reverberations shaking her. Before the maid could protest, Charlotte flew out of her room and hung over the balcony, trying to see who had come in.

The voice she heard made her hurtle down the stairs, her hair flying behind her as her nightcap fell off, her feet striking the firmer carpet on the stairs. She raced along the landing on the main floor and down the stairs again to the marble-floored hall.

"Val!"

Laughing, he caught her headlong rush, halting her and drawing her close.

Charlotte did not allow him to speak but put her hands on his shoulders and drew him down, pressing her lips to his. He returned the embrace, his arms going around her, locking her to him. His soft gasp when he came into contact with her scandalously thinly clad body made her moan and move closer. His warmth enveloped her and she lost her terror as she met his lips and the magic of his embrace.

He drew away gently, drawing his thumbs under her eyes. "Why, sweetheart, you weren't concerned, were you?"

She thumped his chest weakly. "What do you think? I could not tell them—"

"Could not tell them what, Valentinian?" His mother's voice echoed from the floor above. "What have you been up to now?" Her voice was more resigned than angered. "Child, get back to your room before people think I allow women to wander around my house half naked."

Val drew her closer and stroked her shoulders. "Beautiful," he murmured in her ear. "I can't wait for tonight." With great reluctance, he set her aside, his hands lingering on her near naked skin. "Unfortunately, the reckoning is upon me. Darius, the coward, stayed away until I confessed the whole. If I do not, they will hear. There were nigh on fifty people present this morning, all betting on the outcome, so the word will be around town by breakfast time."

"Hervey? Did you…" She licked her lips.

"Do you care so much?"

"Only that you do not get into trouble."

A wicked smile curved his mouth. "I will not. I proved my point, but he is not badly hurt. At least, I don't think so. At any rate, I haven't killed him." He lowered his voice again. "It does me good to hear you care more for me than for him."

"How could I not?"

He kissed her again, a hard buss that sent her senses reeling.

"Val!"

His mother's sharp reminder brought her back to earth, and she glanced up, quailing at the sight of the marchioness, resplendent in gauze nightcap and a fetching lace-trimmed wrapper leaning over the stairs.

"In my chamber, now!"

Taking Charlotte's hand, Val led her upstairs as if she were a great lady. The maid allotted to her waited. With a last glance at her, he touched his fingers to his lips in a fond gesture and meekly, or as meek as he could ever be, followed his mother to her rooms.

* * * *

Charlotte wore the gown that Val had bought for her for her wedding. In fact, she had little choice. Her possessions had shrunk drastically in the last day.

Standing before the mirror in her borrowed bedroom, she couldn't remember ever being happier about her appearance. She wore no powder, and the maid had arranged her hair in a softly flattering style. Her gown had been enhanced with petticoats and a fine lace edge, and the fichu was sheer, so her skin glowed through. It didn't strangle her, either, which had to be an improvement. The maid stood behind her, wreathed in smiles.

Did other people really live like this? From the family's obvious fondness for each other and the informal way they conducted themselves, Charlotte was still unsure. She did not know what to do in many situations. Before yesterday, she'd considered herself well trained and capable of behaving appropriately anywhere. She was very wrong. She would have to learn spontaneity, for one thing.

She would learn, because there was no going back, even if she wanted to.

Except that her husband was a two-edged sword. He could hurt her badly if he lost interest in her. That had stayed the same. He had rescued her, seen her as a damsel in distress, but now that was over, would he move to the next challenge, the next mistress, the next adventure?

Her fears were not unfounded. She had seen him do exactly that a number of times. Even before they had become betrothed she had watched him move on, leaving a trail of broken hearts behind him.

Would hers become yet another?

Last night the maid had brought several items to her—necessities like shifts, stockings and neckerchiefs—but even they were of a finer quality than she was used to. The kindness of her hosts overwhelmed her, but she had a feeling she could get used to it.

A gentle tap came at the door. Was that the summons for her to go downstairs?

It appeared not. The maid returned with a small parcel wrapped in silver tissue paper. "I'm to inform you that this is a betrothal gift." She looked up with a smile. "His last, I am bidden to tell you."

Val had given her gifts in the past, not least the clothes she stood up in, but until then they had been careless, even thoughtless in nature. This was not. When she opened it, she caught her breath. A large sapphire surrounded by small diamonds hung from a delicate gold chain. This exactly the kind of jewelry she'd have chosen for herself, simple and understated, though fine. The stone reminded her of the brilliance of his eyes. She would recall them every time she looked at it.

The maid removed the ruffle of lace around her neck, replacing it with the necklace. Then she was ready. The stone grew warm, because she had touched it so often, before another tap came on the door. This time it was the summons for her to go downstairs and be married.

Charlotte felt no hesitation. Well, only a little. Her stomach tightened and her mouth dried. She had tried for a calm existence with Hervey, but that was denied her. Life with Val would be anything but smooth and untroubled. And to her utter shock, she discovered she wanted that.

Adventure stirred something inside her, gave her a feeling she barely had words for. Excitement was the nearest she could get, but it wasn't quite that. Anticipation, the thrilling pleasure of not knowing what would happen next—that fed into her emotions.

She had no time to explore further. Picking up her skirts, relishing the fine silk under her hand, she quit the room and went downstairs to meet her fate with a joyful heart.

The drawing room was filled, at least it appeared so to her dazzled senses. Every Emperor in London stood or sat, all waiting for her. The son of the Duke of Kirkburton, the startlingly handsome Lord Winterton, stood behind his wife's chair, holding a carefully swathed bundle that she guessed was their newborn son. The presence of a child surprised her, even though the baby was a much-loved and anticipated one.

Charlotte had avoided Lord Winterton for years. He'd always unnerved her, with his foppish appearance and perfect manners; even though he was all male, easily discerned by the powerful musculature under the pale green satin he wore today. But his expression when he gazed at his wife and child was one she had never seen on him before. Fond, not to say loving, the man appeared changed. Or maybe it was because he was en famille, clear of the society mask so many people here habitually wore. While not as rigid as hers had been, they all preferred to keep part of their lives private.

When she dared to glance in the direction of her intended husband, she found him similarly shockingly openly affectionate in expression. A new revelation shook her. She was about to become an Emperor of London, a member of a close extended family. She had never known anything like that before. She had heard that the reason her father was not more influential, despite his status, was this lack of a large family, but she had only thought of it in terms of influence and power. Not in personal relationships. Her future husband had five brothers and sisters. He had so many cousins Charlotte didn't know where to begin counting them.

At last someone she knew. Her sister, sitting next to Lord Devereux and his wife, her husband standing behind the sofa. Sarah smiled and nodded. Next to Aunt Adelaide sat her admirer, Sir Lucas Shapcott. Charlotte was glad of that. In time, perhaps they would marry.

As she faltered, unsure of this new world and where she would fit in it, Sam strode to her side. "I would be honored to escort you," he said, his characteristic smile firmly in place. Her father was, of course, not present.

Swallowing, Charlotte put her hand on his arm and let him take her the few steps to where Val waited for her. He nodded to Sam, who stepped back.

The cleric smiled benignly and began the service.

Twenty minutes later she was Lady Valentinian Shaw, with a gleaming gold band on her finger to prove it. She made her responses with heartfelt earnestness, while Val was quiet but clear when he spoke. The event she never imagined would actually happen was here, and it had passed flawlessly.

Val shook hands with the celebrant while his brother and Ivan signed the registry after they'd had their turn. "Thank you, Uncle Frederick."

So even the man who had married them was family. Val introduced them, and she learned that Uncle Frederick, the marquess's brother, was also the Bishop of Carrick. Then Val took Charlotte by the hand and led her around the room, introducing her proudly as his wife. By the time they had greeted everyone, and Charlotte had received a number of flattering compliments, she was beginning to accept the situation. The knowledge sank into her being and settled deep.

Outside in a larger drawing room in the enfilade of public rooms a group of guests waited for them to go in to their wedding breakfast. As they moved to the door, Charlotte saw a group of pleasant welcoming people turn into grand society lords and ladies.

She felt a strange reluctance to do it herself. She longed for a new mask, one that reflected her current state, not the old worn one that no longer fitted her properly. But she would need time to find it and discover how to use it. What would Lady Shaw be like? Even she didn't know yet.

Her old, rigid polite cover would do for now. It would have to, since she had no intention of parading her feelings for her new husband in public. If her heart broke, that would happen in private. As far as anyone else was concerned, she and Val were fulfilling their contract, and her father was having another of his pets.

They went up the short corridor. At their approach, two immaculately attired footmen flung open the double doors of the dining room. This was not the room where the family generally took their meals. The spacious room, half-paneled in mahogany and half in red damask, with a huge mahogany table in the center was for dining in state. The table could hold fully fifty guests with all its leaves in place, which they were today. People stood when they entered, and Val took her to the head of the table.

Turning her head to greet the other guests, Charlotte received a severe shock. Sitting at her right was her father. He gave her a tight nod and she managed to return it. She could tell nothing from his appearance, but then, she never could. Her father would insist on the correct protocol even on his deathbed. Not that she wished that fate on him. He had treated her cruelly, but she would not respond with the same behavior.

She offered a slight smile. "Welcome," she said.

"Daughter."

That was the extent of their personal conversation. The rest was the usual comments on other members of society and political matters. However, certain remarks taught her one thing as her acute sense of reading the currents under what was actually said took over. Her father wanted the Emperors on his side. His acute awareness of the title and what he owed it had triumphed over his personal feelings, whatever they were. He was here for public show.

That knowledge did not hurt as much as it should have, but how could it? Affection was a foreign concept to the Duke of Rochfort.

The meal took forever. She lost count of the number of courses laid out, but she only took from four. Her appetite had gone at the first sight of her father.

Only her experience kept her smiling and conversing, as if this were yet another normal meal. Her husband's parents sat on the other side, but the contrast between them could not have been greater. While the marquess and his wife displayed entirely proper behavior, the private touches remained. Lord Strenshall clearly knew the dishes his wife preferred and ensured they were sent her way. Every now and then he paused to smile at her with every signal of pleasure.

Charlotte longed for a marriage such as theirs, one where the participants loved and respected each other, where the wife did more than obey her husband or receive him between mistresses. She did not subscribe to the view that when a husband strayed, the wife was at fault. Some wives openly encouraged infidelity, for it put less pressure on them to entertain their husband's carnal desires.

Would she, Charlotte, feel that way? From the kisses and caresses she had exchanged with Val, she thought not, although that would save her.

The toasts started. First the King, of course, and then the happy couple, and then the exalted guests, of which they were many. Charlotte took a bare sip at each one but privately wondered how long this would take. Then she would go to the drawing room and they would go through the tea serving. Would she ever be alone with her husband?

The meal ended midafternoon. From where she sat, Charlotte could not see the hands of the clock on the elaborate mantel, and the chimes were consistently drowned out by the chatter. However, years of attending formal functions had given her an internal clock, and she assessed the time to be around three in the afternoon when the marchioness rose and gently indicated that the ladies would withdraw.

To her surprise, her husband rose with her and escorted her from the room. Outside, he embraced his mother. "We'll leave now, Mama," he said.

The marchioness did not appear the least disconcerted but smiled and nodded her approval. "Have a good journey."

"How did you persuade the old man to agree to appear?"

Nobody needed him to explain who he meant. The marchioness gave a particularly smug smile. "He could not afford to continue his objection."

"Ah."

They had bribed him, or perhaps offered him a business proposal. At least Charlotte had the semblance of respectability for her marriage, something that seemed fadingly distant when she'd woken that morning.

"We're leaving?"

Val caught her hand in the impulsive way he had. "I'm taking you away for a while. Somewhere we can be private. Unless you object?" The raised brow promised much.

Her heart beat quickened. "Of course not."

"There's no 'of course' about it. If you want to stay, perhaps speak more to your sister, we will wait."

Now she knew Sarah was well and happy, and Louisa too, Charlotte was content to leave them for a while. She shook her head. "I'm delighted to do as you ask." More than delighted, if she told the truth.

The part of her marriage that she anticipated with both fear and excitement loomed. Like a badly trained horse, she wanted to rush at it. She would most likely fail the jump, but she wanted it done, so that she knew what she would be contending with.

She knew very little about what would happen next, what he would want. Her father had, naturally, never discussed the matter with her, and her aunt had as much idea as she did. Perhaps if she'd been in touch with Sarah, she could have asked her, but she did not. Sarah was there, of course, but she sat farther down the table. Louisa and Aunt Adelaide sat by their side, honored guests. Louisa smiled at everyone and behaved much better than Charlotte had expected, considering her lack of experience and limited understanding. Charlotte's heart eased to see her beloved sister so content.

She smiled as a maid helped her into gloves and her hat and kept smiling as her husband helped her up the steps into a sleek post chaise. The coachman touched his whip to his hat as they climbed in, and then they were off.

"Where are we going?"

Val frowned. "Hmm. It's a warm day. I want you out of these." He started work on her gloves. "We aren't going far, only to a house I own by the river at Richmond. The journey shouldn't take above an hour."

He cast her gloves aside without noting where they fell and gathered her hands in his.

"I didn't know you owned a house by the Thames," she said numbly. She wanted to ask other things, but she didn't know where to start.

"We still have a lot to learn about one another, despite our long engagement."

That brought a tremulous smile to her lips. "Yes, we do."

"The fault was entirely mine. I did not listen to you or take notice of you." He bit his lip.

Charlotte had never seen him so uncertain.

"I regarded you as a convenience, someone who allowed me to get on with my life without hindrance. After our betrothal, I could spend more time doing what I wanted to. I had fewer obligations."

His mouth tightened, in a way she'd seen when he was exasperated or angry. But with her?

"I was a fool. I looked everywhere but at you."

She blinked. "You looked at me often enough."

"Not in the way I saw you the first night I kissed you."

"That was just after we were betrothed." She remembered that night. Her father had held a ball in her honor, although in reality he had used it to progress a business arrangement with the Duke of Kirkburton, Val's uncle. She understood, but the highlight of the evening for her had been when Val raised her hand to his lips and actually kissed it. Men generally kissed the air an inch or so above the skin. The contact had thrilled her.

"Not that time." His voice thickened. "Like this."

Despite the streets they were passing through, he tugged her hands so she lost her balance. He slid his arms around her and brought his lips down on hers. The broad brim of her hat caught on the upholstery behind them, but that did not stop her returning his kiss. Shocked and thrilled in equal measure, she met him, and when he opened his mouth against hers, she followed suit.

He tasted her, licked in deep, and explored her at his leisure, occasionally teasing her tongue with the tip of his. When her hat loosened, she let it fall. He must have watched where the maid put the pins, for he drew them out without hesitation before tugging the bow under her chin undone and letting the hat tumble to join her gloves.

Now she could rest her head on his shoulder while he drew her into the shelter of his arms and delved deeper. He enticed her into a kiss more lascivious than anything she had experienced before. He kept his hands still, but despite that, she felt the imprint of his fingers on her breast, where they had been once before, and she shuddered with half-understood longing. As the kiss went on, her body tingled, and she yearned to get even closer to him.

He changed the nature of his caress, gentled her, and changed the kiss of yearning into more playful, affectionate caresses, small kisses, touching his lips to her mouth, her nose and her cheeks, before returning to her mouth. "Am I forgiven?"

"For what?" She was breathless, as if she'd run a mile.

"For nearly losing you. For taking you for granted."

"I wasn't aware that you did. You were always kind to me when we met."

He snorted. "My mother urged me to persevere and set a date. She never stopped, and now I know why. She has known great happiness with my father. She wanted me to experience the same thing."

"Happiness?"

"You make it sound like an unattainable ideal. Has it been so bad?" He brushed his lips over her forehead.

She frowned. "I'm not sure what you mean." Happiness was an aspiration, not a natural state. She had rarely known it, and treasured the few times she'd attained it.

"You were not always happy. I shall try to change that."

She basked in his attention. Even if his concentration on her turned out to be ephemeral, she would enjoy every minute of it while it was hers. "I am happy enough. I never wanted for clothes or food, unlike the poor in the streets."

He toyed with the pendant at her throat. "Happiness is not having enough to eat. Or it should not be." He kissed her softly. "You deserve much. I should not have turned my back on your plight for two years. I will never forgive myself for that."

She did not like the turn this conversation was taking. Straightening up, she folded her hands in her lap and faced him. "I was not a poor creature. I managed to create enough for my sister and myself. I even have savings—poor, I am sure, by your standards—but I made plans. When Louisa came of age, we would leave. The only reason I did not was because of her."

"I know. I know." When he tried to pull her back, she resisted.

"I am not to be pitied. I am not so unusual, either. Plenty of women in my situation put up with more, and worse." She spread her hands, palm up. "I came to London every season. True, I provided my father with a useful hostess, but he would have brought us anyway." Because he liked to have them under his eye, but she need not tell him that. "Did you marry me because you felt sorry for me?"

He shook his head.

"Because I am not a charity girl."

He regarded her in silence. She was forced to reach for the grips when the carriage jolted over a rut, but he caught her instead, and she found herself back in his arms.

"You are right, of course." He kissed the top of her head. "Perhaps I overstated my case. I have often done so. I still curse myself, thinking of what I could have missed. If Kellett had been a more admirable man, I might have released you. I agreed to do so, after all."

He must have felt her shudder, because he held her tighter.

"Is it over then? Has he gone?"

"Yes. This morning I drew blood, but that is all. Honor was satisfied." He grunted. "I would have preferred to put an end to his existence, but then I would not have met you at the altar. I would not come to you with a man's life on my hands."

"What will he do next?"

"What *can* he do? We are married. He can hardly argue with that." He paused. "He was angry, but if he has any sanity at all, he'll let us alone now and hunt down another heiress."

"I'm not an heiress."

"You were." He kissed her forehead. "You will probably be again. Your father has settled a considerable amount on you, and as matters stand, I doubt he will renege on that. Does it count that I married you when you were penniless?"

She laughed. "I think it does."

Chapter 16

"We've arrived."

The moment after he said that, they swung into a private drive. Charlotte caught a glance of a stuccoed exterior before the carriage blocked her view and she had to wait to see it properly. When she did, she caught her breath in delight.

"This is exactly the kind of house I always wanted."

The white stucco covered a house of moderate proportions. Not a huge palace of a place or a rambling Tudor edifice, but a pilastered building of three or four stories with a Palladian-columned portico. "What is its name?"

"I shall call it Charlotte's Villa."

"Val! Be serious."

He laughed. "Why should I? Life would be tedious without a little levity. It's currently called Verdant Place, which seems a foolish name, but I like it."

"Did you inherit it?"

"No," he said, as the footman opened the door and let down the steps. "I bought it."

Her eyes rounded as she turned to him instead of drinking in the house's facade. "You did?"

His chuckle warmed her. "I see more questions. What a curious woman you are, sweetheart."

Disdaining the steps, he leaped to the ground and helped her to descend. They stood, her hand tucked in his, and studied the house. It would have six or eight bedrooms, something of that nature, perfect for her. The grounds were well-clipped lawns, with an edging of late spring flowers. She tested the grass with the tip of her foot. "Do you plan to live here year round?"

"That is up to you as well as me." He watched her, still smiling.

She liked his smile, especially when there was no trace of cynicism about it. He appeared entirely enchanted.

"I have another house in Leicestershire, and I spend a lot of time at the family seat, too." He tugged her hand. "Come. Let me show you inside."

Four columns set in a square held up the pleasant hall, and a staircase wound its way upstairs. A butler stood just inside the door and bowed low first to her and then to Val. "My lord, I have made everything ready, as you requested. Would you care for refreshment?"

Val glanced at her. "Our journey was hardly arduous." At Charlotte's slight headshake, he said, "Not now, thank you, Bunson. Leave us to find our way around. I'm anxious for my wife to see the house."

With every room, Charlotte declared herself pleased. The house was delightful. "Anything less like a mausoleum is hard to imagine," she said as they left the music room upstairs and walked to the rooms at the end of the sunny corridor.

"Have you visited many mausoleums?" He paused, his hand on a doorknob.

"I have lived in them for most of my life."

He opened the door. "Your father's houses?"

"Yes. He prefers everything placed precisely in its place. After we finished with our embroidery, or whatever we were doing, we had to take care that no trace of our activity remained when we had done. Every thread must be picked up and the work box arranged properly."

He paled. "Dear Lord, I would never have survived. None of my family would."

She had walked into the room watching him, not the contents. While the house delighted her, having Val all to herself delighted her even more. Every chance she had, she'd drunk him in, his shape, his height, and the way he talked to her alone. "We had to survive. We had no other choice. Until Sarah met Sam, and even then it took her two years to come back for us."

"I'm sorry."

"What for?"

He gave an awkward laugh, not one she had heard before from the assured urbane Val. "For not asking sooner about your personal circumstances. For taking too much for granted. You are a brave woman. Your father could not have been easy to live with. I knew he insisted on formality all the time, but not that it extended so deeply into the private part of your life."

Suddenly shy, she looked away. "I may disappoint you. I know no other way." It choked her to have to admit it, but it was better he knew. "There is nothing more to me. I am as you see."

They were in a bedroom and she was staring at the bed. The gold-colored drapery enhanced rather than hid the softness of the mattress and the silkiness of the cover. No heraldic beasts proclaimed his lineage in the head of the bed, no proud portraits of ancestors hung on the walls watching every move she made. Instead, landscapes and a conversation piece, a painting of his family decorated the Chinese paper on the walls. The tallboy and the cabinets shone with polishing and a touch of gilt, just enough to catch the sun, gleaming when she moved her head.

"Is this...?" She could say no more. The room she had considered spacious seemed to draw in, stifling her.

"It is. If you wish it," he said. "I took this room for my own because of the view."

She hadn't even noticed the view, but when she followed his gaze, she choked back an involuntary cry of delight. The large sash windows looked out over a swath of lawn and flower beds. Beyond them was the river. The Thames flowed along in majestic glory. A swan sailed graciously over the greenish gray water. "It's perfect."

Impulsively, she turned around, but he was standing directly behind her. He caught her in his arms and gazed down at her, laughing. "Indeed you are," he said, and bent to her lips.

Every time he kissed her, he took her into his own world, made her helpless to resist. She opened her mouth to him when he touched her chin, and he took possession. Here, now, wrapped in him, she could not imagine anything else half so good.

He broke away, gazing down at her, his eyes hot and wild. "I have to stop. I'm in danger of losing my resolve."

"What resolve?" She'd lost hers half a minute ago.

"I meant to ensure you ate and rested before I fell on you."

The phrase amused her. "Fell on me?"

"Like a rutting stag." He growled the words against her mouth.

His clarification forced a laugh out of her. "I imagine you have more finesse than that. You do have a reputation as a magnificent lover."

"You've been listening to gossip."

"I've been listening to Lady Cresswell."

He gave a slight shake of his head. "That was a mistake." He clamped his mouth shut.

She waited.

"What?" he demanded eventually. "You want to discuss my past lovers with me?"

It was her turn to shake her head. She couldn't think of anything she wanted less. "Only your future ones." She wasn't entirely sure she wanted to know about those, either, but better she found out from him than from ballroom gossip. When that happened, she would cope. She had to.

"You will, I promise." He was smiling.

Charlotte didn't want to talk about that now. Not on her wedding day. Neither, it seemed did he, for he released her. She moved closer, wouldn't let him retreat. "Fall on me, husband. I want everything you have."

"No, no, you don't."

If she had to wait any longer, the stress would kill her. But how did a woman seduce a man? She'd read about it, seen flirtatious behavior, although she'd never taken part in that herself. Her father would have punished her for behaving like a wanton, even though half society did so. So she had an idea, but the thought of initiating a seduction filled her with terror.

And something else, she discovered to her surprise. A challenge, like a duel between lovers. Desire rose in her, tensed her muscles, increased her sensitivity. She wanted this and she wanted it now.

Lifting her hands to her neck, she pulled out the fine kerchief and tossed it away. "I'm not sure I have a maid here."

"I engaged one for you." A smile in his eyes, he watched her.

He must know what she was about. Would he think her poor efforts funny rather than arousing? She would have to learn if she wanted to keep him.

Daring his derision, she persisted, unhooking the front of her gown from her stomacher. Intent on her work, she did not look up until she'd completed the task.

A flush had risen to his cheekbones, and his eyes were the most intense blue she had seen them. The color of aquamarines, they displayed all his emotions, when he allowed it. He was allowing it now. "Who would have thought I'd be so instantly aroused by a virgin removing her gown?" He spoke with wonder in his voice. "But I cannot deny it. Are you sure you want this now, sweetheart?"

"Perfectly sure."

"Is this in the spirit of getting it over with?"

She nodded before she could stop herself. "I don't know." For a second she let her uncertainty show, and then she smoothly covered it up. "I want you."

With a soft groan, he stepped forward and reclaimed her. "I meant to do this properly, to share a meal with you, and let you come here and prepare yourself."

"Like a virgin sacrificed to the beastly dragon?"

"Andromeda lashed to the rock," he said with a smile. "But perhaps this is better. Besides, I've been waiting for this for a long time. A long time for me, that is."

She would accept that today. Perhaps later, she wouldn't allow it, because he had certainly taken little notice of her for the first two years. He had acknowledged that himself. "Not as long as I have."

He curved his large hand around her cheek, making her feel vulnerable and cherished at the same time. Gazing into her eyes, he touched her, stroked her from waist to arm and back again. He pushed his hand under her gown and eased it away. Now she had unhooked it, he could ease it off her shoulders. She let it go, dropped her arms so the fine silk slid off her shoulders. She would have liked to let it fall to the ground in a fine, dramatic flourish, but unfortunately her maid had tacked triple ruffles to it, and she had to give them a tug to ease the sleeves away.

He took hold of the gown at the top, near where her robings ended, and pushed, helping her rid herself of the gorgeous garment. It slid away, the whoosh of the silk echoing the rush of blood that made her stomach swoop and her senses heighten. With nothing to hold it in place, her stomacher followed, leaving her in petticoat and undergarments.

His comprehensive visual sweep was frank and heated. "I want you naked. Totally, completely stripped." Quickly, he shrugged off his coat and reached up to his neck, pulling the pearl pin away from his neckcloth and unraveling the length of fine starched linen.

The sight of his throat struck her as deeply intimate. She had never seen it before, but she'd felt it under her fingers when they'd kissed. A couple of buttons and loops fastened his shirt. Watching her, he pulled it undone, not bothering to unfasten it properly but tugging until the loops snapped. The front placket gaped open. He reached for her. "Your turn."

He made short work of her petticoat and then her side hoops. Charlotte felt more vulnerable, as if her armor had gone.

"Turn around," he said.

She did so, pirouetting like an automaton, jerky and unsure. Lowering her head she watched her stays as he untied the knot at her waist and loosened the cords. At his command of "Up," she lifted her arms and he pulled it over her head. It stuck on the bun in her hair, but she worked her head from side to side, and it came away. So did many of her hairpins.

Strands of hair drifted down, brushing the nape of her neck, sending shivers through her oversensitive body. While she was standing with her back to him, he undid the cords holding up her remaining petticoats and her pockets. He pushed everything away.

"I can see you," he said. "Your skin glows." He touched her, so lightly she nearly missed it, but she was attuned to him now. A finger brushed down the length of her spine through her shift. "You're so lovely."

Gently, he turned her with a touch to her waist. "You still want this?"

"Don't ask." She paused, surprised by the sultry tone in her voice. That had never happened before. "Just do it."

"It doesn't work that way. You have to be with me." Lifting his hand away from her waist, he circled a nipple with the tip of his finger, laughing softly when she shivered. "You're beautifully responsive, sweetheart."

In a swift move that made her gasp, he swept her shift up and over her head, pulling her arms back up. He paused while the garment was still wrapped around her. "Oh, you are so lovely."

He finished discarding her last garment he bent and lifted her, carrying her to the bed. Holding her with one arm, he dragged the covers down and laid her tenderly on the sheets. When she bent to deal with her shoes and to stop him gazing at her with such hunger, giving herself a moment to try to compose herself, he pushed her back down.

"Let me." He nimbly unfastened the buckles and let her satin shoes drop to the floor with two thumps, one and then the other. Her garters and stockings were equally cavalierly dealt with.

She was naked.

He stood, staring down at her, the hunger in his eyes deepening. Bending over her, he pressed a kiss to her lips, but straightened. "Do not cover yourself. I want to look at you."

When he fumbled with the buttons on his waistcoat, she smiled, but he disconcerted her by saying, "You are my downfall, sweetheart. Completely and utterly."

How could she huddle under the sheet when he said that? The mirror on the dressing table reflected her torso when he moved away to drop his waistcoat on a nearby chair. Hastily, she looked away. She needed no reminder. Her skin prickled with the knowledge. Val was undressing as quickly as possible.

When his upper half emerged from the folds of his shirt, she caught her breath at the sight. She had not realized Val was so powerful. Fashionable clothes were designed to display the peacock male, but Val could have shown to advantage as a prizefighter. His shoulders and upper arms bulged with muscle, and his chest heaved when he took a deep breath. After his shoes, he disposed with the rest of his clothes in short order, shoving them away, careless of where the fine fabrics fell.

She cared even less. Her gaze fell to his groin, and the length of his erection, the head tight and shiny.

"Look your fill," he purred, putting one knee on the bed. He took his shaft in his hand, curling his strong fingers around the column. "This is yours, as is the rest of me. Claim it, my sweet."

How was she to do that? With a deep gulp, she opened her legs.

"Oh, yes. Kiss me, sweetheart."

He moved on to the bed and over her, prowling like an animal tracking its prey. And like a rabbit held still by a fox, she lay there, waiting for him. When he kissed her, he rolled his body over hers, propping himself up on his arms so she felt him but did not take his weight. His shaft kissed her belly, leaving a damp mark of possession.

Charlotte had never seen a man's naked body before, and now she was feeling one, so close to her that if she breathed she would touch him. When he bent to take her mouth, her nipples brushed against the firm muscles of his chest.

He groaned deeply, the sound vibrating against her body. Her response was electrifying, her body knowing what to do, even if she did not.

Her husband kissed her lips, followed to her throat, where he'd kissed her before and made her shudder, down over the upper slope of her breast, and farther. He licked her nipple and she yelped, startled at the intensity of her response.

"Val...?"

"Lie back, sweetheart, let me do this. Let me taste you. I'll take care of you."

"Is it always like this?"

He chuckled, his lips against her skin. "No." But he didn't elaborate further, only continued to kiss and lick her breasts, gently sucking at the tips, driving her arousal to near unbearable levels. Spikes of need tormented her, but so deliciously, she never wanted them to end.

He continued down, exploring with mouth and tongue. Shocked, she lay back as he'd told her to. What was she supposed to do now? Her sigh and moan seemed to work for him, when he growled against the soft skin of her belly, and then—then he touched her.

Opening her folds gently, he slid a finger between them, sliding them over a part of her that responded instantly with sharp arrows spiking through her innermost being. She jerked up as if he'd slapped her instead of treating her with care. What would that feel like? Her mind skittered in different directions, trying to find references, collecting the sparse bits of knowledge she had about what he would do next.

He slid his finger down until he breached her, but only with the very tip. Charlotte lay back, afraid to move. "Is that it?" she managed to ask.

"Is that what?"

"Where—what…?" Tongue-tied, she couldn't vocalize what she meant.

Removing his finger, he came back up the bed to face her, his arms either side of her head, boxing her in. She had nowhere to look but at him. "How much do you know?" he asked her.

"About this?" She swallowed, nervousness tightening her throat. "Not a great deal."

"How did you remain so innocent?" When she would have turned her head, he kissed her forehead. "No, sweetheart, look at me." His shaft pressed against her belly, hot and demanding, but he ignored it and kept completely still. "I thought you'd have known something. When I undressed you I was pleased with your reaction, but I am not a man who appreciates too much maidenly modesty. Mainly because I have never encountered it before this day. Women pretend, you know, but your response is sincere. Are you ready for this? Truly?"

She had to tell him the truth. "If you stop, I don't know if I'll have the courage to let you back." It would be a rejection, one of many in her life, but this would hurt more than any other. "Don't stop, please, Val."

He let out a long breath, as if her response meant everything to him. "I'm not sure I could, but I don't want to behave like a brute." He kissed her again, as if gathering strength from her. "I've never known this before. We're going into this together, sweetheart. Shall we treat this as our new adventure?"

She liked that. Tentatively she slid her hands over his shoulders, feeling his power for herself.

"Hold on to me, lovely woman. Let's take this to its inevitable conclusion."

Rising up, he took his shaft in his hand once more, his knuckles brushing against her skin. He guided it to where he had put his finger. It felt surprisingly good, notching into her crease like an arrow into its bowstring.

Charlotte did as he bade her, held on and watched him, gathering strength from the care in his eyes, the furrows between his brows.

He pushed, but all she felt was tension. He tried again, and something gave, just slightly. He was inside her, a giant protrusion entering her untried body. It did not feel pleasant. Perhaps that was why wives were often happy to let their husbands stray.

"Dearest?"

"What?" Pulled from her speculation, she met his gaze.

"This first time might not be entirely pleasant for you, but I'll try to show you something of what is to come. I will give you joy, Charlotte, I swear it."

When he said it, she believed him. She'd given way before, letting her body sink into the soft mattress. He pushed into her, gently at first, but she was learning what to do. When he thrust for the third time, she dug her heels in. Bracing herself, she pushed back.

A sharp pain pierced her, and he surged into her, invading her. Now she knew why they called it a taking, because he took her, claimed her as his.

Her cry broke the peace of the room, but Val didn't hush her. Relentlessly he drove deep and didn't stop until he was fully embedded inside her. Then he stopped.

They watched one another, learning their intimacy.

He pulled back, but her body gripped him, unwilling to let him go.

"Pull up your knees," he murmured.

She slid her heels up the bed, tucking them into his thighs and letting her knees fall open. He was right. The sense of tightness eased, and when he pulled out this time, he slid nearly all the way back in with ease.

As she was wondering if that was all, he thrust back in. She moaned, the sound taking her by surprise. "There's more?"

"Much more. Oh, sweetheart, so much more." His voice shook, but his movements were steady as he drew out and then back in.

A spot inside her responded, sending waves of pleasure through her. "Oh!"

He smiled. "That's it. Feel it. Watch me, don't close your eyes. I want to know what you're feeling."

"I want that too." Shyly, she opened her eyes.

His thrusts, at first gentle, grew deeper as her body eased, accepting him. Pleasure rippled through her with every stroke, increasing in intensity. Charlotte clutched him, digging her fingers into the firm flesh at the back of his shoulders, pulling him, urging him to carry on.

They were going somewhere, but she didn't know where or how, except she had to put all her trust in him. He would take her there and ensure no harm came to her. He would keep her safe.

Except she wasn't sure she wanted to be safe.

A streak of wild adventure, unsuspected, burst free. Hungrily, desperate for more, to know what happened next, she held on as his thrusts grew harder and faster.

A pause that lasted both a lifetime and no time at all made her catch her breath.

Then everything broke free, and she threw back her head and screamed as thrills racked her body, rippling up and through every part of her. Her body clenched, pulsing around his in hard, wrenching spasms.

He cried her name and clenched his teeth, gazing at her with stark intensity as his shaft pulsed inside her, pushing her back up the mountain she had just tipped over.

Chapter 17

Val lay in his bed, his wife tucked by his side. She was sleeping like a baby, as she should be at this time of night. The moon was up, a sliver lighting up the sky outside the bedroom window, the stars bright in the cloudless sky.

He had never known such contentment in his life. This, their second night together, had been passed like the first, even though he insisted that she rested after he'd taken her virginity. They were naked, and if he had his way, they would never come to bed in any other state.

His reaction to her still left him numb, as had her beauty when he had first laid her bare. Without the hair powder that dulled her creamy complexion and the enveloping clothes that had hidden the lovely curves of her body, Charlotte was a beauty. From now on he would ensure she enhanced it instead of trying to hide her loveliness. It was a positive crime to shroud her in unflattering colors and swathes of fabric.

Her clothes would arrive today. That was another crime, because now he'd seen her naked, he'd prefer to keep her that way. She truly had no idea how lovely she was, but since he'd prefer to keep her naked form to himself, he'd ordered several new gowns for her. They were to be his wedding gift, but matters had turned out somewhat differently, and now she needed them. Her father had kept her deliberately plain.

If her father had appeared at this moment, Val would gladly have murdered him. He had deliberately kept his daughters ignorant of intimate matters. At least he had not frightened them. Knowing Charlotte as he did now, he doubted she would be afraid for long. She had steel in her spine, a ramrod-straight courage that must have taken her through the horrors of living with her father.

He would have to thank his parents for finding him such a perfect bride. If it were not for them, he would have walked past without remarking on her. Her father had worked hard to keep his daughters from finding husbands, but thankfully he had failed.

Charlotte's older sister was right. Their father didn't want them to marry. He'd wanted them as ladies-in-waiting to him until the day he died, obeying his beck and call.

Charlotte would never do that now. Val had a powerful dislike of toadies and obsequious servants. He wasn't above using them if he needed to, but they left him with a feeling that a snail had crawled over his stomach.

When she stirred, he murmured and settled her back into his arms until she fell into deeper slumber. They had spent yesterday either naked or garbed in his robes. He lent her a particularly fetching one of emerald green. It swamped her, which made them both laugh, but later, when he'd disrobed her, the robe had proved singularly convenient. At first, she'd shown a great deal of modesty, but he laughed her out of that attitude. Charlotte deserved much more laughter in her life. She was his now and he would ensure she was happy and safe. Besides, he'd made that promise to her at the altar.

When he pressed his lips to her hair, she stirred and grunted in a way that endeared her to him even more. She delighted him when she curled into him and planted her open hand on his chest as if claiming him. She had already done that, but perhaps she hadn't fully realized it yet.

He had made love to her carefully, twice, but already he longed for more. After their first night, he'd insisted she took a bath with salts in the water. Again, modesty had reared its head until he pointed out to her that she was only doing her wifely duty. "I'm not used to such intimacies," she'd said. He'd told her to get used to them because he didn't intend to stay away.

"Are you awake?" she asked him now.

"Yes. I've been waiting for you."

"What do you mean?"

He answered her question with another one. "How do you feel?"

"Much better than I ever imagined I would." Leaning up on one elbow, she bent to kiss him. He curved his hand around the back of her neck and made the most of it, licking in deep, tasting the elusive flavor of strawberries and apples that was such a part of her.

As far as he was concerned, the claiming had only just begun. He had so much to show her that his mind reeled.

"Are you ready for adventure?" he asked, when he'd pulled her over him. His cock was at attention again, and he intended to make good use of it.

"Yes."

He loved her readiness to follow him. In time, he'd lie back when it was her turn to lead and watch her discovering the joys of controlling their lovemaking. Already she was freer with his body, initiating caresses that he delighted in.

She laughed when he rolled her on to her back and eagerly reached up to respond to his kiss. He pushed his hand into her hair, loving the soft silky mass. He set to exploring her body again, kissing his way down to her breasts, pushing his hair roughly behind his shoulders so it would not impede his progress. He loved her nipples, soft and round as pennies when he started lavishing them with his affection, tighter and smaller, crinkling into hard points when he'd done kissing and caressing them. She had lush breasts, a good handful, something else she'd kept carefully hidden behind the formal gowns and the rigid stays.

Her soft stomach with that tempting little indentation awaited him, and then her hips and the shallow dips inside, where she squirmed when he kissed her. After that, he kissed down to her feet, making her laugh. He would make her wriggle deliciously. Her feminine scent awaited him. It had driven him mad since he had first sensed it, but she had not been ready for such intimacies then. She was now. She had better be.

He took his first lick. Her mingled aromas and tastes flowed into his senses and became one with them, as if they had always been there, waiting for him to awaken them. He absorbed them, taking them into him at this place where her flavor was at its most intense. Where her honey gathered.

When he kissed her mouth, a trace of her remained on his tongue, and now here it was again. The honey of his childhood home, made from bees that had glutted themselves on his mother's roses. His hair tightened when she gripped it, but she could pull it out by the handful if she wanted. He was going nowhere.

Her strangled cry of "Val!" drove him on. Another lick and then another, from front to entrance, and then he concentrated on the most sensitive part, the pearl of her clitoris.

"Val, what are you doing? I can't...oh, Val!"

Her voice transitioned from alarm and shock to bliss, as his actions had their desired effect. He feasted on her, putting every ounce of his hard-earned experience into giving Charlotte everything he had. He would take her, make her completely his without stint, show her how glorious lovemaking could be.

Placing his hand on her stomach, he felt her tension, the way her muscles fought him. He lifted his head. "Give it up. Let me take you there."

Her muscles tightened in unison, and then her breasts lifted with a deep breath. Satisfied with her reaction, he went back to work. He pulled and tugged at that little nub and then brought his fingers into play, sliding one into her and then two, caressing and learning her as deeply as a man could.

Her channel tightened, a precursor of her orgasm. Then she came, hard and fast, her body clenching in reaction. She wailed her cry to the heavens, and precious liquid poured over him.

Val rose up, wiping his mouth with the back of his hand. He barely had to guide his cock to her. It found its own way as he slid his arms to either side of her and bent to kiss her. He didn't want his wife unaware anymore. Her father keeping her so innocent had given him the burden of educating her, but it had become a joy, not a chore.

They would have no limits. Anything she wanted to do or learn, he would show her. Perhaps learn with her, who knew?

Instead of marriage becoming a burden, it had become the best event of his life.

When he plunged deep and her wet heat surrounded him, Val's thoughts scattered, and he sank himself into their lovemaking. Each thrust became a new world, a different sensation. He adjusted his angle of entry, and her reaction was instant. Arching her back, she cried out wordlessly, a sharp "Ah!" of instant response.

With a growl of triumph, Val quickened his strokes until he was pounding into her, the sounds of wet flesh slapping together and their gasps and cries echoing around the room. Harder and faster until—

Val gave her everything he had, flooding her with the essence of life. As it drained out of him exhaustion engulfed him in a great wave, drowning him, but he was happy to stay under the water for a while yet.

Pressing his right knee against the mattress, he rolled on to his back, taking her with him so her head was pillowed on his shoulder and she tucked her leg between his.

She curved her arm around his waist as he pressed a kiss to her forehead. "I'm glad it was you I married."

"So am I." If there was a better time to make his declaration, he didn't know it. "I love you, Charlotte."

A stifled sob answered him, abruptly broken off.

His heart sank as he tucked a finger under her chin and pushed her head up. "What is this? I'm not asking for a response, sweetheart. I wanted to tell you."

"I love you too."

Well, that was good. "So why are you crying?"

"Because I love you so much." She swallowed, making an effort to control her emotion. Maybe that session of lovemaking had produced the response. "Val, I know who I married."

He smiled. "That's good."

"I married a man with a brilliant mind, but one that does not remain in one place for long."

His pleasure-numbed mind took a moment to process what she was saying. Not that brilliant, then. He lifted himself up on one elbow, easing her to her back. "Are you expecting me to stray?"

She shook her head, her glorious chestnut hair clinging to the pillow, but then nodded. "I don't think you will do it intentionally. At one time I did, but I don't now. You will just..." Her voice faded.

That was just as well. What kind of man did she think he was?

The next moment his innate sense of justice came into play. He had spent the two years of their betrothal dashing from one mistress to the next, sampling as many as he could before matrimony. Now he wondered why he had waited so long. She had not seen him consistent or sober much of the time.

"No, I will not." He would start at the beginning. He wanted to kiss the tears from her eyes, but she had to understand what he was saying. "Did you ever know me unfaithful to any woman?"

Her brows rose slightly. Of course she wouldn't know that. "Unfaithful?"

"I prefer to have one woman at a time. I find one woman has everything I need."

"So for now that is me?"

He hated her tremulous smile. "Forever." But she didn't believe him; he saw doubt in her eyes and the slight shift of expression. He doubted anyone else would have noticed the way her eyes narrowed the tiniest bit or a frown came and went, but he did. He'd spent the last few weeks in concentrated study. Inspiration struck. "I keep my promises." He watched her, waited for that piece of information to sink in before he went on to the next. "Two days ago, we made promises to one another. Do you remember?"

She nodded.

"I promised to forsake all others and keep you only unto me, so long as we both shall live. Do you remember that part?"

He received another nod.

"I meant it. That is why I don't make many promises. It's why I avoided marriage for so long, because I knew I would not know any other woman for the rest of my life." He let his smile come. "The difference is, my heart's darling, that I don't want any other woman. I cannot imagine wanting one.

I've fallen deeply in love with you, Charlotte. You are the most important person in my life."

Her tears flowed freely, but she seized him and pulled him close, so she nearly ended up with his full weight. He managed to get his elbows on the mattress and did his best to support at least his upper body. He crooned affection into her ears, touched featherlight kisses to her face and let her cry it out.

His horror that she had carried this fear around with her affected him badly, so much that if she wept much longer he would join her. Until she wailed, "I'm so h-happy!" against his neck and drew a reluctant laugh.

"Sweetheart, tears of relief I can bear, but tears of happiness? Let me fetch us something to drink and we can begin to behave as if we are truly happy."

Thrusting a large handkerchief into her hand, he quit the bed and walked to the boudoir next door to locate a decanter. He found burgundy, collected two glasses, and brought them back to prop them on the bedside table. Thankfully, Charlotte had mopped her eyes and mostly recovered. She gave him a beaming smile, her eyes shining.

She was sitting up with the covers loosely draped over her lap, and the light from the setting sun streamed over her, gilding her ivory skin and turning her hair to pure fire.

As she turned to put the handkerchief on her nightstand, a small mark on the side of her ribs gleamed palely, a contrast to the creamy skin around it. Climbing on the bed, he traced the line with the tip of his finger. "What happened here?"

He had expected her to describe a childhood accident. He had a long scar on his leg from an altercation with a tree when he was nine. "The whip curled too far," she said calmly.

He tensed. "What whip?" Still kneeling, he turned her so he could see.

The scar was faint, only noticeable in a raking light, but what he saw made him feel sick. "Who did this?"

"My father." She made the abuse sound normal. "He preferred to administer our punishment himself."

"He marked you until you bled." He left his voice deliberately plain, leached it of expression. Otherwise, he might frighten her with the intensity of his reaction. Children were beaten, caned, even whipped, but not like this. Six strokes to the backside, not a whipping severe enough to leave scars. The only way she could have been marked like this was with a bare back or with the lightest covering.

His recent experience at the House of Correction made him feel worse. Had he really considered giving her up to Kellett, who would doubtless have given her the same treatment? Worse, because Kellett would have left deep ridged scars. Or a dead woman.

A tear slid from the corner of his eye, but this time he was not ashamed. This deserved tears. Tears of contrition from him. "How could you let him do this?"

"How could I not?"

Her too-bright tone made him pull his horrified gaze from her back and turn her around, so he could fold her in his arms. He could not feel the lines with his hands; indeed, they were so faint he might have missed them altogether had the sun not caught them.

"Disobedient children are whipped, are they not?"

"Not like that." Not to leave marks. "My father beat me when I ran away from my tutor or taught my sisters to say rude words in French. Six of the best, on the backside." Over his breeches. The marks had stung for a few days, but no more than that. And they had left no marks. He kept coming back to that. How hard must her father have struck her to leave those marks? "When did he stop?"

"When I left the schoolroom."

She would have been seventeen or eighteen. That didn't bear thinking about, but he would. "I'll ruin him. Destroy every connection he has."

"No!" She pulled away, staring up at his face. "Please, no, Val."

"His cruelty to you sickens me. Even to keeping you innocent, so you can't long for what you don't understand. He would have given you up to Kellett."

"I asked him to."

"Any father would make detailed enquiries about a future husband. Surely he knew—" He bit his lip, cutting off his words abruptly. In his anger he had let out more than he meant to.

"What is it? Knew what?"

"Never mind. I am merely shocked by his severity. Not for the first time, I might add." He would not say what he thought, would do nothing to distress her.

After laying her gently down, Val reached over to the nightstand to pour the glasses of wine. He needed a drink, even if she did not. He handed her a glass and touched his to it. "To us, sweetheart. May we have a long, successful, happy marriage."

The shy smile she gave him as they touched their glasses together made him vow not to allow cruelty to touch her again. And he would discover more, because his instincts screamed at him that there was more to be told.

Chapter 18

Overwhelmed by the half dozen gowns she found in her room the next day, Charlotte made her selection with pleasure, instead of the sense of dull duty she usually experienced. She could wear what she liked now. Not that she would count that as the major benefit of marriage.

She had been lucky. Once dressed, in a light green gown that took account of the hot weather, she tripped downstairs to explore her new domain. After she had spent an hour with the housekeeper, she turned in her chair to find her husband standing behind her. The big scrubbed deal table held a collection of books—recipes, inventories, and the household account books, which she'd been absorbed in. The familiar scents of spice and cooking beef surrounded her, but she started when he touched her shoulder.

Already she knew his touch. His presence wreathed around her before she turned her head to smile at him. His smile was equally warm. "I thought you might like me to show you the garden," he said.

She turned in time to see the housekeeper's warm gaze. Although she should perhaps have scolded her for her effrontery, at least her father would have punished any servant for looking at him so, she smiled back at the woman. "Perhaps we can resume tomorrow."

Because she would have a tomorrow here. As many tomorrows as she wanted.

Val took her hand and led her upstairs and outside. The day was fine, the sun beating down on them but she refused everything but a hat. "I've had enough of gloves and kerchiefs and warm woolen stockings that itch," she told him. "I will wear them only when I have to."

Lifting her hand to his lips, he kissed it. "Then I will ensure that only the finest silk and linen touches your body. And me, of course."

Oh, yes, and him. Already he could send her into ecstasy with a few careful touches in the right places. She had woken up in his arms for the last two days, and already it felt so natural she didn't know how she'd managed without it for so long.

They walked along winding garden paths, pausing to examine the spring blooms the gardener had brought into perfection. "You're blessed with your servants."

"I treat them well," he said.

"You treat me well, too."

He jerked her roughly back to him, so she landed against his chest with a soft "Oof!"

"I do more than that with you. You are my wife, not my possession, not someone I pay to do my will." His gaze softened. "One advantage is that you can never leave me." He bent his head and kissed her. She responded, marveling how easy this was, passing a fleeting thought to her father, who would have locked her in her room if he'd caught her doing this.

The Duke of Rochfort had no more jurisdiction over her. If she wished, she could ignore him completely from now on.

"Come." He led her toward a small pavilion at the rear of the garden, overlooking the river. Did he remember that night when he kissed her at the ball?

"Of course I do," he said as if she'd voiced her thoughts aloud. "I will never forget. Oh, but now I think of it, perhaps I need a reminder after all."

When he kissed her this time, it was with playful teasing. She opened her lips, as she always did now, and he touched his tongue to hers, and then outlined her lips, drawing away a little to add the sensation of cool air to their embrace. Perhaps she should thank his past mistresses for making him such a wonderful lover.

No, she wouldn't go that far.

He drew back, smiling, but tension put fine lines at the corners of his mouth. "What is it?"

"I have to tell you something. I don't know how to begin, but the woman I know you to be would want to know."

"Oh." That did not sound good. She settled on the bench inside the pavilion within sight of the river, folding her hands in her lap. He sat next to her, his attention wholly on her, but not in the way she preferred.

"I believe I might have been remiss in sheltering you. You are so much stronger than I imagined."

That meant as much to her as any declarations of love. He knew her now, and he was proving it by telling her something that was obviously uncomfortable for him to say.

"Have you heard of a place called the House of Correction?"

"In Covent Garden?" she answered immediately and then recalled where she had seen it. "I remember, it was early in the season, before April was out. I was bringing the household accounts up to date, entering a pile of bills into the books, when I saw one I did not authorize or recognize, so I took it to my father, since his name was on it. It had that name at its head. He took it from me, said it was a private account and should not be in the household books. It was his manner I recall. He appeared almost shamefaced, which was so unusual I thought on it for a while afterward."

"Ah. Then we have the final piece." He took off his cocked hat and put it on the seat next to him, lifting a hand to smooth his hair back. The hand shook as he turned to face her. "I had suspected as much. I meant to make enquiries when we returned to London. It was what you told me about your punishments that made me wonder." He met her gaze directly. "Your father probably met Lord Kellett at that place."

"I did not think they had met until Hervey asked me to speak to my father about breaking the engagement with you. Why, what is the House of Correction?"

"Do you know what Covent Garden is famous for?"

"A market, a theater and…" She broke off, her eyes widening. "Houses of ill repute."

He nodded. "It's a house, a brothel that specializes in a particular preference." He heaved a sigh. "I cannot think of a delicate way of saying this. People who take pleasure in inflicting punishment or having it inflicted on them. I already knew that Kellett was one such. Now I believe your father might enjoy such practices also."

Recognition hit her, almost as hard as her father's whip. Yes, he took pleasure in beating her, but before today she'd imagined it came from his control over her, the way she was forced to bow down to his will. He did enjoy ordering the house, using her sister Louisa to manipulate Charlotte and Sarah. "I didn't know." She felt stupid. Why did men keep so much information from them? "When did you find out?"

"Darius told me I should not let you go to Kellett and showed me why…"

"Does Darius like…?"

"No. However that house caters to men and women with that inclination, and they have rules. Killing the person you have paid to spend time with is not one of them, but Kellett did so."

Her hands curled in and she gripped the fine fabric of her gown. "He killed someone?"

He nodded. "She was alive when we left, but she died later. Darius ensured her death was recorded, instead of her becoming just another poor unnamed unfortunate lost at the bottom of the Thames."

That showed true compassion. At least the girl didn't pass unmarked.

Slowly, events slotted into place. Her father's acceptance of her request to break the contract with Val had seemed a far easier victory than it should have been. Had he boasted of her obedience and the way he'd schooled her to Hervey, told him he had readied her for marriage to one such as Kellett? She felt sick. She closed her eyes.

"My love?" Val touched her hand tentatively.

She opened her eyes, showing him she was not crying. Nowhere near. In fact, anger was closer than sorrow. "I doubt I will speak to my father again." She swallowed. "Even if you had been the rake I thought you, even if you had chased every woman in London, my fate would have been better with you. That it was so much more than that is not something I looked for. But I am glad. So glad."

"Your father is not without connections or influence," Val said. "He could do serious damage to our family if he wished. But I don't care, and if I tell my family, they will not, either."

She shook her head. "No, please do not. It's not kindness or consideration, since he deserves none. Not for him, at any rate. We may be polite to him in public and avoid him in private. That will serve." She didn't want to cause another feud. She'd had enough of those. "I would prefer to know that he is not causing harm to anyone else."

"My love, far be it for me to speak for your father, but as far as I know, he has never killed anyone or lost his temper with them. I am angry that he was over-severe in his discipline of you, but he did not leave you damaged beyond healing." He paused. "Some men—women too—know how far is too far and when their activities become too much."

She shook her head. "I cannot believe it is right." What he had told her shocked her to the bone. She was learning too much, too quickly, but she appreciated his needing to tell her.

"He is better at a place like the House of Correction," Val said. "The madam is careful of her girls." He paused. "And the male employees. This vice is not one that is exclusive to one sex. The madam trains her people well, and they are more valuable than the average..."

"Whore," she added helpfully. "Please speak frankly. I know most of the words, and I know what they mean. At least I thought I did." Heat warmed her neck when she recalled how much she had not known until a few days ago. "I assumed my father had mistresses or employed whores. He did not remarry after my mother died, although he might have done so."

"His wicked pleasure in controlling his daughters was probably enough for him. However, he has his just reward. He has lost all of you."

"When our brother returns from abroad, he will probably lose his heir, too." George would treat their father with the revulsion he deserved. They were innocents and unwilling. While Charlotte could not understand why anyone would want treatment such as people like her father and Kellett were only too eager to bestow, she could accept that they existed. But she had never wanted it.

"Did you ever believe that your father would kill you with his blows?" Val had withdrawn into himself, but Charlotte would allow it this once. He was trying to control his reaction to his discovery.

She shook her head. "Looking back, I believe he enjoyed it, but that day, when he inflicted the mark you have seen, he stopped immediately and sent me to my room instead. I think he has enough control to know when he has gone too far."

Val nodded. "I am glad for that, at least." His gaze strayed to where her scar lay, the one he had first noticed.

She had spent hours studying her back in the mirror, noting how light at a particular angle highlighted the mark. It had faded over the years. It might go altogether, but she would keep that one, if only to remind her what she'd nearly lost. Recalling that day, something she generally avoided, she pictured the expression on his face. That was the only time she'd ever seen her father horrified. He'd licked his lips and said, "You must not scar," in a quiet voice, almost as if he spoke to himself, before he sent her away.

"What about Hervey? Lord Kellett," she asked.

"He is more dangerous than your father. His temper is more volatile, and he has less control. We must move to destroy him, my love." His lips firmed. "Kellett has killed more than one woman."

Terror struck her dumb, but Charlotte forced herself out of her stupor. "What will you do?"

"Take him down. And out." He shook his head. "Darius is working on the answer. We want him to pay for what he did, so do not fear we will take underhand measures."

"You will tell me." She made it a statement rather than a request.

He got to his feet. "What I've learned of you made me want to tell you sooner rather than later. If you'd been a shrinking violet, I would have sheltered you and ensured you came to no harm. But you are not. You have withstood so much, my love. Much as I wanted to protect you from this, I consider you my partner, and I know you are strong enough to bear the knowledge. You will be stronger for it and know why we do what we do."

"I wonder you did not kill him when you fought him."

"I considered it." A flicker of a smile threatened. "But I had too much to lose. You, sweetheart. How could I have lost you? I would not bring a death to your door."

She let him help her up and they left the pavilion. At its edge, just as they stepped into the garden, he caught her shoulders and turned her to him. Over his shoulder the river flowed, a small boat bobbing at anchor a little further up. "Let's create a tradition," he said, drawing her into his embrace. "A garden pavilion deserves a kiss."

Gladly she went to him. He framed her face with his hands and kissed her. Their lips parted reluctantly, and he was smiling. He glanced back. "I forgot my hat. I won't be a moment."

Gazing out over the river, Charlotte let her new knowledge sink in. Her father enjoyed pain, enjoyed torturing people mentally and physically. Now she knew, now she understood, the last trace of guilt left her. That had been one of his favorite things, to make his children feel guilty for something they could not help or wasn't their fault.

Someone moved behind her, probably a gardener. Before she could turn and discover who it was, a cold, hard circular object was slammed against the back of her head.

Val stood in the opening to the pavilion, his eyes wide with horror. "Let her go," he said.

"Not until you give me what belongs to me," Hervey Smithson, Lord Kellett said.

* * * *

Val glared at his nemesis, thinking more rapidly than he had ever done in his life. He did not trust Kellett. The man would kill Charlotte just for the pleasure of seeing Val's pain. He did not see people as anything but objects, to be used for his pleasure. Or maybe just to make him feel alive. That would explain his extreme violence. If he lived in a cage, forever reaching out and not touching, then he would take any opportunity to force emotion on himself.

Val had met one such person before.

Therefore, Val could not let him know how much this woman meant to him. Leaning against the central pillar holding up the pavilion, he crossed one foot over the other, a study in negligence. How much had Kellett heard of their conversation? If he heard Val tell Charlotte that he loved her, this act would be harder to pull off.

"What do you want?"

"The garment you stole from me."

Kellett wanted the shirt. Kellett knew as well as Val did that it was the one item that could prove what they asserted, if the matter came to a court of law. The madam who witnessed the crime would be tainted in the court, and Val's grudge against Kellett was well known. Their evidence could be discounted if it were not for the bloodstained shirt.

"What will you give me if I let you have the item?" he asked, by way of opening negotiations.

"Her. You can have your wife back."

Kellett appeared wild, not at all his usual tidy self, but Val supposed the rowboat moored a little way up the river had something to do with that. It would not have been an easy task to row all the way here. If Kellett committed murder today, he could get back to London and nobody would be the wiser. He had another gun stuck in his belt. That meant he probably planned to kill both of them. Even if he got the shirt, they wouldn't live.

At least he could get them to the house, where there were witnesses. "You'll have to come up to get it."

Kellett's lips moved back, baring his teeth in a feral snarl. "Do you take me for a complete fool? Bring it to me. Then you can have your wife back."

Val curled his hands, relieved to see they weren't shaking, and examined his fingernails, as if the conversation bored him. "I've had her. I've spent the last three days rutting. You can have her. If you kill her, you'll be guilty of murder. That saves me a job."

"Don't tell me you'd kill her."

Val shook his head. "I have more sense. No, I'll leave her in the countryside. I've only worked my way through half of society. I have the other half to go yet." He grinned, and glanced up. "I don't even have to produce an heir. Younger sons don't have that burden." He daren't meet her eyes. Did she believe him?

Better she hated him and lived than loved him and died.

He needed to separate them. "How's your wound?"

Kellett lifted a shoulder in a half-shrug, the opposite shoulder to the one Val had injured. He wished he'd killed him in that duel now. "I hardly notice it. Healing well." He was using his good arm to hold the pistol. The other hand was tucked in his belt, close to the handle of his second pistol.

Val could make his move, but if he did, he could risk Charlotte's life. For all his words, that was the last thing he would ever do. He was too far away to leap for him, and the bastard had his weapon cocked and ready. The guns were quality, well made, which meant they had good responses. He couldn't depend on a misfire or a jam.

Thoughts raced through his mind, but not in a haphazard way. As he always did, he was assessing the risks and the odds, with one difference. Where Charlotte was concerned, there were no odds. There was only win or lose.

He would not lose.

Kellett moved the gun he was holding against Charlotte's head in a way that made Val feel sick. "Come on, I'm waiting. Go and get the shirt. That's all I want."

Val made some swift calculations. If he went in the house, ostensibly to fetch the shirt, they were both dead. When Kellett had sight of him, he'd kill Charlotte and then he'd draw the other weapon and shoot Val. He couldn't do it. He had been waiting for a gardener to notice them, or a boat passing by on their part of the river, but so far everything was infuriatingly tranquil.

He could go to the house, get a pistol, race to the top floor and shoot Kellett. No, he couldn't do that. The only way he'd get a shot from the house was to climb up to the roof and hang off the eaves. Even then he was too far away to be sure of getting his man. And by that time Charlotte could be dead.

"You'd risk this morsel?" Kellett took his eyes off Val long enough to give her an insolent, raking visual scan. "If I'd known what was hidden under that hair powder and dowdy clothes I wouldn't have let her go so easily."

Although it killed him to do it, Val shrugged. "There are other morsels, some even more delectable."

"But none as well trained as this one. Her father brought her up exactly the way I like. I never intended to let her go completely. She's most likely loving this. You know they like it, don't you?"

As if Charlotte were a creature, a thing. From the way she'd sobbed in Val's arms, he would not have said that she liked what was done to her.

He could only find one solution. He had to take the first bullet and pray he had enough stamina left to reach the other before Kellett did.

He could brush past Kellett, hurt his injured shoulder and shove his wife behind him. That was all he could think of.

"Go and get the shirt," Kellett said, as if he were talking to a child, patiently and slowly. "Tell nobody and alert nobody. I swear your wife will be alive when you return if you do that, but if you alert anyone or call for help, she will be the first to die."

He could return to the house and fetch something. Kellett wouldn't kill Val until he had the shirt, and likely he'd keep Charlotte alive until he was sure of the garment. A pity Val had left it in London, locked up in the safe in the City office. But he could fashion something, ask the cook for some animal blood, and call the alarm at the same time.

He couldn't risk his wife.

Charlotte had said nothing through this exchange. She had shut down, adopted that mask she always used, the one that had kept Val at bay for so long. She stood as if she were in the middle of a ball, utterly composed, her back straight, her face revealing nothing.

He glanced at his wife. Her eyes gleamed as she looked down to the ground and then at him again. She was obviously trying to tell him something, but what?

Yes, he had it. And she was right—that was their only chance. She would collapse. The sudden laxness in her body would shake Kellett's hold.

Standing here, too far away to do anything, did not help. Kicking away from the column he was leaning against, he strolled down the steps, watching Kellett carefully. The silence was palpable, stretched tautly between them. Nobody else seemed to exist.

Until a shout came from the end of the garden. Even at this distance he recognized his brother's voice, calling his name. "Here!" he cried back, and at the same time, he lunged.

Charlotte dropped. From where she stood she went down, as if she were a silk balloon pricked with a pin. As she collapsed, she reached up and grabbed Kellett's arm, the one that held the gun. When his grip loosened, she snatched it out of his hold. At the same time, Val went for the other gun tucked into the man's waistband.

He missed it. Kellett jolted back, pulling the pistol out with one hand. He cocked it with the other. The sights were firmly on Val. He breathed a sigh of relief. Charlotte was free.

His next move took him to Kellett, wrenching his wrist, twisting, trying to grab the weapon and turn it into the bastard who had hurt his wife. A wave of red fury engulfed him but Kellett threw him back. Val prepared to spring at him once more.

An explosion next to his ear and a scream had him reeling, but not for long. Before his brother reached the spot, Val had the gun in his hand and his arm around his wife. Kellett lay on the ground with half his head blown off.

But Val hadn't been the person who'd pulled the trigger.

Chapter 19

"They're coming for you," Darius said.

Val took a few impulsive steps across the morning parlor toward the window. Charlotte sat outside, ostensibly enjoying the sun. Neither had ventured anywhere near the pavilion since the terrible incident of a week ago, but the garden was still beautiful and she needed the peace.

Her decisive action had saved their lives, but it had taken something from her, too. He wanted to devote himself to her, helping her to recover from that devastating blow, but every time he saw the haunted expression in her eyes he knew what she was thinking and he knew he couldn't take that burden from her. She had killed a man.

She refused to talk about it, which worried him more. Now, it seemed, there was another distraction in store. "Who are coming for me?"

"Kellett's family. His mother, his sister, and his heir."

Val glanced over his shoulder at Darius. "What are they doing?"

"Bringing a private prosecution for murder."

"Murder?" Val turned his attention back to his wife. He shoved his hands in his pockets, watching the way she sat, her back straight, her gloved hands folded in her lap. She barely moved. He slotted the new information into his mind and went to work on it. "At least they are basing their accusations on me. But it wasn't murder."

"We have to tell Charlotte."

"I know." He shook his head. "How can they believe it? At the very most it was self-defense."

"They have a case," Darius said grimly. "They will collect evidence of your arguments with him. They'll say you took the woman he and her father wanted her to marry. They'll bring the card game and the duel into court." Darius moved closer and put his hand on Val's shoulder. "And you did not do it."

"How can you say that?" Furiously he turned to confront his brother. "I killed him."

Darius shook his head. "You did not. You held the gun when we caught up with you, but only because you had taken it from Charlotte. I saw the movement and the way she looked at you after you'd taken it. Besides, when I went over events in my mind, she was on the right side to take the cocked and loaded weapon. You took the other."

"One bullet each," he said dully. "That was what he planned. After that, he would row back up to London, or far enough away to distance himself from us."

"He is better dead," Darius said, "but his family is rising up. They never did when he was alive, but they smell blood. His heir is a straitlaced man who spent most of his time at his family estates in Yorkshire, but he doesn't want the taint of his predecessor to touch the title. He is a lawyer, but I do not know how good he is."

Val grimaced. "Straitlaced," he repeated. "At least that has to be better than the last incumbent." But not, perhaps, for him.

"Ivan is going to Yorkshire to see what he can find about the man. A way to clear the title of any stain is to accuse you of initiating and planning the last viscount's murder. He will claim that what appears to be self-defense is in truth the result of a calculated plan."

He was right, damn him. The new Lord Kellett had a case. That meant they would expend considerable energy and money on it. And it meant one more thing. "So I'm to stand trial in Bow Street?" He was not a peer, merely the son of one and not in the direct line, so he would be treated as a commoner in law. Otherwise it would have been the House of Lords. He wasn't sure which option would draw the most crowds. "Probably Newgate Prison, too."

"You should think about telling the truth," Darius said.

Furious, Val lifted a hand but his brother caught his wrist before it reached him. Their faces were close, glaring at one another.

"Listen to me," Darius said. "With the case they have, they will bring it to court, but they will lose. They must. We will use every weapon we have."

"You will not tell anyone who shot him, do you hear me?" Val said furiously. "Charlotte is in no state to stand trial." He gave Darius a moment to absorb what he was saying. "Even if she were, I would do everything I could to prevent it. It is immaterial who killed Kellett. He was threatening both of us, and he had every intention of killing us both." He frowned. "How did you know he was there?"

"I wasn't sure. I went to his house and his butler told me he wasn't available. His servants are not very loyal. It only took two guineas to elicit the information that he had taken his carriage to the docks. From there, I guessed why he would want a boat. If I was wrong, I'd have stayed for dinner and left." He grimaced. "I know we don't make much of the twin link, but I felt you were in danger."

Val dropped his hands and stepped back. "Perhaps we should. Your shout distracted him for the few seconds we needed." Their likeness was close and staring into eyes so like his own brought reason back to Val's turbulent thoughts. "But I don't want to leave Charlotte. If they arrest me, I will have to. She is suffering badly." He paused. "If I can't get her to return to me, she will retreat into herself." If he had to cope with this new problem, he must trust his brother to care for her. To do that, he needed to know the whole story.

He crossed the room to a chair by the unlit fire, where he could keep his attention on his wife. "I have something to tell you."

Darius took the chair set opposite the fireplace and crossed his legs. "Go on."

Typical that he didn't question Val. "Charlotte was ill-used by her father," he said bluntly. "In fact, I have every reason to assume that the Duke of Rochfort met Kellett at the House of Correction."

Darius's quickly sucked-in breath told Val what his brother thought of that. He swore, long and colorfully. "I had no idea. I have more knowledge of that area of London than perhaps I should, but I have never heard even a whisper that Rochfort was involved."

"Charlotte was unaware of it, too. But from what she told me of her father's behavior, I saw a pattern. I have not confirmed my suspicions. I had more important things to do."

"I will confirm it." Grim-faced, Darius sighed. "I have work to do. I'll confirm the link, and I'll find witnesses to what we saw that night."

"Won't that show that I had a grudge against Kellett?"

"An understandable one. It's a risk, but I will collect every scrap of evidence that I can."

Having a brother like Darius was worth ten fortunes. "Rochfort is not as dangerous as Kellett. He has a sense of self-preservation and some self-control."

"That might be why he imposed that rigid control on his children."

Val nodded. He hadn't considered that aspect before. If Rochfort considered his unusual tastes a sin and unnatural and worked hard to control his natural urges, he might want his children to have armory. Not that the knowledge made Val feel any better disposed toward the man. "He was certainly of the same frame of mind, so it seems likely that was where they met. I have been thinking and made a few suppositions that work. Kellett wooed Charlotte and persuaded her to go to her father and ask to break the contract. And to me. Kellett would use that to control her, to tell her that he was her choice." He swallowed back his anger, although for two pins he would have stormed outside and punched the ash tree near the side of the property hard enough to break his fingers. To think they had nearly fooled him made his stomach roll.

"That sounds like the kind of thing he would do." Darius's face was made of stone. "One way or another, we will prevail. We have enough. I will return to London and make enquiries. If he persists with the suit, we will do our best to destroy him."

Val nodded. "Can you persuade the bawd in Covent Garden to stand witness?"

Darius paused before he said, "If I can find her. I will do everything I can."

Val lifted his chin belligerently, accepting the challenge as he might a challenge to a duel. They would win. They had to.

His gaze went to Charlotte again. She had not moved, still sitting as still as a marble statue, watching nothing. The other challenge came first. Unfortunately he could no longer give her the time she needed. He needed help. "Charlotte has withdrawn. She is more than troubled, and unless I can find a way to persuade her to open to me again, I fear I'll lose her forever." She was perfectly capable of locking herself away. At the moment, she spoke to him and discussed household matters. He'd been trying the gentle approach. As soon as the inquest into Kellett's death was over, he planned to take her to Leicestershire and give her the peace of the county for as long as she needed it.

They went out to her. Charlotte's smile was polite, almost vacant. "Should you not come in now? The day wears on."

"Is Darius to stay to dinner?" When he responded in the affirmative, she appeared almost glad their intimacy was to be interrupted, her words brighter than they'd been for days.

Val tried not to take her reaction personally. When he held out his hand to her she ignored it, pretending to be busy gathering her skirts. She rose gracefully, and stood before him as he dropped his hand. He knew better than to touch her, but his palms tingled with the effort not to take her in his arms.

Before Val could stop him, Darius stepped forward and lifted her hand to his lips.

Her reaction was instant and terrifying. Leaping up from the garden bench, she took a step back and caught her heel in her skirts. Her face contorted and tears sprang to her eyes. As she stumbled, the sound of tearing fabric came to his ears, but she righted herself by gripping the arm of the bench. Her bosom heaved as she regained her breath and Val knew her heart would be beating so hard she could hear it. But he could not help her, could not sweep her into his arms and carry her away. If he did, she would only grow worse.

Charlotte closed her eyes. Val watched, appalled, but unwilling to leave until her breathing slowed and she opened her eyes again.

The frozen expression of Lady Charlotte Engles returned, clamping down over the agitated woman who had shown herself. If anything, that hurt Val more than her upset, for she was shutting him out, closing him down.

"Good afternoon, Darius, it's good of you to come. Won't you stay to dinner?"

A shaken Darius accepted her invitation, and she went indoors, sweeping past them like a queen.

Val swallowed. "She will not let me touch her."

Darius's mouth straightened. "So I see." He watched Charlotte go inside.

Last night Val had tried to make love to her. His mind veered away from what happened, but the vision remained burned into his brain. The cry she had given was distress, and she'd shrunk to the far side of the bed, whimpering in terror.

He'd spent the night elsewhere, once he'd called her maid to care for her, telling the girl that his wife had experienced a bad dream.

"When I picked her up after Kellett's death, she'd gone completely rigid. I ignored her response. I thought it was shock. I carried her to our room and laid her on the bed. When the maid came down later, she told me she'd had the same response from Charlotte." He recalled her words. "She won't let me touch her, sir. She insists on tending to herself. All I could do was pour the hot water for her, lay out her night rail, and tidy up when she had done."

That she hadn't wanted even a maid to touch her worried Val deeply, but considering Charlotte's reaction due to crippling shock, he let it be and took care not to touch her. He slept in the same bed the first night, but when he'd discovered her huddling at the very edge of the bed, he'd spent the intervening nights elsewhere. Until last night.

"I must do something. The authorities could arrive any day. Once the new Lord Kellett and his family have a case, they will waste no time coming for me."

Darius nodded. "You cannot force her reaction. I have heard of that phenomenon before. I know you will not take advice from anyone, but listen to me this once, Val. Let her touch you."

He listened. How in the devil's name did he do that, when he yearned to fold her in his arms, to surround her with his love? But he couldn't do that now, and time was running out for him. Once they came for him, they could well lock him up, separate him from her. Then she would truly be lost to him. She might never come back.

* * * *

Charlotte came down to dinner, once again her serene self. Over dinner, Val explained what was about to happen. As he expected, his redoubtable wife protested. After a glance at Val, she said, "But I shot him, not you!"

Darius dropped his fork with a clatter, apologized, and restored it to the side of his plate. "Charlotte, I know, but Val and I are the only people who know. Do not tell the authorities."

"It was an accident." Tears sprang to her eyes.

Val lifted his hand, reaching out to her before his reason caught up with his desire. He did not touch her. He could not bear to see her flinch away and freeze. The more he touched her, the worse her reaction. He was terrified that if he tried too much, she would leave him and never come back, in mind if not in body.

Val had never been so circumspect before. His wife was teaching him some salutary lessons, although he wished they were not quite so brutal.

Darius softened his voice. "If they accuse you of murder, do you think Val would survive it?"

She turned a stricken gaze to him, and Val felt even worse. That wasn't the reason he was preparing to take the brunt of the accusation. Charlotte was in no state to take that kind of pressure, and if they had her locked up in Newgate, people would be jostling and touching her all the time. She would lose her mind.

Besides, if she had not pulled the trigger, he was sure as he was sitting here that he would have. Kellett had gone too far with his final action. The minute he'd threatened Charlotte, he was a dead man. If Val had not killed him, Darius would have ensured it was done. The small technicality that had prevented him from doing the deed mattered little.

"To be blunt my dear, the Emperors have more friends and popularity than your family. Your father is resented in many circles, and not a few people would take this opportunity to get their revenge on him."

He knew she would understand that, and she did, nodding.

They had sent the servants away so they might talk, but at that moment, someone knocked on the door. "There are three men outside who are insisting on seeing you, my lord," the butler said sonorously.

Val noted the use of "men," and not "gentlemen." "Very well, Bunson, show them into the drawing room. We will be through when we are ready. Did they leave their names?"

"One is a Bow Street Runner, my lord, a Mr. Dunmore. The other is our parish constable, who appears deeply uncomfortable. The third did not speak, but he is a large man."

They found out exactly how large he was when they walked into the drawing room. His hulking form dominated the comfortably spacious room.

The man with the red waistcoat, marking him as the Runner, executed a short bow. "Lord Valentine Shaw?"

Val gave his wife a reassuring smile and nodded. "Close, but it's Valentinian. Why do you interrupt my evening?"

"My lord, I have the task of informing you that you are arrested for the heinous crime of murder. I must request that you accompany me to Bow Street, where you will be placed in custody pending your trial."

Although he had expected it, a cold chill seared through Val. His memory went back to the day when he'd rescued Charlotte from the Tyburn crowds, and a sense of gloom descended on him like a smothering blanket.

"You will not incarcerate him in Newgate," Darius said, as if stating a fact.

"Our instructions are to take him there," the constable replied. He tucked his thumbs in his waistcoat and stuck out his chest, as proud as a turkey cock.

Darius looked from Val to Charlotte, but Darius shook his head. "Take care of my wife, Darius. I will shift well enough."

"Do you have money?"

Val grimaced. He had not thought he wanted it, spending a day at home, but he would need money to pay for a room of his own, even decent food. The guards at Newgate Prison thrived on them. They could hardly live on what they were paid.

Without a pause, Darius drew out his purse and handed it over. "I'll see you tomorrow."

"Look to my wife first," Val told his twin. "Above everything, take care of Charlotte."

Chapter 20

Charlotte wanted to go with Val, but Darius stopped her. The men had gone, taking Val in a closed carriage with the blinds down and she could not even let him kiss her. The thought of doing it sent her into a blind panic.

How could she be so unfeeling? Except that she wasn't. She felt as if she were battering against the walls of an impregnable room, locked up there for all time, unable to escape. Her isolation was as real as if it had been physical and she could not break out of it.

When Darius offered to take her back to London that day, she accepted with alacrity. "I cannot stay here without gossip spreading, you know that," Darius told her. "We have time, and to be truthful, I would rather start work tonight."

"They're taking him to Newgate," she said numbly. "He could catch gaol fever."

"He will not spend above one night there," Darius vowed. "I will find a way. He may not have to stand trial by the time we're done. It is fortunate that the family came to London for your wedding, because I intend to put every one of them to work."

"Yes." Charlotte gathered her skirts in one hand. "Give me an hour, and I will be ready. Or I can come now, and send for my things."

"No, bring what you must. But no longer than an hour, mind."

Charlotte's maid seemed relieved to have something useful to do and proved her worth by having Charlotte's clothes and her dressing case packed in half the allotted time.

Since Darius had ridden here, they took the carriage Charlotte and Val had arrived in, and left his horse for a groom to bring into town the next day.

At the door, the butler bowed low. "I trust we will see you soon, my lady? If I may venture to wish yourself and his lordship all the good fortune in the world."

That meant a lot to Charlotte. Servants rarely gave opinions, and the ones in her father's house generally crept about like mice, so to have the loyalty of a London servant was something indeed. She nodded and smiled. "Thank you."

Darius held out his gloved hand to help her into the carriage. When she paused, he dropped his hand and she made shift to climb into the vehicle on her own.

Her reaction to touches began immediately after Kellett's body lay on the ground next to her. Blood and bits of bone had spattered her, but it wasn't until the pool of blood had reached her face that she'd felt the full horror of what she had just done. It was warm, touching her like fingers of liquid.

Almost immediately Val had scooped her up. His touch, so soon after Kellett's, had done something to her senses. Still in deep shock, she'd reacted instinctively from somewhere deep inside her. At the time, she'd assumed she would recover after the shock had worn off and she'd had some rest, but it was not to be.

When Val had tried to make love to her—even now, her mind shied off from her horrific response, fighting as if her life were at stake, screaming and pushing him away. Another man would have forced the issue, but Val left the room, telling her not to worry. Her reaction shamed her.

She'd wept when he left, but she could not help her reaction. Her body had reacted before her mind had. And now she might lose him forever without knowing the joy of holding him again. For all his brave talk, he had his enemies, and they would use this to try to destroy him. The whole family had enemies.

Charlotte refused to be bowed, although she'd be an idiot to deny her fear.

They reached the London house of the Shaw family in just over an hour. At this time of year, the days were drawing out, and darkness would not fall for some time yet, so anyone who wanted to see her could. Darius descended from the carriage, and waited for her to descend. "We will take the greatest care of you."

"I know you will."

Within another hour, the Emperors still in London arrived en masse and gathered in the drawing room. Darius contrived to protect her from touches by guiding her to a sofa at the edge of the room, and sitting next to her. The room, when it was not cleared for balls, contained several casually arranged groups of chairs and sofas, which as they arrived the guests had no compunction in dragging around to suit their purposes. Julius, Lord Winterton, arrived with his wife; Lord Devereux and his lady; Ivan; and Ivan's brother Lord Ripley, who did not spend much time in town these days. Four of Val's five siblings, his parents, and nine of Val's cousins, with spouses, made for a full drawing room.

Charlotte sat very still and rigid, trying to keep her wayward emotions in control. She was not used to suffering so many at the same time, nor was she accustomed to the strength of her passions. She was constantly on the edge of tears or edgy, uncontrollable laughter. The only way she knew how to cope with such emotions was to retreat inside herself, as she had done so often before. Quell everything, tamp it down. She had developed skill doing that. She put it into play now, and disappeared behind her facade.

The meeting passed in a daze. However hard Charlotte tried to concentrate on the vital business at hand, what they said slipped away from her even as she was grasping it.

At one point, Darius leaned over and spoke to her. "Don't worry. I'll take you over the salient points another time."

Was her bemusement so obvious? She hardened her expression, remaining still and calm, trying to look as if she knew what was going on.

Watching them, she finally understood why the Emperors were successful. Even the new members of the family circle contributed to the discussion. Nobody was excluded. The marquess acted as unofficial head, ensuring everyone had his say and the more promising ideas taken forward. Their reach astonished her. They had tentacles in every part of society and the underworld.

They were prepared to take as long as it took. At one point, Julius's wife, Eve, quietly left and returned half an hour later, having fed and put her baby to bed herself in the nursery upstairs. Charlotte had heard of fashionable ladies feeding their babies themselves, but that was the first time she had come across the phenomenon.

She could be pregnant with Val's baby. Although they were under no compulsion to set up a nursery, Charlotte surprised herself with the longing that temporarily pierced her numbness. She wanted Val's child.

They had each their assigned tasks. She cleared her throat. "May I coordinate?"

She thought they hadn't heard her at first, but then Lord Winterton's head swiveled in her direction. His cool blue gaze, his eyes several shades lighter than Val's, swept over her thoughtfully, making her itchy in her skin.

"I am used to running my father's households, so my organizational skills are very good."

He held up a hand. "I have no doubt, ma'am. Your offer is most welcome. If you set up an office in the book room here that would work very well. Keep it locked, and lock the jib door, too. Dust will have to gather while we are busy." He meant don't let the servants in to spy. Charlotte was fully in agreement with that.

When he came toward her, she tried not to shrink back, but of course he would not touch her.

Except that he did. He lifted her hand to his lips.

Charlotte snatched her hand back with a cry of alarm and moved so convulsively the substantial sofa scraped back on the floor.

Reaction was instant. Julius straightened as Darius leaped up to stand protectively in front of her.

"I have to tell them," he said regretfully. "Everyone here feels your pain, Charlotte. We will do everything we can to protect you." He addressed Julius directly, although he spoke loud enough for everyone to hear. "Charlotte does not like being touched at the moment. Please give her this time."

Sympathetic murmurs and a soft cry of dismay from her mother-in-law followed Darius's statement.

He moved aside and sat down again. Charlotte folded her trembling hands in her lap. "I did it," she said. She could not bear this group of people to be under any illusions. It was clear they would move heaven and earth for her. Would they do so when they knew the truth?

They fell silent and stared at her. "Hervey—Lord Kellett, that is—held a pistol to my head. He told Val to get the shirt, the one we told you about. We knew that his word was worth nothing, and as soon as Val left, he would kill me. Or perhaps he would do it when Val returned, so he could take the shirt and see him watch me die." She closed her eyes and took a deep breath. She pictured the scene in her mind as if she was sitting in a box at Drury Lane watching a play. "But if Val did not go to the house, he might kill us both anyway. He had two pistols, so our only chance was when he paused to cock the second. But by that time one of us would be dead." She swallowed, recalling the risk they took. "I tried to signal Val, and I think he understood what I planned. When he made to walk past me, it was our only chance. I dropped to the ground and grabbed the pistol. Kellett's hold loosened, and I managed to take it. I turned it and fired." She did not continue. If she had, she'd have admitted that she shot to kill, that she did not intend Hervey to leave that garden alive.

The guilt crippled her, especially when she'd seen the result.

"I want to tell the authorities. Val should not suffer for my sins."

"No!" Darius, Ivan, and Julius spoke at once.

"Newgate is no place for you," Darius added.

Julius frowned. "From what you say, either of you could have killed him. He clearly intended to murder you, so I cannot see this case being anything but self-defense. It cannot be murder."

"They can make a case," Darius said gloomily. He'd already outlined the events leading to Kellett's death. He was right, the public nature of the card game, the rivalry and the duel could have led to a planned killing. But not by Val. Except that Val had a reputation for reckless behavior, and hadn't he shot at Kellett before?

Charlotte felt sick. She swallowed, but even that small move was noticed by Julius.

"Are you growing tired?" he asked her gently, so softly Charlotte finally understood why Eve was so deeply devoted to him. The care and consideration in those words belied the reputation Lord Winterton carried of a haughty, proud man whose first name should have been Perfection. He had accepted her problem without a blink, and now he was treating her with care. He would never run roughshod over her, as her father had done.

"I'm not at all tired, thank you." She sounded prim, but she could not help that. She wanted to get to work.

Shortly after, the group broke up.

Charlotte found she felt much better, having a task to perform, and a place in this family.

* * * *

When her father called, Charlotte was busy in the book room. Although small, the room was furnished with everything she needed to keep the different strands of the case together. She'd stacked papers in neat piles on the large circular table and set up a sheet of paper with all the details on it on a table with carefully ruled lines. Frankly, she loved that kind of work, detailed and precise, when she could sit back and see what she had done.

However, she'd never done anything this important before.

The butler knocked and stayed at the door, as she'd instructed him. "My lady, your father, the Duke of Rochfort, has called. Are you available to see him?"

So that was why he was speaking softly. She could behave like a coward and refuse to see him, but she would not, although she might in future.

But she would not see him alone. "Is anyone else at home?"

The butler nodded. "Lord Darius is abed. He was out all night, but I believe he is stirring. His valet went up to him half an hour ago."

"I would appreciate you telling him that my father is here. Would you offer the duke refreshment, please, and let him know I'll be in directly?"

She didn't have to ask where the butler would put him. Only the grand drawing room would do.

She gave him five minutes, taking the time to compose herself. Her father could not distress her anymore. She had been through too much recently to allow him to drag her back into his particular version of hell. Whatever happened next, she would not go back.

Darius met her outside. He reached out, but dropped his hand before he touched her. "I have news. I could not see you before. I was not fit for anyone to see me, but I would have come to you next. I've had Val moved from Newgate. He is now in Sir John Fielding's private residence at Bow Street."

She clasped her hands together. "May I see him?"

"Perhaps." He paused. "He wants to bathe and make himself decent for you. And sleep. He hasn't been well." As her stomach twisted and she turned around to race up to her room and fetch her hat and gloves, he continued quickly. "He could not sleep. He needs rest. The news I gave him helped ease his mind. I am to care for you, which I intend to do anyway."

"He is not truly ill?"

"No, merely tired and worried."

"Very well." Feeling heartened, she lifted her chin and nodded to the footman to throw open the doors to the drawing room.

Her father had settled on a sofa, a relief to the housekeeper who might have feared for her chairs. As it was she could swear that the delicate-seeming piece of furniture bowed under his weight. This drawing room was very different than the one she was used to. A portrait of the marquess and his wife were hung either side of the fireplace, but in the center was a painting of the family home, surrounded by carvings Val had told her were by Grinling Gibbons. The twisted ribbons and flowers in bloom were miraculously carved in wood, the motifs repeated in the plaster ceiling. Yet this was a family room. For all the treasures it contained, it had a warmth and welcome Charlotte had never felt in any of her father's houses. Even now she felt it, reaching out to hold her in a protective circle of warmth.

The duke did not get to his feet. He nodded to Darius. "You may leave. I wish to speak to my daughter alone."

"I am charged by her husband to remain with her." Darius was at his grandest, every bit the son of a premier peer.

"Humph. He won't be her husband for much longer."

Charlotte sat in the chair by the fire. Her father's frown deepened, but he said nothing. Probably reserving his battles. Charlotte could not remember ever sitting in his presence before. Ever, except at meals and never without his permission. Darius sat in one nearby.

The maid brought a tray of tea, and Charlotte had to go through the ritual of pouring it and handing it out. She had no desire for tea. She wanted to know what he wanted and get him out of the house. "He is my husband until I die," she said quietly.

"When you're a widow, you come back to me," her father said. "I regret I cannot provide the husband for you that I chose, but there it is. You would behave stubbornly, and this is your reward. A disobedient child is anathema to me."

"The last time I saw you, you declared you had no daughters," she pointed out, keeping her voice sweet.

"You were too untrustworthy to be any child of mine." He cleared his throat. "However, I would be unnatural if I left you in your time of distress. I have come to fetch you home, daughter."

Horror filled her, making her heart quicken at the mere suggestion. "I *am* home."

"Now we are on different sides of the dispute, your loyalty belongs to me." He took a slurp of his tea and set the dish back on its saucer with a hard click. He was not pleased.

"I am naturally loyal to my husband."

His lips firmed. "Not for long. He murdered a man. It is not the first, I believe."

What did he mean by that?

Darius took a hand in the conversation. "Val has never killed a man before, much less murdered one. I would take care what you say, your grace." Never had a title sounded more like an insult.

"I do, and I do not need a person like you to remind me of it. You are not here of my will, sir."

"Nevertheless…" Darius gave a gracious wave of his hand, indicating his presence. "Sir, I am devastated to inform you that your daughter will not be returning to your house, now or at any time in the future."

"When her husband is hanged—"

Darius held up his hand again, this time with more firmness. "He will not be hanged." He had clearly seen Charlotte's flinch even though she had done her best to control it. "If he is otherwise detained, which we are also not prepared to accept, he has provided handsomely for his wife."

"I am retaining her portion. She will have nothing."

"On the contrary, she will be a wealthy woman. She *is* a wealthy woman, since my brother has already settled an amount on her."

The duke's lip turned in a sneer. "What money does he have? He's a wastrel. What money he has, he squanders."

"Apart from the fortune he has made in partnership with me." Darius shrugged.

"Pandering?"

Fury seethed brought Charlotte's blood to boiling point. "How dare you speak of any man so?" The bitterness of years poured out. "You, with your disgusting habits? We know of your proclivities, sir, although I did not when I lived in your house. If I had, I would not have remained there. I would have lived on the streets rather than taken your abuse and your dictatorial behavior. We went in fear of your moods, sir, but no more. If you insult my husband, if you think to appear in court against him, I will tell them everything I know of your unnatural practices and your visits to the House of Correction."

She had never seen her father shaken before. He knew what she meant, she saw it in his red-rimmed eyes, and in the way his mouth hardened. He got that look just before he was about to beat her, but the anticipatory gleam was missing. "I was right to cast you off," he said quietly. She once trembled at that tone. "You are an ungrateful daughter. I will be leaving for my estates tonight. I will acknowledge you in public, but no more. Do you understand? You are nothing to me."

"I wish I could say the same," she said, alarmed at the calmness that settled over her.

Darius escorted the duke to the door and then returned to find her sitting still and calm. "You did well," he said. "Without your father's testimony, Kellett's case is considerably weakened."

Charlotte heard the words, but she was locked inside her cell once more. With that flash of temper she had felt like her old self, but the freezing barrier had descended, a curtain of stillness.

She was back with her own company, sealed in her own living tomb of solitude.

Chapter 21

The Emperors had done their work and scheduled Val's trial for the fastest turnaround they could contrive. Ordinarily Val would have had to wait at least a month, but they had compiled his case and brought it forward several weeks to take their enemies by surprise.

Charlotte had visited him several times in the humble room John Fielding had put at his disposal. Each time he had been left in an agony of wanting her, unable to think clearly for the haze of longing that blanketed him the minute she entered the room. Only when she had left could he make sense of what she had said.

The instinct to take her in his arms blazed through him, but he'd clenched his fists tightly by his side and showed her a smiling face when she left. She was not ready for what he wanted. He prayed that one day she would be, and that he'd be there to experience it.

The amount of work his family had done in the last week staggered him, but Charlotte's careful accounting of the evidence did not. He knew and loved his wife's methodical mind. She had cross-referenced every statement to the pieces of evidence that supported it. The lawyer Julius had engaged, one Andrew Graham, had built the case for him, step by logical step.

But he could still lose.

Other members of the family had been collecting gossip, discovering what the opposition was preparing, and while the Smithsons had been surprisingly closemouthed, they'd found that they had been making particular reference to his more outrageous exploits. He had no excuse for those, other than high spirits. Now they were coming back to haunt him. The time when he'd won a wager to chase a fox around Grosvenor Square at full gallop in the early hours of the morning read like foolishness now.

And that was the least of the exploits. He had no idea which they would choose. He hadn't exactly made a secret of them.

His valet prepared him for the trial. He debated the red and gold, the coat he'd worn when he'd claimed Charlotte from her father's house, but decided he might be too blatant. Not that Mr. Fielding would care. He was as blind as a bat, and liked to emphasize the fact in court. He had stayed scrupulously away from Val during his time in the house, which was a pity, because Val would have appreciated a conversation or two with the magistrate. Not just this case, but Fielding was possessed of a fine mind, by all accounts.

How ironic that the moment Val had everything to live for, he became at greatest risk of losing his life. He had risked it recklessly many a time, but not now. He would do nothing to reduce his chances of losing Charlotte.

So he dressed grandly, but soberly, in a coat of slate gray ribbed silk, embroidered with silver at the pockets and buttonholes, and a waistcoat of white, embroidered with silver and gold. His buttons of engraved silver caught the light, but did not glare.

Standing before the spotted mirror in the modest room his reflection appeared incongruous, as if he didn't belong here. After a week confined to this place, he was heartily sick of it, but this was the last time he would see it. If he went free, he would go home. Otherwise tonight he'd sleep in the condemned cell across the road at Newgate Prison and become the latest attraction for tourists who could bribe the guards enough to gawk at him through the bars. But not for long. He'd be the central attraction at Tyburn, probably break the records for crowd attendance. Of all his ambitions in life, that was the one he wanted the least.

He was putting the finishing twitch to his neckcloth when the summons came. "My lord," his valet said quietly.

Val nodded. "Pack up my belongings." One way or another, he would not be returning here tonight.

The man bowed and nodded.

The guards entered and Val suffered his legs to be put in irons. He shook his foot and let the links clank. Prisoners wore these all day. The sores they caused were often marked by the recorders of court proceedings. Had Fielding left Val in prison, he would have the marks, and he'd stink like a prisoner, of damp, dirt, and despair.

The braces around his ankles clinked annoyingly against his shoe buckles when he walked, or rather, shuffled. He walked between the guards who were remarkably uncommunicative, his folder in one hand, down the stairs, where one of the guards kindly took the weight to spare poor Mr. Fielding's staircase, and down a private passage to the court.

As he passed through the main door, a roar went up, and simultaneously, his nervousness left him. Holding his head up, he walked to his place in the dock, looking neither to right nor left. A highwayman would have acknowledged the crowd, but he wouldn't have had the opportunity for long.

Magistrates were notorious for the speed with which they could get through cases, and Fielding was no exception. In his capacity as judge, he sat in the chair of honor, the royal coat of arms on a painted panel hung above his head, a wide black band across his eyes in a deeply dramatic way. In the normal course of events he wore a thin black band above his eyes, a symbol of his blindness, but the thick ribbon made a statement that was hard to miss. His assistant, a young man of delicate appearance, leaned down and murmured to him.

The public gallery was packed, so full Val feared for the people crowded into it. Anyone of his family not due to be called as witness was up there. The jury, twelve soberly dressed men, sat to one side, close together so they could discuss the case. They would not play their part until the end.

Val's lawyer and counsel for this case, Andrew Graham, came unhurriedly to his feet and strolled across the court to stand by Val. He had a slim folder in his hand.

He glanced at the jury, who sat in their appointed places, to one side of where Val stood, their faces eager and expectant.

He gave Val a curt nod. "My lord."

"Good morning," Val said, not to be outdone in coolness.

The clerk of the court cleared his throat and made the announcement. "Valentinian Shaw, you are indicted for the willful murder of Hervey Kellett, in firing a pistol at him at close range with an intent to kill, on May the twenty-seventh, 1757. How plead you?"

"Not guilty, my lord." Val stepped back, his work done for the time being.

It said much for the authority of John Fielding that the court fell relatively quiet. Clearly they did not want to have their entertainment spoiled.

Charlotte would be sitting in another room, waiting to be called. Val prayed the case would be cut short and she would not have to appear.

The new Lord Kellett was called first, as he was the accuser. He had a lawyer, too, a man who stared at Val down his long nose until a dewdrop formed there and he was forced to find his handkerchief.

Kellett was a tall, thin man, dressed in the country style, in a frock coat of tobacco brown and a fawn waistcoat. He stood up and glared at Val. Then he stated his case. "I had no desire to become viscount, but when

I was unexpectedly called, the news sent me into a severe paroxysm. I wish for justice for my predecessor. Murder should never go unpunished."

"I agree." Graham smoothly got to his feet. "However, Lord Shaw did not murder the late Lord Kellett. I wonder how well you knew him?"

The new Kellett blustered. "I knew him as an upright and honorable man. He spent most of his time in the city, and I went about my work elsewhere, but we corresponded."

"Frequently?"

"Often enough."

Graham glanced at the jury and spread his hands in a "what do you think?" gesture.

This man was good.

Next came Kellett's mother, who declared her son to be an upright and good man. Graham showed that she had kept her distance. When asked why, the lady pleaded her health, or lack of it, although she appeared perfectly healthy to Val.

"Do you know where your son spent his nights?"

Lady Kellett lifted a shoulder in a shrug. "He was a healthy young man. I spent most of my time caring for dear John in the country." She glanced at the new Lord Kellett, a look of fondness passing between them, but of the mother and child variety, Val was relieved to see. He could do without the mental pictures anything else might have contained. "But he was diligent in business and considerate to us."

"So you do not know the details of your son's life, except what he vouchsafed to you in his letters. I can hardly suppose he told you about the notorious house in Covent Garden that he was fond of frequenting?"

Not even Mr. Fielding could prevent the excited murmur that rumbled from the public gallery.

Relaxing a tiny amount, Val leaned back and prepared to listen, go through the notes Charlotte had left him, and make sure Graham left nothing out.

While most people did not have lawyers speaking for them, the fact that both sides had chosen to do so created a stir in itself. Once they realized Andrew Graham was not the usual caliber of lawyer to appear, the buzz increased. The Old Bailey did not generally attract the better legal minds. Graham's name floated back down from the gallery. The son of a minor branch of a noble family, he had connections and far more lucrative business than an appearance at the Old Bailey would indicate. Of course, they ran the risk of putting Mr. Fielding's nose out of joint, but so far he'd listened with interest, rather than snapping in a way visitors to this place were only too familiar with.

The stench of the prison drifted to Val as he listened and watched, a stink that had made him ill the one night he had spent there. The brawling and cacophony of anxious people living in close proximity to one another sickened him as much as the smell had, so he'd been relieved when Graham had secured his release to private accommodation. But that smell would remain in his nostrils until the day he died. Greasy, cloying, with the pungency of strong, raw alcohol and beer mixed with putrefaction from the wildlife that fed on the prisoners, the whiff of disease and unclean human bodies, it would always remind him of this time in his life.

More prisoners were gathered in the cells downstairs, waiting for their time in the court.

As if aware of this, Fielding banged his gavel. "Proceed a little faster, please."

And then, as if summoned by magic, Charlotte appeared in the witness-box. Val forced concentration.

Charlotte glanced at him then away nervously. She brought a reminder of spring with her, in her pale cream gown printed with a pattern of spring flowers. Had she done that deliberately? She was delicately lovely and beautifully poised.

"Could you tell the court how you came to know the late Lord Kellett?" Graham asked her.

She wet her lips. "Lord Kellett courted me when I was betrothed to my husband, and I considered asking for my contract to be broken, but I decided against it."

"Why was that?" Graham asked. His voice had gentled considerably from the crisp, sharp tone he'd used to question the other witnesses.

"Because I preferred Lord Shaw," she said softly. "I have considerable affection— I *love* my husband." The way she said it and lowered her chin, speaking softly, sent a wave of appreciative purrs through the audience.

Val was taken by a powerful urge to hold her close, to protect her from the speculative eyes. To make such a confession in open court must have cost his wife a great deal. He knew how private she was, how carefully she kept her inner emotions hidden from everyone around her.

His love flowed out to her and as if she felt it, she turned to him. A faint flush stained her cheeks, and although she didn't smile, he saw a glimmer of pleasure in her eyes. Impatience spiked his skin. He wanted to get her away from this place and to somewhere private, where he could care for her and—what?

Even if he never touched her again, he would remain with her. He needed to escape the shadow of the noose before he could even think about that.

"Lord Kellett was not pleased when I turned him down," she went on. "I learned that it was partly this, and partly because my husband has an item of clothing belonging to him. He took a pin from the same place but gave that back."

"In fact," the prosecution said, cutting into her speech with no preamble, "that was the item your husband threw into the late Lord Kellett's face when he challenged him to a duel, was it not?"

"Yes. They had returned from the house in Covent Garden and the terrible scenes there."

"Does it concern you that your husband frequents a house of ill repute?"

Several people in the public gallery sniggered.

Charlotte kept her peace. "No, because he does not."

"Are you sure about that?"

"Positive." She sounded so certain, nobody could doubt her. And she spoke the truth. Even when he'd returned from the Grand Tour, full of explosive energy that needed dissipating, he had not concerned himself with brothels. He'd preferred to gamble thousands at the tables, or engage in reckless wagers, but they had not asked him about those. Of course he'd had mistresses, but he kept them to himself until he was done with them. Now he'd done with them for good.

"You were betrothed for two years. That is a long time, is it not?"

"I cannot say," she answered.

"Did your husband's reputation make you hesitate?"

She paused. "His reputation for what?"

"Whoring and gambling."

"The date of my marriage was not my decision. My father would have considered it his privilege."

"So your husband's reputation deterred your father?"

"I cannot say. You will have to ask him."

The prosecutor's jaw set. Her father had refused to come to London, as everyone knew. He had claimed illness, but he must know that Graham would question him about his activities at the House of Correction. The prosecution could have tried to compel him, but they would not have had a willing witness. The Duke of Rochfort would have perjured himself rather than admit to the habits he had successfully kept quiet for thirty years or more.

"I wish to ask you about the afternoon Lord Kellett was murdered," the prosecution said now.

Her hands, gripping the edge of the box in which she stood, tightened, the knuckles turning white. "I know of no such afternoon."

Clever girl. "Very well, the afternoon Lord Kellett met his bloody end."

Val concentrated, willing her not to confess that she killed him. She must not, or they would lock her up, perhaps insist on putting her in the dock. That would not happen. He'd take her abroad, flee the courts, if he had to.

"Describe the events, if you would."

"Lord Kellett appeared unexpectedly in the garden of my husband's house on the Thames. He threatened me, held a gun to my head."

The prosecutor held up a hand. "Have you not missed something out?"

She shook her head. "No. There was no warning. He threatened my life. My husband tried to take the gun from him, and Lord Kellett was shot in the struggle." She glanced down, and plucked a handkerchief from her sleeve. "It was a severe shock."

"I see. When you refused his hand, was he upset?" The man was trying to steer her away from the House of Correction.

"I believe he was angry, but he didn't mention that when he was threatening my life. He wanted the shirt my husband took from him." She glanced at Val. He sent all the love and courage he had to her. "The bloodstained shirt," she said.

The court exploded in shouts and speculation again, and it took Fielding some time to calm the cacophony.

Graham interposed, standing and declaring, before anyone could stop him, "What do you know about the bloodstained shirt?"

"He obtained it from the same place as the pin. From the bedroom of the girl whom Kellett whipped to death."

There was little that would have quieted the gallery now. Until Mr. Fielding, in stentorian tones threatened to have the public gallery cleared, the noise was almost unbearable.

Val's head swam. He had lived every moment of that session with her, urged her on, encouraged her, and prayed that she would not be forced to open her vulnerabilities to public glare. And best of all, she had not confessed to the killing.

Under the sound, he said to Graham, "Don't let her go on. We have other witnesses. I do not want her connected in any way with those events."

Graham raised a brow, but Val was adamant. And so, as it turned out, was Mr. Fielding. When he had brought the court under control, he said he would hear no more speculation. Unless Lady Shaw was present at the house of ill repute, he would not accept any evidence from her.

"I can say that my husband had a bloodstained shirt that had the laundry marks and the initials of Lord Kellett," she said, her chin high, in answer to a question from Graham. However, after that, she was dismissed. Her answers were too dangerous for the prosecution. Val was deeply grateful that he had told her the truth.

The man the new Lord Kellett had engaged was good, and he did not give up. He brought witnesses to his predecessor's good character to refute the allegations of bad behavior, and slowly won the tide of regard. He cast scorn on the Emperors of London and their clique, as he called it, making it sound more like a power-hungry club than a group of relatives acting together for their own good.

Graham could not make headway, although he, too, argued cogently. But he had saved the best of his witnesses for last. "Mr. Desmond Trotter!"

Mr. Trotter, dressed respectably in wool and linen, took the stand. He held his hat in his hands, turning it round and round as he spoke. "I am a button maker, sir, presently owning a small business in the City. I employ two men and a boy. Until two years ago I had a wife, three daughters, and a son, but my youngest, Janey, moved away and said she would make her fortune. I confess that I told her to leave, fearing she might corrupt my other children, because she had decided on a life of sin. I never saw her again until three weeks ago, when the coroner called me to ask me to identify her body." He swallowed, and tears glimmered in his eyes. "She looked like my little girl again, but her body was terrible. It was marked by cuts and bruises. She'd been whipped to the bone on her back. If it weren't that she was left outside Mr. Fielding's house, I wouldn't have known what happened to her." He glanced at Mr. Fielding.

Fielding nodded. "I was sorry to find her at my door in that state. The result of the case was that the girl was murdered. There were old marks on her body as well as fresh ones. On enquiry, we discovered that she was kept at a house of ill repute in Covent Garden for the exclusive use of one client. Lord Hervey Kellett."

The court erupted, so much that Fielding couldn't be heard for a minute or two, until he used his gavel and crashed his way into being heard. "We are running late already. Anyone who creates more trouble will be ejected forthwith!" He had to repeat his threats twice more before the crowd quieted enough for him to speak again. "We have no proof that Lord Kellett inflicted the wounds on her that caused her death."

Graham held up his hand. "I think that we might, my lord. I call Lord Valentinian Shaw!"

Finally, Val took the stand.

From his new position, he could see his parents sitting at the back of the gallery, his mother white-faced, wringing her hands, her family around her. The rest of the Emperors were scattered through the audience, but the gallery was packed.

He answered Graham's questions. "Yes, I saw Janey Trotter on the night she died. I had heard that Lord Kellett went to the house, so I went with my brother and my cousin to talk to him. I saw him chase Janey down the stairs. She was bleeding badly from wounds to her back. Lord Kellett was shouting insults at her and telling her to come back. He had a bloody whip in his hand."

The audience gasped as one.

Graham went on to the relationship between Val and Kellett. "I was disturbed that if I broke the marriage contract, my betrothed would find herself wed to a brute. I refused to break it and consequently married her. Kellett was not pleased and threatened me several times." He went on to describe the duel, and then he felt it. He had the audience with him. Whether Mr. Fielding would agree was another matter but the mob had been known to change the outcome of a case. He went on to describe the day of Kellett's death, as well as he could. With Graham's expert guidance, he described the scuffle and the nature of the weapons. When he'd finished, he went back to his place. He was shaking.

Mr. Fielding banged on his desk. That bench must be covered with dents. Someone had put a polished inch-thick piece of wood over the surface, but he missed it more often than not. "Are there any other witnesses?"

"I have signed affidavits from Lord Darius Shaw and Lord Ivan Rowley, corroborating the events. They are available, should you wish to question them, sir."

"Hmm. I've had the documents read to me," Fielding said. "Are there no other witnesses?"

"No, sir. The house is empty, and its occupants have disappeared."

They would no doubt appear again after the trial was over, probably to set up shop somewhere else. When he'd heard the news, Val had fallen into deep despond, but despite Darius's diligent enquiries, he could find no trace of the madam or her staff.

The court tensed. Val felt sick with relief.

Fielding asked his assistant for the time. "I've heard enough," he said. "For the benefit of the jury, I will sum up. There is no doubt that passion had much to do in this case. Lord Kellett went to the house of Lord Shaw with the intent to kill, wound, or threaten him. Lord Shaw considered his wife was under threat, and with good reason. That much is clear. Lord Shaw, by his own account and that of his servants, was unarmed. He tried to attack Lord Kellett to disarm him, he says, and I see no reason to disbelieve him. The guns were dueling pistols, weapons with fine responses. Lord Kellett had cocked one. In the tussle to gain control of the weapon, it was somehow discharged. I will leave it to you, gentlemen, to decide how. You may wish to consider reducing the charge to manslaughter, perhaps with the mitigation of self-defense. I will not speak to Lord Shaw's discoveries that had led him to believe his wife was in danger. I do not believe it had anything to do with the sequence of events after Lord Kellett held the weapon to Lady Shaw's head, only for motivation. They fought for control of the pistol, and it discharged." He motioned to the jury. "Come to your decision, sirs."

The men who'd been sitting listening to the evidence moved together. If they retired, they would receive no comforts until they delivered the verdict, but that would not stop them.

Val wrung his hands together, but he did not have to wait long.

The spokesman stood. Fielding's assistant murmured to him, and the magistrate nodded. "Your decision please," he said.

"Not guilty," the man said promptly.

Cheering began in the gallery, and Fielding had to raise his voice to be heard. "The present Lord Kellett has brought a frivolous case, and I do not take it kindly that he has taken up my valuable time. The prisoner at the bar is acquitted of all charges."

Waves of relief swept over Val and he sagged. Graham gently pushed him back into his chair. He knew how close he'd come and in cases like this, it was acquittal or death. He could have chosen to lower the charges to manslaughter, and then he could have suffered this ordeal all over again.

The judge had given him his life back. He bent his head, and the tears came.

Andrew Graham shoved a handkerchief under his nose. "I take it you want to leave this place? Best we do so before the public has left. I am told there is a carriage waiting for you."

"Thank you." He tried to get up, but his shaky legs wouldn't hold him. He was forced to grab the rail for support. He bowed his head, breathed in and lifted himself upright.

His life had changed. His marriage had begun it, or perhaps his lighthearted engagement in investments and insurance had become more important, but this event, this trial was a gate between one section of his life and the next.

First he would devote himself to his wife, use everything he had to help her back to the light.

Val took one step and then another, and went to discover what life brought him.

Chapter 22

"You specialize in lovely houses." Charlotte stepped through the door of the Leicestershire house, and felt the cool peace. This house was older than the villa by the Thames, built in the last century, but again of a comfortable size rather than palatial. After her childhood spent in houses where she could go for days without seeing anyone but her governess and the nurserymaid, she preferred this. She would never subject a child of hers to that upbringing.

Not that she seemed likely to have any children. Her courses had come and gone since the last time she'd allowed her husband to make love to her, and still he hadn't touched her. Of course, he had his own recovery to make. By mutual consent they had carried on as they were, neither forcing the issue, until he declared his intention of taking her to his other house.

They had traveled up here in comfort, but occupied separate rooms at the inns where they'd stayed. In a month they would set out for Haxby Hall, the family seat of the Shaws, for the summer gathering of the family, but for the rest of June and the beginning of July they were together, husband and wife.

Charlotte felt more like Val's sister than his wife. He had treated her with the utmost courtesy, but it was as if his shield were greater than hers. She wanted to reach out to him, but she didn't know how, and every day that passed she felt more distant from him. She had tried so hard, and now she could allow her maid to dress her hair and lace her into her stays. That was progress.

Were the all-too-few nights they'd spent in the villa by the Thames all that there was for them? As he'd told her, there was no great pressure for him to set up his nursery, so there was no reason for them to share a bed ever again.

She still shook with fear when someone touched her. She could control it better if she initiated the touch. As she did now, when he held out his arm and she laid her hand on his sleeve. Even now he hadn't offered his bare hand to her. She wanted to try it, but she was deathly afraid that this time he would reject her.

"Wait," he'd told her after the first day's journey. Now they'd arrived in Leicestershire, the lovely county of lush green fields and flocks of sheep, timber-framed cottages and elegant manor houses, of which this was one.

The domestic staff gathered in the hall, and Val introduced them with a disarming charm she had discovered he could switch on and off at will. Like his town finery, which he'd discarded for simpler country wear. Val was always on point. She couldn't imagine him ever inappropriately dressed. He'd even worn the right outfit in court. At the memory of that horrible day, both the best and the worst in her life, she shuddered.

Immediately Val turned to her, his face a picture of concern. "What is it, my love?"

She shook her head. "Nothing at all." She forced a smile of reassurance. "I cannot wait to see the house."

"Wouldn't you like tea first?"

"Not at all. Afterward, I would love it." She nodded to the housekeeper. "In the sunniest room, please, Mrs. Baker."

Mrs. Baker, a homely woman with an almost perfectly round face, smiled, curtsied, and led the kitchen maids back downstairs.

Val took her on the tour. If not for the circumstances, she would love this house. It was set perfectly in a modest estate, and the furnishings were neat, but not showy. Charlotte was discovering she preferred that kind. "I hate the old solid way my father prefers, but I am not too fond of the French way of gilding everything, either," she said. "I had no idea I had any taste at all, since everything was selected for me."

"Even your clothes?"

She paused. "Well, I chose them, but if my father disapproved, he'd have them sent back. So in effect, he ruled there, too. The gown from Cerisot was the first I had chosen for myself. I enjoyed that. Does that make me completely frivolous?"

When she turned to him, he was close enough to kiss. She could see desire in his eyes, the widened pupils with their rim of bright blue, the way his mouth tightened a tiny bit and his lips reddened. He moved toward her but then jerked back, as if remembering he could not. "You have many years of frivolity to make up for, and I'm just the man to show you." But the words sounded wrong, as if he'd been about to say something else.

Never one to shirk an issue, she said, "Val, what are we to do?"

"You mustn't worry."

"I worry all the time. I can't do it, Val. I can't let you touch me. I've tried, but it's as if that part of me is locked away." Finding a nearby window seat, she made use of it, sparing a glance at the pretty garden below. A gentle breeze stirred the leaves on the rosebushes. At least her enjoyment of gardens had not disappeared.

He sat down next to her, and where he would once have taken her hands, he laid them on his thighs. "I know." He followed her glance. "Would you like me to sell it?"

At the thought of the house where she had known happiness for the first time in her life, she shook her head. "I will not allow him to taint my memories of that place. I would like to go there again."

"I have ordered the pavilion in the Thames-side house torn down. We'll restructure that part of the garden, or we can rearrange it completely."

"Yes, that would be for the best." She liked that idea, so the place where Hervey had died would be completely obliterated. "He was a terrible person, wasn't he?"

Val nodded. "Overindulged as a child and taught to believe that everything he wanted was right. By his father, I understand, not his mother, which was why she fled."

"Then why would she support him at the trial?"

The shoulders of his brown country coat moved in a shrug. "Loyalty, or perhaps she loved him but couldn't live with him. That's not unknown. I do not know. I didn't ask."

Stricken, she clenched her fist into folds of yellow silk. "Will that happen to us?"

"No, never." He closed his eyes, sitting very still. When he opened them again, his eyes were clear once more. "I have a plan. Are you brave enough to try it?"

"Yes." She paused, recalling Val's reputation. "That is, if it's not dangerous."

"Everything in life worth having carries a little danger with it. Will you try?"

She nodded. If he could find them a way out of this torture, she would take it.

Looking at him every day, longing to touch him, to love him as she had so briefly and being unable to do so was killing her. If she touched him, he would want to touch her back, but when anyone did so, visions of blood and death and the utter blackness descended on her, having its inevitable result.

"I thought it would wear off, but so far I cannot bear to be touched. I'm so sorry."

"You think it's your fault?" His voice rose as if he were angry. "No, love, it's not. It is an obstacle we will overcome. If we don't win tonight, we will do so another day. Believe it."

She dared do nothing else. His express was so fierce she would have believed anything he said.

"Take off your ring," he said abruptly. "Read what's inside."

Her attention went to her hands. She only wore her wedding ring. She slid it off. The plain gold band gleamed in the sunshine, but she noticed writing inside. "What is this?" She held it to the light and slowly read, "Cert a Mon Gre." Sliding it back on her finger, she shook her head. "What does that mean? It's French, and it's something like 'certainly my...'"

"It's old French. It's a medieval posy ring, and it's been in the family since the first earl gave it to his countess."

"Shouldn't it go to the heir?"

Val shook his head. "They have their own troth ring. This is ours. It means 'Certainly my will,' or 'For sure my choice.' I mean it, Charlotte. If I had not, I'd have not used the ring without telling you. It's a very quiet, very personal pledge. My parents' marriage was arranged, so at the time he chose not to give her the ring. Otherwise my mother would have it."

"I thought they were devoted."

His smile disappeared. "They are, now, but it was not always that way. They fought for their love. Just as we will." He glanced around at the pretty room. "This house has a romantic history. Perhaps we can add to it. I bought it a few years ago, but it was built for a minor mistress of Henry the Eighth. She fell in love with a local man, and they had to hide their love for two years, until the king met the Boleyn sisters and lost interest in her. Her love had to watch her with their monarch or lose his head. They waited, and when the king tired of her, she married the man she loved. They lived long and happy lives and never went to court again."

"That is lovely." Leaning forward, she lifted her hand, as if to touch him.

Val froze and watched her, but said nothing. She hovered her fingers over his hand, waiting for the profound shock that accompanied even this much proximity.

It came, but it was muted. She could control it. She grazed her fingers against his skin, not sure if she was actually touching him or not, but snatched them back.

He had not moved. "You can trust me," he said. "If this is what it takes, we will do it."

"Was that your plan?"

He shook his head, smiling. "No. Wait until later, my love."

She leaned back into her corner of the window seat, glad he could smile. "Thank you for bringing me here, and thank you for marrying me." She shook her head. "I asked you to release me. I was foolish."

"You were duped. Anyone can be duped. Your father wanted you to give yourself to Kellett, so nobody was to blame but yourself. At least, in his perverted way of thinking, that was what he'd planned. But that is done with, over."

"Yes it is." She drew back, marveling at what she had just discovered. If she gave herself time, worked through the initial shock of touching, she could prolong it. The feeling faded, and the visions of horror went away. Perhaps, with a little determination, she could do this.

She could place exactly when the horrors began to diminish, but before, with the trial and its aftermath, the bustle of London and the constant visitors coming to the house to see them, she had not had time to let her mind and body settle.

The moment was when Mr. Fielding had said, "Acquitted."

* * * *

Charlotte let the tranquility of this place sink into her bones. As she went through the rest of the day, exploring her new domain, the garden, and afterward ate dinner with her husband, her body unwound like a clock does as the day passed.

Val had taken care of her at every turn, even in gaol. He'd made his will the day before the trial. Whether her father provided her portion or not, whether he'd been condemned or not, she'd be a wealthy woman, able to make her own decisions. The thought of that fate made chills run through her, even on this warm day.

She would not have allowed it to happen. If the verdict had gone the wrong way, she'd intended to stand up in court and claim that she shot Kellett, that she had aimed for that despicable man.

After dinner, they read and chatted in the drawing room, and Val played a new air on the harpsichord, laughing when he realized it had not been tuned recently and turning the melody into a discordant jangle, pretending to sing along to it. Val had a pleasant baritone singing voice, but he turned it harsh for her, making her laugh more than she had done since—she didn't think she had ever laughed that much.

They had separate adjoining rooms. With a simple turn of the knob on the connecting door she could be in his chamber. Hers was hung in blue silk, with similar drapery around the bed, a charming place to sleep. But she would sleep here alone and yearn for him.

She changed into her best night rail made of fine linen and lace, with a delicate wrapper of pale blue silk over the top. She'd refused to let her maid put her hair in its usual braids, but brushed it out, dismissing the woman to do it herself. She was sitting at the dressing table, brushing her hair when she heard the communicating door open.

She kept her strokes steady until she found the brush being taken from her. Even then he was careful not to touch her hand. She let it go, and he took over.

"Close your eyes," he murmured. When she didn't, he said, "Do you trust me?"

Of course she did.

His strokes were smooth, a little firmer than hers. Opening her eyes, she met his gaze in the mirror. He was smiling, the kind of open, happy smile she remembered from before his trial.

He raised a brow. "How is it?"

She swallowed. He was touching her. Yes, he had a brush in his hand, and he was doing what she could now allow her maid to do. As she watched, her tension rose, but not so much that she could not quell it. This was a beginning.

His robe was black with dull gold figuring tonight, more somber than his usual choice of bright colors. It seemed appropriate. "Sweetheart, I want more. I want us back where we were, but I know that will take time."

Before he masked it, she read the desperation in his eyes. She had not realized how much her reaction to him was pushing him toward the brink, but now she did. She felt sick, but also determined to put an end to this state of affairs. "We don't have to live in the same house. Would you be more content if we parted for a while?" That might kill her. Her spirit, her heart, everything about her that mattered would shrivel and die.

Her father had taught her how to hold herself up when she was dying inside and that to face a problem was better than to avoid it. "I want to try. If I cannot do this, I don't deserve you." He had stood trial for her, offered his life for hers. The least she could do was give him his life back.

"You deserve it all." Quietly, he put the brush down and stood behind her, his hands on the back of her chair.

Still she did not turn around. Speaking like this, so close and yet separated by the mirror, gave her the confidence to say what she needed to. "I don't." She caught her breath on a sob, refusing to allow it to break free. "I deserve nothing, because I have earned nothing. Please, I want to try making love. Tonight."

"But I can't touch you when you react the way you do. It destroys my spirit." The words, spoken so softly, with such sincerity, broke her heart. "I do have an idea, but we will both have to take courage."

She meant what she said. If she could not manage to resume relations with him, she would leave and let him take his own path in life. So she had no choice, none at all. "Yes." She didn't need to think about her decision. "Very well."

He walked to the bed. Dipping in his pocket, he came out with a sharp knife and four long strips of cloth. Neckcloths, if she was any judge. He dropped them on the nightstand. Then he stripped off the black and gold robe. He was naked beneath.

His glorious buttocks tensed as he bent and climbed on to the bed, sitting in the middle. Taking one cloth, he bound it around his wrist and used his other hand and his teeth to make a tight knot. He did the same with his other wrist, and then he sat up and mirrored his actions with his ankles, so he had a length of white cloth suspended from each of his limbs.

Sitting up, he nodded. "Come here, sweetheart. Tie me to the bed."

The words were stark, her reaction the same. "What are you talking about?"

"I learned a few things in the House of Correction, and by talking to people afterward." He sat up and scanned her thinly clad body.

Her tension rose, but this time it was a good tension. She wanted that hunger, to see it more and to stoke it. His lean, muscled form tempted her beyond bearing, warring with the now-familiar terror that threatened to freeze her limbs.

When she rose from her chair, she stripped off her robe and draped it over the back of the chair.

He groaned. "No more. I can see the shape of you beneath that gown, and the adorable cluster of curls decorating your mound."

Heat rushed over her face, but she didn't try to hide herself. "What did you learn?" She went to the side of the bed and picked up the first binding, bringing it to the bedpost. Step by step, that was how she'd take this.

"That control is a stimulating addition to intimacy for many. Giving up that control to another person can prove immensely arousing. I am giving my control up to you."

She walked to the bottom of the bed and secured his ankle. The neckcloths gave enough length that he could lie on the bed, and although he had to stretch out, he was not put under too much tension. But he would not be able to move. He was giving her even that much power, and his trust humbled her.

"You may leave me here, if you wish." He smiled. "I am trusting you not to, but if you wish, you have the power to do it. Tie the knots tightly, use the knife if you need to release me. Like this, you can touch me all you want to, without the fear of me reciprocating." His voice shook. "I want you badly, Charlotte."

By the time she had knotted the fourth strip of linen around the sturdy bedpost, he was erect, his shaft red and straining. As she stared at it, a bead of clear moisture glistened at the tip and she was taken by a strange urge.

Leaning forward with one knee on the bed, she swiped the liquid on her finger and tasted it, closing her eyes to savor it. It tasted of salt and musky male, concentrated Val. At his groan, she opened her eyes. "You look blissful."

"It's good."

Emboldened by his helplessness, she climbed on to the bed and studied him. Longing to touch and taste overwhelmed her. Still in the thrall of need, she took his shaft in her hand. The pulse in it throbbed, each one a heartbeat. She caught her breath, and when a chill crept over her soul, she fought it down, letting her desire for him help her. Her body was at war with itself, two strong emotions, unreasoning terror and powerful need battling for control.

Forcing control, she studied his erection—the large central vein, the hair-covered balls at the base, the sac tight now with their weight. She traced her finger over the shiny head, unable to resist testing its heat and silky strength. He gasped and flinched, his rod moving in response.

Her attention went briefly to his face. He looked as if he were in pain, his lips drawn back over his teeth, his head thrown back. His dark hair was spread over the pillow, wild as his expression. She drank in the sight.

Lowering his chin, he met her eyes. They shared an unspoken lingering regard before she went back to work. Closing her eyes, imagining he was a dish to be savored, she licked him, exploring the delicate dimple at the center with the tip of her tongue and tracing the flanged head, learning its shape. She cupped his balls, cradling them in her hand. The living example of the images she had seen in marble statues fascinated her.

She would have remained there forever, but she wanted more. Touching him still gave her a shock, but it was nothing she could not control. Not like when *he* came into contact with *her*. She could explore and push away all visions she didn't want.

"Take your time," he murmured. "Think about what you're doing, savor the pleasure."

As she traced one finger over the groove from his hip to his groin, she concentrated on the smooth skin under her fingers, and the soft hair surrounding his most intimate parts.

Her own intimate parts were unashamedly wet. She rubbed her thighs together, trying to bring herself some relief.

Every time she stroked him he gave her a response, either a gasp and a cry or a murmured purr of pleasure. She learned how she could drive him mad and how she could pet him to please him. To have such power under her hands excited her, but to have him helpless increased her enjoyment.

"I can touch you," she said in wonder.

"You can. Stop whenever you wish." His voice tightened.

She knew without him explaining it that stopping would torture him. The barrier between her and the rest of the world had thinned. She could almost reach out and punch through it. But not quite.

"Let it go," he murmured. "Don't think about it. Let's take what we have."

He was articulating her thoughts again. He was doing that a lot recently. But it was good advice.

Slowly, Charlotte moved up his body, discovering that when she brushed her nipples against his skin, they both received pleasure.

"Bring them here," he said. "Let me suck them."

A mixture of delight and embarrassment set up a strange feeling; pleasure and guilt made for a potent mixture. Propping herself at either side of his head, her legs either side of his, she gazed at him. His eyes were almost black, his lips open, waiting for her.

He pulled and sucked at her breast when she dipped and let him reach it. His erection pressed into her stomach, but she didn't want it there, so she lifted and let it nestle between her legs, nuzzling the moistness at her center with an eagerness that matched her own. Touching, using her fingers hurt the most, she discovered. So she would use other parts of her body.

He let the nipple leave his mouth with a pop, and she presented the other one, eagerness pushing aside her pain. Tingles swept over her body, pushing her higher and driving her from want into need. She needed him, and she had the means to fulfill that.

Wriggling, she made the adjustment that brought them into alignment. He bit and sucked her breast, his movements more frantic as she tried an experimental push. His erection slid past her opening. She would have to do something different.

Desperation seized her. She wanted him so much she could not bear any further separation. Desire roared through her, urging her to do more.

He kissed around her nipple and drew back, gazing into her eyes. "Sit up. You can control it better that way." His voice was ragged. "I want you so much, sweetheart. Take me."

His words emboldened her. Watching him, she drew her knees up to hug his sides and then sat up. She glanced down to see his shaft harder, if it was possible, than when she'd kissed him there. She wanted to do that again, but she needed more. Lifting on to her knees, she took him in her hand and guided him to where she wanted him. His gaze went from her face to her groin as she pushed and took him inside her.

They both groaned. Easy as silk, she slid down on him until he was fully embedded inside her. The intimacy widened her eyes, made her gasp. But they had never done this before, never made love this way. The newness of the experience helped her. They were creating fresh memories that had nothing to do with anything that had gone before.

He sucked in a breath, his chest heaving. "Move."

Leaning down, pressing her hands against the mattress either side of his big body, she raised herself and slid down on to him again. He held rigid for her, providing the resistance she needed when she plunged down on him.

He cried her name and dragged a breath in noisily as if he found the task difficult. Urging her on with his voice and his body, he sent her mindless. She wanted him, and nothing else mattered. Nobody else existed. They collided in a rhythm that became instinctive as hers rippled with sensation. Pursuing the goal, she quickened her pace and heard him laugh. She joined in, for the sheer joy of it. She was laughing when she came, right until the laugh became a long drawn-out scream.

The glass screen shattered. She was back, and alive.

* * * *

Charlotte woke up with a bird shrieking the dawn chorus outside the bedroom window.

"We need to work on your knots," he murmured sleepily to her and kissed the top of her head.

She snuggled in to her husband, enclosed in his arms, and it didn't hurt a bit.

Author's Note

The Duke of Rochfort is based on two real-life Georgian dukes—The Duke of Somerset and the Duke of Richmond. Somerset was known as "The Proud Duke." He was a notorious stickler for pomp and carried etiquette to the extreme, when it suited him. He insisted that his children always stand in his presence, and he only gave them permission to sit if necessary, like at dinner. Famously he disinherited one of his daughters for sitting; she'd fainted after six hours standing in attendance on him.

The Duke of Richmond wasn't so pompous, but he was the father of the Lennox sisters, beauties who captivated society, even to a royal level. At one point, serious negotiations went on when the future George III fell passionately in love with the second daughter. This duke also disinherited his daughter when she ran off with Henry Fox the politician, but she was later allowed back into the fold when her husband became successful and influential. Of course, I exaggerated him a bit and added some characteristics that neither duke had, although both were believers of "spare the rod and spoil the child."

There really was a House of Correction in or around the vicinity of Covent Garden. It specialized in flagellation, which was known by the French as "The English Vice." Of course where sex is concerned, nothing can be taken for granted, but it seems that a mixture of children being brought up with the "spare the rod and spoil the child" discipline may have led to the plethora of prints, stories and accounts of houses that specialized in it. The house (or to be more precise, houses) led to an exploration of the darker side of sexual practices, and later in the century, de Sade and Sado-Masoch.

As for the abduction and that theme—I use it a fair bit because there was an epidemic of abductions in the 1740s and 1750s. Men abducted heiresses to force them into marriage, and it got so bad that a law was enacted in 1753, laying down the rules of marriage much more clearly than they had ever been before. However, abductions still occurred. If a young woman was despoiled, the abductor would expect her family to marry her to him to save her good name.

That was why a young woman of good family, especially an heiress, was surrounded by servants and had a chaperone.

In the sex scenes, I try to use only terms that were available to the people at the time, so "climax" and "having sex" weren't possible, but some others were. Until the advent of the family planning movement in the early twentieth century, terms were more direct.

John Fielding, the magistrate of Bow Street Magistrate's Court, aka The Old Bailey, had claimed the job after the death of his brother, the author of *Tom Jones*, Henry Fielding. The brothers were as clean as a magistrate could be at the time and presented several White Papers to Parliament on the subject of law reform. In 1749, they established a group of thief-takers, who were partly salaried but mostly got their remuneration from rewards.

The law was very different then than it is now. Most crimes were punishable by death, though in practice many were commuted to transportation or imprisonment, but in the main, prisons were places a criminal was kept until his or her trial. Newgate Prison was close by, and the prisoners were brought directly to the court.

John Fielding was knighted in 1761. He was blind, caused by an accident in his youth, and he was fond of wearing a black band over his eyes in court, to emphasize his state, and point out that justice was supposed to be blind.

Meet the Author

Lynne Connolly was born in Leicester, England, and lived in her family's cobbler's shop with her parents and sister. She loves all periods of history, but her favorites are the Tudor and Georgian eras. She loves doing research and creating a credible story with people who lived in past ages. In addition to her Emperors of London series and The Shaws series, she writes several historical, contemporary and paranormal romance series. Visit her on the web at lynneconnolly.com, read her blog at lynneconnolly.blogspot.co.uk, find her on Facebook, and follow her on Twitter @lynneconnolly.

Printed in the United States
by Baker & Taylor Publisher Services